The yellowbacks... classics of popular fiction

The yellowjackets or yellowbacks were a great series of bestselling adventure and crime thrillers that had its origins in the mid to late 19th century following on from the 'penny dreadfuls'. They virtually began the mass market revolution of the early 20th century with a clear standard format and imprint/series livery (what would today be called branding). Hodder & Stoughton published the yellowjackets in two main series with series run dates of: 1923-1939 and later 1949-1957.

As the tagline ('where thrillers really began') on the back cover implies, the imprint and series focused on thrillers that were the bestsellers of their time. This current reissue or retro revival if you will, brings back many of these masterpieces, now classics in their own way and extends it further by including key titles from that period that were either great crime or thriller or even general commercial fiction (including sub-genres of noir, horror, gothic, romance, westerns, etc.) influences of their time. There are some perennial favourites and many rarities either lost or not easily available being revived in the current series. Writers and characters ranged from adventure heroes like Bulldog Drummond, Allan Quatermain, Richard Hannay or the Saint through thriller grandmasters Edgar Wallace and E. Phillips Oppenheim, crime and mystery maestros like Patricia Wentworth, GK Chesterton, Agatha Christie and the Detection club, to western and swashbucklers like Zane Grey, Max Brand, Captain Blood and even romance or general fiction classics like Hermina Black, Denise Robins, Marie Corelli or Stella Morton. These were books that had storytelling at their heart and always entertained.

The yellowbacks had both hardback (with varying design elements) and paperback (which built the series look) versions with the latter still carrying the imprint 'yellowjacket'. The current reissues pay tribute to both and use an amalgam of elements from both editions while retaining the complete yellow (or 'mustard-plaster') livery with the author's name in blue beveled type with a 'simulated emboss' effect and a white outer 'outline', and the book title in black. These reissues retain the distinctive size of the original mass market paperback and follow the three main category variations—the thrillers (crime, westerns, mystery, adventure) had blue lettering for the author's name, while Romance and softer general fiction had red; and other categories like humour had green.

For more detail and a full list of titles visit https://www.hachetteindia.com/home/yellowbacks

THE MAN FROM MANCHESTER

THE MAN FROM MANCHESTER

Dick Donovan was a pseudonym used by Joyce Emmerson Preston Muddock (1842–1934). Muddock was also a journalist and author of mystery and horror fiction. For a time his detective stories were as popular as those of Arthur Conan Doyle. Between 1889 and 1922, he published nearly 300 detective and mystery stories.

He was born near Southampton, England, but travelled to India and the Far East as a boy. His series characters included not only Dick Donovan, the Glasgow Detective, but also Russian Secret Service agent Michael Danevitch, Vincent Trill of the Detective Service, private detective Tyler Tatlock and early forensic criminologist Fabian Field among others. Muddock's technique of using his character's name as a pseudonym was also used by 'Nick Carter' and later adopted by his American counterparts such as Ellery Queen and Hank Jansen.

THE MAN FROM MANCHESTER

Dick Donovan

HODDER AND STOUGHTON
YELLOW JACKET

hachette

The Man from Manchester
First published by Chatto & Windus in 1890

1

The texts in these editions in most cases have been reprinted as is, with minimal editorial changes and by and large no bowdlerizing for political correctness; though in some editions, a few words and phrases considered archaic, or those considered offensive now, along with archaic punctuation may have been modified in places to make the text more accessible to today's readers. The narratives, language, beliefs, social mores and/or cultural depictions, in these volumes are a reflection of their times and must be viewed as such. They may also contain certain cultural, racial and gender prejudices and stereotypes that may be outdated or clearly wrong then and wrong today; but their removal would be tantamount to claiming these prejudices never existed. The Publisher does not endorse or support those depictions or stereotypes; and these books have been made available for a discerning audience that will read it for entertainment value and a chronicle/record of popular fiction of past times.

Cover design by Priya Singh adapted from the original classic yellowjacket by Hodder & Stoughton.

Cover illustration by Ishan Trivedi.

Series note: Some of the books in the series (unless otherwise credited) may have cover or inside illustrations from the original yellowbacks or early editions, and while full restoration has been attempted, some images may be grainy or faded due to the condition of the original material. The end notes or bonus material or blurb details may have been sourced from the public domain or free use publications such as Wikipedia and attribution is hereby made also allowing similar free use reproduction from here. Sources requiring further specific attribution may write in and further detailing and/or corrections shall be made in subsequent printings/editions.

Reprint specifications may be subject to change including but not limited to finishes, paper, colour sections.

ISBN: 978-93-5731-111-3

Hachette Book Publishing India Pvt. Ltd.
4th & 5th Floors, Corporate Centre,
Plot No. 94, Sector 44, Gurugram - 122 003, India

Typeset in Electra LT STD 10/12.5 pt by Manipal Technologies Limited, Manipal

Printed and bound in India by Manipal Technologies Limited, Manipal

MIX
Paper from responsible sources
FSC www.fsc.org FSC™ C043100

CONTENTS

I

THE LONDON EXPRESS

It was a dark November afternoon, and the time within a minute or two of a quarter-past four. The up-platform of the London Road Station, Manchester, presented a busy scene of confusion and bustle, as was usually the case at that hour, for the London express was timed to leave at 4.15. On this particular afternoon there seemed to be an unusual number of passengers, and the train was very crowded. Two gentlemen, however, who were comfortably ensconced in a first-class compartment near the engine, had managed so far to keep out intruders, a judicious tip to the guard having had a magical effect. Excited passengers had repeatedly rushed up to this compartment, but, finding the door locked, had growled out something naughty and gone to another carriage, much to the satisfaction of the two gentlemen, who smiled and seemed well-pleased at the success of their efforts to keep themselves isolated.

These two men were utter strangers to each other, and had come together for the first time in their lives. And it is in the highest degree probable that had a third party, gifted with the power of prophecy, ventured to tell those two men that their chance meeting in a railway carriage on that dark November afternoon was destined to be the beginning of a series of most astounding events that would bring them both into public notoriety, they would surely have laughed the prophet to scorn. In personal appearance the two men presented as striking a contrast as it is possible to conceive. One was a handsome, well-made, burly fellow, not more than thirty years of age. There was something about him—what it is not easy to accurately define—that at once stamped him as representing the better type of the true 'Manchester Man.' He had a round, healthily-coloured face, clean-shaved, save for a somewhat heavy moustache, that was full and round, and curled under to his lips, while his expression was at once frank and pleasing, and gave one the idea that life went well with him, and he enjoyed it. He had dark-blue eyes, that beamed with laughter and contentment. His hair, which was lightish brown, clustered about his forehead in tiny curls, almost like a young boy's. He was well-dressed, and though there was nothing in his dressing that was in the least degree offensive to good or artistic taste, it was obvious that he studied his appearance, and aimed at 'dressing like a gentleman.' His clothes were fashionably cut and fitted him accurately; and a heavy dark-green overcoat, trimmed with Astrakan, imparted to him rather a distingué air, that was further enhanced by his faultless kid gloves, and the crimson silk handkerchief that was allowed just to slightly display itself from the outside breast-pocket of his overcoat.

This gentleman was Mr. Josiah Vecquerary of Manchester. All his people had for many generations been natives of the busy city on the banks of the Irwell, and Mr. Vecquerary prided himself on the fact. And he seemed to take a special delight in making it known to strangers that he hailed from Cottonopolis. I suppose that all men are more or less proud of their birthplaces. But your Manchester man, above all others, seems proud of his. Nor is this pride unjustified, for Manchester in itself is a city to be proud of, and the average middle-class Manchester man is generally an upright, fair-dealing, thoroughly business-like, shrewd, and open-hearted fellow. Blunt of speech and frank-speaking, he strikes you at once as straightforward and reliable. And if you attempt any double-dealings with him you find that you have caught a tartar, for your true Manchester man hates chicanery. He is not suspicious as a rule. By instinct and nature he is very hospitable. He is a staunch friend, but can also be a bitter enemy.

Most of the traits here indicated were prominent in Mr. Vecquerary's character, and he had troops of friends by whom he was highly esteemed.

The Vecquerarys were a very old Manchester family. They had originally come from France, and had then spelt their name Véquérie. But that was at such a remote period that it was no more than a dim tradition amongst the descendants, who had taken kindly to the soil, and become thoroughly imbued with the distinguishing Manchester spirit.

Mr. Josiah Vecquerary was the head of the firm of 'Vecquerary and Sons,' Manchester Warehousemen, whose place of business was in Fountain Street—a thoroughfare long associated with that particular class of business known as the 'Manchester trade.' The firm of Vecquerary and Sons was a very old-established one, and had been handed down from father to son through many generations. Josiah's father had been dead for four years, and Josiah and his younger brother, Alfred, carried on the business. Alfred was single, but Josiah had been married for six years, and was the father of girl and a boy, the latter being five years of age and the girl three.

Mr. Vecquerary's marriage had at first been productive of some little friction and unpleasantness in his family, for he had chosen to marry one of his father's warehouse girls. A well-behaved and pretty enough girl, but as the Vecquerarys were not without pride of race they thought this was a mésalliance, and Josiah's father and mother were particularly annoyed. Mr. Vecquerary, senior, went so far as to refuse to recognise his daughter-in-law; and though when he came to lie on his deathbed he showed some disposition to be reconciled, he died before the reconciliation could be effected. After that, Josiah's mother took to his wife, especially when the first child was born. But most of the other members of the family still manifested a certain disdain for Mrs. Josiah Vecquerary, as they did not consider she was in any way their equal. There is reason to believe that this to some extent influenced Mr. Vecquerary, whose relations with his wife had not been altogether of a cordial character. Not that there had been any serious difference between the young couple, but the husband had occasionally given evidence that he did not consider his wife quite on a level with him. This, however, did not affect him appreciably, and life agreed with him. His business was prosperous, everything went smoothly; he had a perfect digestion, and he loved a good dinner, and knew how to appreciate a choice cigar, and a bottle of old wine.

As we make his acquaintance he is journeying to London on business in connection with his firm. He is in the habit of running up to town once every six weeks on these business matters, and is generally absent four or five days.

The gentleman who so far shares the compartment with him is a very striking contrast. He is a little man, apparently about forty-three. His figure is sparse and shrunken, so that his clothes fit him ill. His face is yellow, with high cheek bones, and he has a very scanty crop of greyish whiskers, and a thin, straggling moustache. His eyes are small and somewhat deep-set, and their expression is not altogether pleasing. He habitually wears spectacles, which tend to make him look a little older than he is. He is slightly bald on the top of his head, and his hair is thin and grey. His general appearance is not altogether calculated to beget the confidence of a stranger, who might in fact experience a sense of shrinking from him, without being able to tell why he did so. The two men have been seated together for several minutes, but with true British reserve neither has yet spoken, The little man at last breaks the ice.

'There seems to be an immense number of passengers today.'

He speaks in a high-pitched voice—a thin and trebly voice that is harsh and unpleasant; and he rubs and twists his hands one about the other as if he was oiling them.

'Yes, but it's been market-day in Manchester, and there is generally a rush for this train on market-day.'

Thus spoke Mr. Vecquerary, and his voice was in no less striking contrast to his companion's than his personal appearance was. It was a deep, round, mellow voice, with a pleasant Lancashire burr in it; while on the other hand his companion's had an unmistakable Cockney twang about it.

'Oh, I didn't know it was market-day,' answered the little man, oiling his hands again. 'You Manchester folk are a busy people.'

'Yes, we bear that character,' answered Mr. Vecquerary with a pleasant little laugh. 'But it's evident you don't belong to Manchester.'

'Oh dear no. It is my first visit. I am connected with the law, and I came down here two days ago on a little matter of business, but I confess I am rather glad to get away.'

'Why?'

'Well, it's a dirty, gloomy sort of city, and the people are very boorish.'

'As regards the city,' answered Mr. Vecquerary quickly and decisively, as though resenting the remark, 'you have seen it under every possible disadvantage, but any city would look gloomy in this filthy November weather. The people, however, are all right. They may seem boorish to a stranger, but when you come to know them you'll find out how warm-hearted and hospitable they are.'

'Ah,' exclaimed the little man with a sceptical snigger.

At this moment the guard of the train hurriedly unlocked the door, and said apologetically: 'Gentlemen, I am sorry I cannot reserve the compartment for you, as the train is so full.'

A porter came up carrying a hand-bag, a railway rug, bundle of umbrellas, and various odds and ends, and having deposited these things on the scat and in the rack, he got out and helped two ladies to get in. That done, the door was slammed to; the guard locked it; the shrill blast of the signal whistle resounded through the station; the engine uttered a shriek, and then the train went out into the fog on its way to London.

II

THE TWO LADIES

The two ladies who had thus become fellow-passengers with Mr. Vecquerary and the lawyer were both of them singularly pretty women. The elder of the two could not have been more than seven or eight and twenty. She was a pronounced blonde, with a complexion like a ripe peach, and a most bewitching mouth, the lips of which, when parted, revealed teeth of the most perfect evenness and whiteness. Her hair, which lay on her forehead in graceful waves, was of that shade which may best be likened to old gold; and it was so abundant that it formed a large knob at the back of her well-shaped head. She had the soft blue and entrancing eves that generally accompany such complexions, and her figure was so shapely that not even a hypocritic could have found fault with it. A neat little boot displayed itself from beneath the snowy frill of her petticoat; and as she removed one glove to take a handkerchief from her satchel and wipe her face, she revealed an exquisitely-shaped hand, white as a lily, with perfectly trimmed and kept nails. Several diamond rings sparkled on her fingers, and she wore a diamond and ruby bracelet on her wrist.

Her companion would not be more than seventeen. She was a brunette, with keen bright eyes, and hair of a very dark shade of brown. There was an arch coquettishness in her expression which was rather an attraction than otherwise. They were both exceedingly well dressed, and conveyed the impression that they were favourites of fortune. They occupied the corner immediately opposite Mr. Vecquerary, and for some minutes that gentleman somewhat rudely stared at these two pretty women, and wondered what relation they bore to each other. They could not be mother and daughter, because the younger one was too old and the elder one too young for them to be so related. Mr. Vecquerary's speculations were soon set at rest, however, by hearing the young girl address her companion as 'Auntie.'

The little man, who had been seated on the same side as the ladies, seemed to be no less interested in them than Mr. Vecquerary was, and in a few minutes he changed to the opposite corner so that he might see them better.

Before reaching Stockport there is a pretty long tunnel to be traversed, and as the train clashed into this tunnel the breaks were applied with such suddenness that the passengers were all but jerked off their seats. Then the engine whistled shrilly, and the train came to a standstill.

'Oh dear, I hope nothing is wrong,' exclaimed the elderly lady to her companion, in evident trepidation. This was Mr. Vecquerary's opportunity to speak to them, and he availed himself of it. He hastened in the blandest tones to assure them that there was no danger. The train, he said, had stopped because the signals were against it, owing probably to there being another train in the station ahead. In a few moments the train began to move slowly, and in due time passed out of the tunnel all right.

This little incident had been an introduction for Mr. Vecquerary, and he made the best of it, and for a long time he chatted pleasantly with the ladies. He had a very pleasant, genial manner with him, and his conversation was of a kind well calculated to interest the fair sex. In fact, he proved that he knew what most men nowadays do not know—the art of talking to ladies so as at once to engage their attention and interest them. For a considerable time he had the field to himself; but during that time his unknown male companion sat in his corner in a manner that was somehow suggestive of a tarantula spider, which sits huddled up in its nest, its glittering eyes fully extended on the look-out for prey. At length the unknown—still like a tarantula when it spies prey—darted forward, and opening a neat little hand-bag, he took therefrom a small round basket, in which, cosily nestled in immaculate cotton-wool, were five most tempting-looking peaches. Extending the basket towards the ladies, he said:

'Permit me to offer you, ladies, a peach.'

His high-pitched, squeaky voice was an unpleasant contrast to the full, round tones of the Manchester man, and as he had not hitherto spoken to the ladies, and his movement and manner of making the offer were somewhat abrupt, his act, kindly meant perhaps, did not make the impression it otherwise might have done. The younger lady gave an uneasy glance at her aunt, who returned it; but at last said, with a gracious smile:

'Oh, thank you, you are very kind, but really we cannot deprive you of them.'

'I assure you, madam, you will afford me great pleasure if you will take them,' urged the little man. 'Pray do.'

Thus pressed, the ladies each took a peach, and the little man, having got his introduction, followed it up and talked incessantly, although Mr. Vecquerary did not allow himself to be driven from the field, and quite held his own against his rival. I say 'rival' advisedly, because the little man, it was unmistakably evident, was anxious to make himself as agreeable and acceptable to the ladies as Mr. Vecquerary had done.

Thus, all the way to London, these four fellow-travellers chatted and laughed freely. The ladies alone were known to each other; the men had met for the first time, and they and the ladies were strangers, and yet these four, engaged in a pleasant little social comedy now, were by-and-by to become actors in a grim and tragic drama.

As the train steamed into Euston, Mr. Vecquerary ventured to inquire of the ladies if they expected any friends on the platform; and the elder lady answered somewhat hesitatingly, and, as it seemed, almost apologetically, saying that they did not expect anyone.

'May I have the pleasure, then, of looking after your luggage and procuring you a cab?'

The offer was accepted with a gracious smile of thanks; and when the train came to a standstill, Mr. Vecquerary sprang out, handing the younger lady out, and the two went off to reclaim the luggage. That done, they returned to where they had left the elder lady. They found her already seated in a cab which the little man had got, and he had made himself useful by handing in the small packages, and was still standing talking to his fellow-passenger when the other two came up. As soon as the young lady had taken her seat beside her aunt, Mr. Vecquerary gracefully raised his highly-polished hat, saying:

'You have made the journey up to London so exceedingly pleasant for me, and I have enjoyed your conversation so much, that I would venture on the liberty of asking to whom I am indebted for so much pleasure?'

The elder lady's face crimsoned a little, and she seemed to hesitate; but it was only for a moment. Then she opened her satchel, took therefrom a pearl and silver card case, and gave him her card. The next moment he was waving his hat in adieu as the cab drove away, and as soon as it was out of sight he moved a little so as to catch the rays of a gas lamp, and he read on the lady's card this name and address—Mrs. Sabena Neilsen, 28, The Quadrant, Regent's Park.

'Dear me, what an exceedingly pretty name!' remarked someone in a squeaking little voice at his elbow.

The someone was his fellow-passenger. Mr. Vecquerary thrust the card into his waistcoat-pocket, and seemed annoyed.

'Yes, it is,' he answered grumpily.

'Are you going to be in town long?' asked the little man.

'No, only for a few days.'

'You stay at an hotel, probably?'

'Yes; the Golden Star, Charing Cross. I always stay there when I come up.'

'Strange,' smiled the little man. 'It's a favourite house of mine, for I live in Craven Street, close by; and I often drop into the Star in the evening for a game of billiards. As we go in the same direction I'll share a cab with you if you like. There's my card.'

Mr. Vecquerary took the card, and found that his companion was 'Mr. Richard Hipcraft, solicitor.' It was a somewhat curious name, and Mr. Vecquerary could not help thinking somehow that the name was suited to the man. However, although he was not very favourably impressed with Mr. Hipcraft, he consented to share a cab with him; having got their luggage, they drove off together.

III

HOT BLOOD

For many hours after Mr. Vecquerary had parted from his lady travelling-companions, his thoughts were occupied with them, or, rather, with one of them; and perhaps it is needless to say that one was Mrs. Sabena Neilsen. Her charming manner, her sweetly pretty face, her engaging conversation, had made a very deep impression upon him, and he could not turn his thoughts from her, although he had a wife and two children in Manchester. But mixed up with his thoughts of the lady was the objectionable Mr. Hipcraft; and irrational, and inconsistent, and ridiculous as it may seem, Mr. Vecquerary actually felt jealous of the little lawyer. Wherefore jealous? it may be asked. Ah, you must know a good deal of the foibles and vanities of human nature to understand that Mr. Vecquerary was not without a certain self-consciousness of his own superiority when compared with Mr. Hipcraft. That is, he was superior to him physically—in personal appearance, and he believed he was also superior mentally and morally. That, of course, was an assumption of vanity pure and simple; but does not every man think himself superior to someone else whom he may know? Mr. Vecquerary had been anxious to monopolize the attention and conversation of the ladies during the time they were journeying up to London; Mr. Hipcraft had, with a fellow-traveller's privilege, intruded himself on the little party, and Mr. Vecquerary was annoyed and jealous accordingly. That was foolish, and also wrong; but Vecquerary was human.

Now what he should have done was this: after having parted from the lady he should have dismissed her from his mind once and forever. She was apparently a married lady, and he was a married man. Therefore his thinking of her with feelings akin to admiration was not compatible with the due regard he ought to have for his position and his honour. Not that he had any dishonourable intentions at this time; but he was labouring under the spell and fascination of the lady's presence, and he had a strong desire to see her again. Many men would, under the circumstances, have resisted that desire; others would not, and perhaps could not, have done so. And in the latter category Mr. Vecquerary must be classed. So he made a resolution, and having dined well, he went to bed after smoking his nocturnal cigar, and slept soundly.

The next day Mr. Vecquerary was engaged in business up to four o'clock. Then being free, he returned to his hotel, washed some of the London grime off him, arrayed himself in a spotless shirt, and a brown velveteen coat—an article of attire he had a great partiality for—and looking very handsome, and very gentlemanly, he jumped into a hansom cab, and ordered the driver to take him to 28, The Quadrant, Regent's Park. Arrived at his destination, he dismissed the cab; and then, with some small feeling that he was not justified in being there, he went up the steps of the house, and rang the bell. The door was speedily opened by a white-capped and white-aproned servant; and he was informed, in answer to his inquiries, that Mrs. Neilsen was at home; and being shown into the handsomely-furnished drawing-room, he requested the attendant Phyllis to take his card to the lady.

It was fully ten minutes before the lady appeared. If she had looked charming the previous day in the train, she looked doubly so now in an evening dress of delicate blush-rose silk, which admirably suited her complexion. He rose, and stammered forth an apology for his presence there.

'Pray be seated, Mr. Vecquerary,' she said, not without some embarrassment, and yet gracefully. 'I did not think when I parted from you and the other gentleman yesterday, that I should see you both again so soon.'

'Both of us!' exclaimed Mr. Vecquerary, opening his blue eyes to their fullest possible extent.

'Yes; Mr. Hipcraft—is not that his name?—called this morning to restore to us a tiny scent-bottle I left in the railway-carriage. He honestly confessed that he purposely kept it in order that he might have an excuse for calling upon me.'

'He is a cunning rascal,' returned Mr. Vecquerary, with something very much like a growl, while his brows were knit with a frown.

'Indeed! Are you personally acquainted with him?'

'Oh no; pardon me!' and Mr. Vecquerary felt very embarrassed.

'And may I venture to inquire if you have any property of mine to restore, for I am very careless when I travel?' asked the lady, with a touch of irony, and yet smiling sweetly.

Mr. Vecquerary felt foolish now, and he was conscious that Hipcraft had scored a point, and from that moment there arose in his breast a positive hatred for the lawyer.

'No, I—I have not,' he stammered; 'but I will be no less candid than this Mr. Hipcraft; he emphasized the name contemptuously. 'I—I wished to see you again,' the lady's colour deepened, 'and,' Vecquerary went on, trying to excuse his conduct to his conscience, 'I thought I might have the pleasure of making your husband's acquaintance.'

Mrs. Neilsen's face became scarlet, and her manners betrayed that she was greatly troubled and embarrassed. She seemed to become suddenly interested in an album on the table, but it was only an excuse to hide her face from him.

'My husband,' she faltered, 'is—is not here. He is abroad.' Then suddenly, and with the obvious intention of changing the subject, she asked: 'Are you going to remain long in town, Mr. Vecquerary?'

'For a few days only.'

Mr. Vecquerary did not altogether feel comfortable. He was conscious of two things—firstly, that he had no right to be there; secondly, that the beautiful woman before him had some mystery in connection with her life. He could not, on his slight acquaintance, venture to question her, and yet he felt he would give a great deal to know her story. She proved herself a diplomatist, however, for she talked delightfully about the theatres, concerts, music, etc., giving him no chance to do more than to get in a monosyllabic response now and again to what she said. And at last she rang the bell, and told the servant to ask Miss Muriel to come there. 'Muriel is my niece—the young lady you saw yesterday.' This to Mr. Vecquerary.

'She lives with you, then?'

'Yes, she is my constant companion, and is a very charming and dear girl.'

Mr. Vecquerary was about to give expression to some complimentary remark, when the door opened, and Muriel entered the room. She looked a picture of girlish sweetness and grace. She wore a cream-coloured dress trimmed with red, and a dark red rose was in her hair.

'This is my niece, Miss Muriel Woolsey,' said Mrs. Neilsen.

Muriel seemed surprised at Mr. Vecquerary's presence, bit she shook his hand and smiled upon him. Then she sank down in an attitude of perfect grace on an ottoman at her aunt's feet, and rested her white hands on her aunt's knees. The two women were a study of grace and beauty, and Mr. Vecquerary was so carried away by his feelings that he paid them the most extravagant compliments. And then, having remained to the utmost limit of time that etiquette permitted, he reluctantly took his leave, having first asked for and obtained an apparently unwilling consent to call again.

Mr. Vecquerary drove straight back to his hotel, for he had invited two friends to dine with him. Usually a very lively and entertaining companion, he was so absorbed and absent-minded on this occasion as to call forth a mild protest from his companions. He pleaded some worrying business matter as an excuse, and at last livened up under the effects of the champagne. After dinner the three gentlemen adjourned to the billiard-room to smoke and take their coffee and liqueur.

'Ah, good-evening, Mr. Vecquerary,' exclaimed a squeaky little voice, as the three entered. The owner of the voice was Mr. Hipcraft, the lawyer.

'Good-evening,' returned Vecquerary with a scowl, and wishing the other at—Jerusalem, or somewhere else.

If the lawyer was conscious of the brusqueness—and no doubt he was—he did not allow it to affect him. But with a certain unctuous suavity he engaged Vecquerary in conversation, and as Vecquerary rather prided himself on his good breeding, he did not like to be positively rude to the man, for which line of conduct he could not have found a shade of legitimate excuse. He was about to take a cigar from his own cigar-case, when the little lawyer quickly whippet out his own case, and said:

'Will you pay me the compliment of accepting one of mine? I can recommend them. They are very choice Havannas, sent direct to me by a relative residing in Havanna.'

Vecquerary could not get out of it, so he accepted the cigar, and then Mr. Hipcraft offered his case to Mr. Vecquerary's friends. And they also availed themselves of the offer. Thus the lawyer established a claim to be considered one of the party. A little later billiards were proposed, and Vecquerary and one of his friends played the lawyer and the other friend. They were an amicable and agreeable quartette for some time, and two or three games having been played, the four adjourned to the smoking-room, where more champagne was indulged in.

It would be useless to deny that each of the four men was more or less excited with what he had drunk during the evening, and in that condition when laughter may suddenly, by some injudicious remark, be turned to curses. Incidentally, during the conversation between Mr. Vecquerary and Hipcraft, their travelling companions of the previous day were referred to, and with a sneer, the lawyer said:

'There is something queer about that Mrs. Neilsen.'

'How do you know?' asked the other sharply.

'I guess it,' said the lawyer coolly. 'I called on her this morning'—this boastfully.

'Yes, I know you did.'

'How the deuce do you know?'

'That's my business. I know it anyway.'

The lawyer sniggered scornfully, as he replied:

'I suppose you have been hanging round there?'

'And what if I have?'

'Oh, nothing. Only it rather tends to confirm my opinion that the lady is not quite what she seems.'

This was an ill-advised remark, although the lawyer did not mean exactly what the words seemed to imply.

'You are an infernal cad to make any such insinuation,' exclaimed Vecquerary hotly.

'Well, if I'm a cad, it's equally certain that you are a blackguard,' answered the lawyer.

The friends interposed to allay the rising quarrel, but without avail. Wine and excitement deprived Mr. Vecquerary of his usual good sense, and he flicked the lawyer's nose with his finger, saying at the same time:

'You are an ass.'

Mr. Vecquerary was a big man, and the lawyer was a little one, but nevertheless he proved that he could resent such an insult as that, and rising to his feet he struck his opponent in the face. Vecquerary was maddened, and before he could be stopped he sprang up, and striking straight from the shoulder he sent his antagonist all in a heap into a corner.

Most of the men in the room cried shame on Vecquerary, who was secured. The lawyer was helped to his feet. His face was white as note-paper, and blood was pouring from a wound on his temple where a ring on Vecquerary's finger had cut him. He was evidently excited, but also it was evident that he had the power of controlling his excitement, for he spoke coolly and with the air of one who was pronouncing a doom. And strangely enough, at that moment Big Ben, with his solemn, deep boom, began to toll the hour of midnight, and somehow the reverberating, sonorous strokes, as they shivered in the night air, seemed to lend force and point to the man's words.

'Vecquerary,' he said, with a sibilant emphasis, 'this blow shall cost you dear, and prove a curse to you as long as you live.' Every word was deliberately uttered, and the man who uttered them might have stood as a model of concentrated hatred and revenge.

IV

VINDICTIVENESS

Mr. Vecquerary was an impulsive and excitable man but, like most such men who are quick to resent an insult but as quick to forgive, he was generous and ready to admit an error. He saw at once that he had been too hasty, no less than too severe, in inflicting chastisement on Mr. Hipcraft, and, being neither frightened nor affected by that gentleman's denunciatory and prophetic outburst, he put forth his hand, saying with frank honesty:

'I am sorry for this. I have done wrong. I apologize, and will make what amends I can.'

As may be readily supposed, the quarrel had caused a great commotion in the room, which was crowded with gentlemen; and it is certain that at first the majority looked upon Vecquerary as a bully, and they were not slow to give expression to their feelings by loud cries of 'Shame,' but Vecquerary's expression of regret and apology caused a revulsion of feeling in his favour generally, though there were still a few who took part with the lawyer. As for Mr. Hipcraft himself, his whole manner and his expression were indicative of concentrated rage and disgust. Some men under certain circumstances seem to show all their character at once and Mr. Hipcraft was one of that sort. If an observer had wanted something to have likened him to, it is almost certain that a snake would have suggested itself. It is not altogether easy to give a clearly logical reason why the lawyer was like a snake, unless it was in an unmistakable malignity that made itself manifest in his whole bearing, and a peculiarly wicked look in his eyes.

As Vecquerary put forth his hand the lawyer drew back, and fairly hissed out these words:

'Take your hand, you brute! I should sully myself if I did. I never allow any man in this world to insult me with impunity, and I repeat, this blow shall cost you dear.'

Vecquerary saw at once that further argument would be but waste of time, and, irritated by his opponent's manner, he retorted:

'All right, do your worst. I defy you.'

This was perhaps an unfortunate remark, but he could not help it, and his friends deemed it wise to get him away. As he reached the passage leading from the billiard-room, a gentleman, who had followed him out, said politely:

'Excuse me, sir, but if you take my advice you will try in some way to appease Hipcraft. I know the man of old, and he is one of the best haters I have ever met. He will ruin you if he can.'

In his then frame of mind Vecquerary somewhat resented this advice, coming from a perfect stranger, as a liberty, and he said snappishly:

'I think you had better mind your own business, sir. What have my affairs got to do with you?'

'Nothing,' answered the gentleman with an ironical emphasis.

'As for Hipcraft,' continued Vecquerary with an expression of disgust, 'he is a toad.'

'So he is—a poisonous one,' added the gentleman who had spoken to him, and who with this utterance went back to the billiard-room.

Vecquerary was certainly not a bully, and it is no less certain he was not a quarrelsome man. He was, as a rule, an even-tempered, rather easy-going fellow, fond of the flesh-pots of Egypt, and not disposed to put too fine a distinction on what constitutes social virtue. Let it not be supposed that he was either a roue or a reprobate. He was fond of his wife and his children, and denied them nothing. But when away from his home he displayed a tendency to forget that he was no longer a bachelor. Being of the world he was worldly in the sense of thinking more of this life than of that which is to come. But then the same thing may be said of nineteen human beings out of every twenty. In so far, therefore, as Mr. Vecquerary could be judged by ordinary standards he was a good husband and father, an equally good citizen, and a highly respectable man; ambitious, too, and with an eye to the mayoralty in the city to which he belonged. As yet, however, he was young, but that would be corrected in time, and he was also good-looking, and of attractive manner—two qualities that are apt to be dangerous to their possessor unless counterbalanced by an absence of vanity and a large amount of self-denial and self-restraint.

His quarrel with Hipcraft troubled him sorely—so much so that for many hours he could not get to sleep. He did not attempt in any way to justify his conduct. He felt, in fact, that he had degraded himself, and gone astray from that line of gentlemanly conduct upon which he prided himself. He had with a generous impulse offered to shake his opponent's hand and confess himself freely in the wrong. But that opponent had scornfully rejected the offer, leaving Vecquerary now no alternative but to stand on his dignity, and urge in his defence strong provocation. But what he really dreaded was publicity. He felt that he would rather give a thousand pounds than that this wretched and disgraceful squabble should become noised abroad. It was the thought of the probability of the affair becoming public property that kept him awake. Had his opponent been a less vindictive man all might have ended well, but Mr. Hipcraft was a totally different man to Mr. Vecquerary. Hipcraft had been for many years what is contemptuously termed an 'Old Bailey lawyer,' and in this particular branch of his profession he had conspicuously distinguished himself, and any case which he took up he fought with a determination and a bitterness that made him dreaded as a foe.

It is said that no one can dabble in pitch without soiling his hands; and it is no less true that a man cannot habitually be dealing with criminals without, unconsciously it may be; catching up some of the mental characteristics that distinguish them. And so Mr. Hipcraft's mind had moulded itself to his particular calling, and having to deal with cunning, craft, greed, and vindictiveness, he had become imbued in a greater or lesser degree with these qualities.

Mr. Hipcraft had many friends and acquaintance, for like clings to like; and whatever a man may be he is sure to find somebody who believes in him; but in a general way Hipcraft was not esteemed. He was considered to be very sharp, and without those restraining feelings of brotherly charity which redeem our common nature. He had been married. He married a lady much younger than himself, and, unfortunately perhaps, the union was not blessed by children. Mrs. Hipcraft, who was pretty and weak, deceived her husband, and that deception brought forth all the innate vindictiveness of his character.

From the moment he discovered his wrong he became her sworn enemy. For years he pursued and persecuted her, until, driven to desperation, the poor thing destroyed herself. So much of the world as knew of the circumstances cried shame on him; but with supreme indifference and scorn he justified his course of conduct by saying 'revenge is sweet,' and that an enemy should never be forgiven. It was a cruel doctrine, but it was a creed with Hipcraft, and he claimed to have a right to form his own opinions.

The foregoing synoptical remarks will enable the reader to understand the kind of man Mr. Hipcraft was, and to see at a glance that Mr. Vecquerary had placed himself in the hands of a very cruel enemy, who would have his pound of flesh to the uttermost grain.

Mr. Hipcraft had certainly been severely punished, using that word in the sense in which bruisers use it. In falling after he had been struck he had strained the muscles of his left arm, and had also extensively bruised his shoulder. The back of his head had likewise come in contact with the wall against which he fell, the result being a large and painful lump. But the most conspicuous, and certainly the most galling, damage was the gash over his eye. With lawyer-like exactitude, the first thing he did when his enemy left the room was to secure the names and addresses of as many of those present as possible. Then he wrote in his pocket-book the particulars and details of the brawl, stating the part he himself had taken with impartial accuracy, and that done, he got two or three gentlemen to sign it. His next step was to wash himself and go home. He lived as a bachelor in Craven Street, off the Strand, an old woman acting as his housekeeper, with a young girl to assist her in the housework, for there was a good deal of work to do, as Mr. Hipcraft did not lead an isolated life, but was fond of a little company.

Letting himself in with a latch-key, he rang his housekeeper up, much to that good woman's surprise and disgust.

'Mrs. Hartley,' he said, 'put on your bonnet and shawl and go to Dr. Turner's house, ring him up, and tell him be must come to me at once.'

'Lor' bless me, sir,' exclaimed the woman, 'have you met with an accident?' as she noticed the wound in his temple.

'Yes,' he answered hotly, and in a tone which she knew too well meant that she was to ask no more questions. So grumbling and shivering she got on her things and went off for Dr. Turner, who lived at the bottom of the street. Mr. Hipcraft being a maladeimaginaire, as the French say, and always imagining that he had something the matter with his internal organs, was a pretty good customer to Dr. Turner, so that that gentleman, although very much averse to turning out on such a beastly cold, foggy night, felt that he could not refuse to do so. He therefore muffled himself in a big coat and woollen scarf, and stepped round to the lawyer's house.

'I'm sorry, doctor, to drag you out of your bed at such an unearthly hour,' said Hipcraft apologetically, 'but the matter is urgent. I've been shamefully assaulted in the billiard-room of the Golden Star by a low cad and bully from Manchester, and I'm going to make him pay for it. Please to examine this wound.'

The doctor drew off his gloves, put on his spectacles, and did as he was desired.

'Umph! An ugly gash, the result of a blow with some blunt instrument, I should say.'

'A ring,' suggested the lawyer.

'Yes, a ring,' repeated the doctor, 'no doubt.'

'That is it, he struck me here, and a large signet ring on his finger made the gash. Now feel this lump on the back of my head. He knocked me clean down, and my head came in contact with the wall. My arm, too, seems to be strained. I can't lift it, and it's very painful.'

The doctor scrutinized the arm, and felt it with professional skill.

'Yes, some of the tendons are strained, and it will be painful and stiff for weeks.'

'Now, I want you, doctor, to make accurate note of my injuries and condition, as I shall call you as a witness. I have been brutally assaulted, and as you know I am not the man to submit tamely to that sort of thing.'

'No, you are not,' muttered the doctor, with what might or might not have been a soupçon of sarcasm in his tone. Then he drew forth his note-book, jotted down some memoranda, and having dressed his patient's wound, and given him a prescription for a liniment wherewith to rub the arm, he took his departure; and as Mr. Hipcraft closed the door after him and put up the chain he muttered:

'I think, my friend Vecquerary, this night's work will be rather a bad bit of business for you.'

With this self-comforting reflection, Mr. Richard Hipcraft went to bed.

V

A LITTLE MYSTERY

The following is an extract from a long letter which was received by a Mrs. Haslam, a widow lady of means, residing in Manchester, and with whom Mrs. Sabena Neilsen and her niece had been staying. The letter was a very womanly letter, with a great many petty details about the journey back to town, and a good deal of gushing sentiment about the 'immense enjoyment' the writer and her niece had derived from their stay in Manchester. The only part, however, that will have any special interest for the reader of this narrative is the following:

'Do you happen, dear Nellie, to know anything of a Mr. Vecquerary, who, I think, belongs to Manchester? Now, pray, dear, don't draw any wrong conclusions from this question. I assure you it is prompted by only the idlest of curiosity. The fact is, Muriel and I had for a fellow-passenger on our journey back to town a Mr. Vecquerary, who was so excessively kind that I became quite interested in him. I was surprised to receive a visit from him the day after we got home. He was full of apologies of course, and said that he had simply called to see if we had reached home safely. What artful creatures men are! Don't you think so, Nell? Muriel is quite struck with Mr. Vecquerary, and I don't wonder at it, for he is very good-looking, and such a perfect gentleman. I could not get rid of him until I had reluctantly consented to his calling again. But when he comes Muriel and I intend to be out. However, I am sufficiently interested in the fellow to want to know who he is. So find out something about him, Nellie, will you, there's a dear old darling?'

Mrs. Haslam was the widow of a naval officer, and though she was under forty she was somewhat of an invalid, and did not go out very much. Her friend Mrs. Neilsen's letter interested her greatly; and she prided herself on not being deceived by the artfully phrased remarks anent Mr. Vecquerary. 'I suppose the fact is,' thought Mrs. Haslam, 'either Muriel or Sabena is smitten with this man. Well, they had better be careful what they are doing, for there is no telling any man nowadays.' It will be seen from this that Mrs. Haslam was somewhat of a philosopher, with perhaps a dash of the cynic in her composition. And a few days later, in answering at length her friend's letter, she wrote thus concerning Mr. Vecquerary:

'You know, dear, that I lead such a quiet and retired life that I have not much chance of learning anything about people who are not included in my own immediate circle of acquaintances. You will, I am sure, readily see, that with every desire to serve you, you place me in a delicate position, because I could not go about openly making inquiries as to who Mr. Vecquerary is. I might compromise myself, for people are so quick to draw wrong inferences, and suspect wickedness where none is intended. I find, however, on reference to the directory, that there is a firm in Fountain Street here styled "Vecquerary & Sons," but beyond that I have not come across anyone who could give me any information about them. Possibly the Mr. Vecquerary you met will be one of the sons, as I gather from what you say that he is young. I should say anyway that there is no doubt your travelling companion is connected with the firm in question, as I cannot find any other Vecquerary in the directory, and the name is a very uncommon one. Take my advice, however, dear, and before you allow this man to form any intimacy with Muriel—for I presume that it is Muriel he is interested in—find out all about him, for men, you know, are so deceptive, and an unprotected woman cannot be too careful. Of course, these Vecquerarys may be highly respectable, and I have no doubt they are, but still one cannot be too cautious in this world. For my own part I should be delighted to hear of dear Muriel making a good match. But do not let her marry merely for money.'

As Mrs. Sabena Neilsen perused this letter, she smiled ironically, for she was not quite pleased at her friend presuming to give her advice, and she was amused, too, at the erroneous inferences Mrs. Haslam had drawn.

'Muriel,' said Mrs. Neilsen to her niece that afternoon as they sat over the cheerful fire in the drawing-room, each engaged in some needlework, 'what is your opinion of Mr. Vecquerary?'

'Oh, well, he's nice enough in his way, as far as one can judge from such a short acquaintance.'

'He's good-looking, don't you think?'

'Yes, passably so.'

'Do—you—suppose that he's interested in you, Muriel?'

The girl broke into a little laugh of derision as she answered:

'Really, auntie, I should say you were his choice, if he has one. Certainly he bestowed upon me no more than the most passing notice, while he seemed to feast his eyes upon you.'

'Muriel!' this severely and in a tone of reprimand.

'Well, auntie, you know it,' retorted the girl, with the most bewitching pout, and speaking in such a decisive way as to leave no doubt as to what her opinion was.

'Well, it doesn't much matter,' remarked Mrs. Neilsen somewhat sharply, 'for I don't suppose we shall ever hear anything more of him.'

'Perhaps not,' returned her niece carelessly, as though the subject had no further interest for her.

A little later Mrs. Neilsen was alone in her bedroom. She stood before the glass, peering at the reflected image of her own sweet self. She smoothed back the soft, wavy hair from her temples; and if anyone had whispered in her ear just then, 'You are really an exceedingly pretty woman,' she would have answered, or at any rate thought, 'Yes, I know I am.'

She turned from the contemplation of herself to a chest of drawers that occupied a position on the opposite side of the room. From her pocket she drew forth a bunch of keys, and selecting one, she opened the top drawer; and after rummaging the things over for a few moments, she produced a photograph in a double case, that closed like a book. This she opened, and revealed the picture of a dark, stern-looking man. This portrait affected her.

The soft, womanly expression of her face changed to one that by comparison was fierce. It was an expression that betokened disgust, contempt, cynicism, disappointment. And yet it was hard to associate cynicism with so charming a woman. But it was evident that, whoever that man was whose portrait she contemplated, she bore him no love. And in a few moments she uttered an exclamation of profound disgust; she shut the photographic case with a spiteful snap, and pitched it into the drawer. Then she closed the drawer with a bang, and drew the keys out savagely, and with a heart-rending sigh she muttered:

'What an unfortunate wretch I am!'

In thus putting her feelings into words, her self-control appeared to be overcome, and sinking on to the sofa, she covered her face with her handkerchief, and burst into tears. Some bitter memory of the dead past had come back, and harrowed her into weeping. But what did she mean by saying she was an unfortunate wretch? As far as outward signs went, she appeared to be a petted favourite of fortune. Nature had made her beautiful, and she did not seem to suffer from poverty, for her house was well furnished, and, though she and her niece constituted the family, three servants were kept, including a cook. That, at any rate, was prima facie evidence of worldly ease. But may not an apple be fair on its rind and yet rotten at its core? A smiling face sometimes masks an aching heart; and often it happens that what seems the most joyous household has the most gruesome skeleton hidden in its closet.

Before Mrs. Neilsen had recovered herself, Muriel came suddenly into the room, and found her aunt in tears.

'Why, auntie dear, whatever is the matter?' exclaimed the affectionate girl in amazement, as, dropping on her knees, she threw her arms round her aunt's neck, and laid her own soft warm cheek against her aunt's.

'Oh, nothing, darling,' answered Mrs. Neilsen somewhat petulantly, as though she was angry with herself for her weakness. 'I'm foolish, and I think I'm a bit hysterical today. I've had a crying fit. There, that's all. But it's over now.' She sat upright, kissed her niece, and added: 'We'll go to the theatre tonight, dearie, if you like. It will cheer me up.'

It was so unusual for Muriel to see her aunt in tears, that, naturally the girl wondered what it meant. But she had the good sense not to irritate with questions; and as she and her aunt were very fond of the theatre, she expressed her delight at the prospect of going.

As Muriel rose to her feet her aunt rose too; and taking her niece's hand, Mrs. Neilsen said with some solemnity:

'Muriel darling, I have a dark secret in my life, and some day I will tell you what it is. The memory of it came back to me this afternoon, and made me weep. It was very foolish, but I could not help it. There now, go and dress yourself, and I will tell cook to let us have our dinner in good time.'

As Muriel sat before the glass combing her beautiful hair, she was very pensive, and she wondered and wondered what the dark secret in her aunt's life was.

Dinner over, the two ladies drove in a hansom—Mrs. Neilsen did not keep her own vehicle—to a theatre where a highly-amusing comedy was being performed; and the way in which the elder lady enjoyed herself—or seemed to do so—was not suggestive of a dark secret that was capable of moving her to hysterical weeping.

The next morning, immediately after breakfast, Muriel unfolded the Standard newspaper. She had got into the habit of reading the day's news to her aunt immediately the breakfast things had been taken away. She ran over many items, and at last in an excited tone she exclaimed:

'Oh, auntie!'

'What is it?' asked Mrs. Neilsen, looking up from some work she was doing.

'Whatever do you think?' continued Muriel. 'Mr. Vecquerary has been had up for an assault.'

Mrs. Neilsen's work dropped from her fingers, her pretty face became pale, and with manifest agitation she gave vent to the one word:

'What!'

Then Muriel in an absorbed way read the following paragraph:

'AN ASSAULT CASE.—Yesterday, at Bow Street, before Mr. Jones, a gentleman who was described as of Manchester, and whose name is Josiah Vecquerary, of the firm of Vecquerary and Sons, of that city, was charged with committing an aggravated assault on Mr. Richard Hipcraft, the well-known solicitor. The prosecutor, who appeared in the witness-box with his head bandaged, and his left arm in a sling, stated that he was in the smoking-room of the Golden Star Hotel in company with Vecquerary, when some words passed between them about a lady whose acquaintance they had both made while journeying up from Manchester the previous day. Vecquerary, who is a big and powerful man, called the prosecutor a cad, and he retorted by calling Vecquerary a blackguard. This irritated Vecquerary, who struck the prosecutor a violent blow, knocking him down, and seriously injuring him. Several witnesses were called to prove the prosecutor's case, including his family doctor, who was summoned late on the night of the assault to attend to Mr. Hipcraft's injuries. The doctor described the condition in which he found the prosecutor; and stated that besides a deep incised wound over the temple, that was within an ace of being dangerous, he was suffering from severe contusions, and sprained tendons of the left arm.

'For the defence it was urged that the prosecutor had really begun the quarrel by speaking lightly of a lady of whom he really knew nothing; that on the defendant resenting this, the prosecutor called him a blackguard, whereupon the defendant tweaked his nose. The prosecutor retaliated by striking the defendant in the face, whereupon Vecquerary knocked him down.

'In spite of the provocation the defendant had received, Mr. Jones characterised the assault as one of the most brutal violence, and he felt in doubt whether he ought not to send the defendant to prison. In fact, he would not have had the slightest hesitation in doing that, but for the provocation the defendant had received. But whatever his social position might be, such blackguards as the defendant represented would have to be taught that respectable citizens were not to be assaulted with impunity. The defendant, therefore, would be fined ten pounds, and would have to pay the prosecutor's medical expenses. The fine was at once paid, and the defendant, who seemed to feel his position acutely, left the court with his friends.'

'There, what do you think of that?' asked Muriel, as she ceased reading. 'Whoever could have believed that such a quiet, gentlemanly man as Mr. Vecquerary seemed could have so disgraced himself? I declare, there is no trusting anyone now.'

'Muriel, dear,' said her aunt quietly, as she bent over her work, and betraying by her voice that she was a little agitated—'Muriel, dear, don't you think it possible that Mr. Vecquerary must have received very strong provocation indeed? The report says that the quarrel arose from Hipcraft speaking insultingly of a lady they had met the day previous on their way from Manchester. That must refer to me. I did not like the look of that Hipcraft at all, and I rather think it redounds to Mr. Vecquerary's credit that he was quick to chastise a man who had the audacity to speak insultingly of a lady that he knew nothing at all about. Is that not your opinion?'

This argument placed the matter before Muriel in a somewhat different light to what she had first seen it in, and she answered thoughtfully:

'Yes, aunt, you are right.'

'Poor Mr. Vecquerary, I feel quite sorry for him,' sighed Mrs. Neilsen, in a way that left no doubt that her sorrow was something more than mere words.

A little later some friends called and took Muriel off shopping, and Mrs. Neilsen retired to her room to dress. Presently a servant entered with a card on a salver, and as the lady glanced at the card she saw with surprise that the name on it was Josiah Vecquerary.

VI

ENDEAVOURS TO EXPLAIN IN WHAT WAY MR. HIPCRAFT WAS LIKE A SNAKE

The disgrace of figuring in a police-court, to say nothing of being called a 'blackguard' by the presiding magistrate, crushed Vecquerary with a sense of the most absolute degradation. The record of his life—so far as such scenes as that at the Golden Star Hotel, in which he had figured so prominently, were concerned—had been as a tabula rasa. The Vecquerarys, in fact, claimed to be considered eminently respectable, and their claim was generally allowed. Strictly honourable in their business transactions, and liberal in all their dealings with their fellow-men, their reputation—in Manchester, at any rate—was very high. Josiah, as the chief representative, was proud of the family traditions, which he endeavoured to sustain with honour and dignity, and there is no doubt he was very popular with those who knew him. Now, however, a little forgetfulness, and a miserable squabble in a hotel, had led to his appearing as a defendant in a police-court case, and to being described by a metropolitan magistrate as a blackguard.

Unhappily for Vecquerary, his opponent was one of those outrages on our common nature, a man with whom vindictiveness was a creed, a man who believed that it was noble 'never to forgive.' As Vecquerary left the court covered with shame and humiliation, he passed his enemy in the corridor. The lawyer had evidently posted himself there purposely, and in tones of the utmost scorn he squeaked out:

'How do you feel now, Mister Vecquerary? I wonder what your friends in Manchester will think when they hear of your little escapade. And they will hear of it, Mister Vecquerary. And I further wonder'—here he lowered his squeaky voice a little—'what the lady, who is not quite what she seems, will think. Eh?'

This latter remark so galled Vecquerary that the blood rushed into his face and the fire flashed up in his blue eyes. He turned quickly on the speaker, and seemed about to make some stinging retort, when his arm was seized by a friend, who said:

'Do not notice the wretched little cad. Come away.'

'Yah,' hissed the small man, as though he was spitting out venom; 'the "little cad" and your dear friend Vecquerary will perhaps meet again some day.'

Vecquerary showed his good sense by keeping silent, and hailing a hansom, he drove off with his friend.

In trying to find a prototype, as it were, for Mr. Hipcraft amongst the lower orders of creation, it has been suggested that in a certain sense he approximated to a snake. We are in the habit of speaking of some men as being 'cunning as foxes,' 'as bold as lions,' 'as relentless as wolves.' It is, therefore, not straining the privileges of similitude too much to say that a man has some of the characteristics of a snake. That is, when aroused he may be vicious, using this word in the sense of being wicked as applied to animals, and more than vicious, he may be venomous in so far as seeking to do his enemy every harm within his power. This trait was a leading one in Mr. Hipcraft's nature. In so far, then, he was like a snake. And he was possessed of another quality which still further justifies the comparison. It is well known that the male and female cobra de capella, one of the most deadly snakes of India, rarely stray far from each other. If a person kills either of the two the survivor when it misses its mate becomes furious, and it is said never forgets its loss. And so revengeful does it grow that it will attack any living thing that comes in its way not of its own kind. Herein, then, the reptile displays that quality of hatred which was so conspicuous in Mr. Hipcraft. Cunning, too, is associated with the snake, and Mr. Hipcraft was cunning. Said he to a friend as they smoked together on the evening of his day of victory in the police-court:

'My revenge is not satisfied yet. I wanted to have got the brute locked up in a common police cell. I wanted to have put the brand of the gaol-bird on him, but I failed. A fine of ten pounds to a fellow like that is nothing. I'd swear an affidavit that he would have given a clean thousand to have kept this matter out of the court, and I might have bled him, but money would not satisfy me. I am a good hater, as you know.'

'Yes, I know you are,' his friend assented.

'I believe in hate,' the lawyer went on. 'If a man wrongs you, hate him, and never let your hate die until you've ruined him. To love your enemies and do good to them that hate you is a parson's doctrine, but it doesn't work out in real life.'

'No,' mumbled the friend mildly, as though he did not altogether feel as if he could endorse, the sentiment.

'I've ascertained,' continued Hipcraft, 'that this fellow Vecquerary has a wife and two children in Manchester. Now I know nothing of human nature if, in spite of that trifling circumstance, he doesn't go fooling round that Mrs. Neilsen. And I'm utterly ignorant of womankind if she doesn't draw him on till she has got him fast. He is well off, and she is an adventuress. Do you see the connection?'

'Not quite,' responded the friend, with a simple expression of countenance.

'Good Lord: then you must be obtuse: Don't you see, she being an adventuress, and he having money and being a family man, she'll keep up a constant drain on his purse, and he'll submit to it to avoid scandal. A fellow like that has to assume an appearance of virtue, or he would be ostracised, and his business would go to pot.'

'Ah, just so,' responded the friend sententiously and gazing up at the ceiling.

'Now, I shall watch him like a hawk, and when I find that he has been trapped by the siren spells of his charmer, I'll blow the scandal all over Manchester.'

'But that would be injuring his wife and children,' the friend ventured to remark a little timidly.

'And what the deuce do I care for that?' squeaked Mr. Hipcraft, in his objectionable treble, like an angry rat. '"The sins of the father must be visited on the children." The brute has injured me, and in seeking to have my revenge I cannot take his belongings into account; I'll leave that for your philanthropists. I am not a philanthropist. I am a hater of those who injure me, and I hate sentiment also.'

'I tell you what it is, Hipcraft,' said his companion, 'I would far sooner have you as my friend than my enemy.'

'I should think you would,' exclaimed the lawyer, with a dangerous curling of his lips so that his uneven teeth were revealed; and then with a wicked snarl he added: 'Better to have the devil to deal with than Richard Hipcraft as your enemy. I tell you.'

The friend did not seem quite comfortable, and to steady his nerves he took a deep draught from the glass of whisky and water that stood near him, and thus fortified he said, as he wiped his moustache with his hand:

'Hipcraft, I hope I never shall have you as an enemy. You've got a dangerous sting in you.'

'I hope you never will,' was the rounding off remark—which seemed to suggest an ellipsis which might be filled in with 'God help you if you do.'

From the foregoing fragment of dialogue the reader will get another insight into Mr. Hipcraft's character, and even the most charitably disposed amongst us could not honestly say that this gentleman was anything but a most objectionable person. Perhaps he himself did not think he was any worse than the majority of his fellows, He acted according to his lights, and his lights led him to the conclusion that living in a crafty and wicked world he must meet wickedness and craft with their own weapons.

Mr. Vecquerary, on his part, was without craft. He was in many respects weak, if you like; but he would far sooner have done a generous deed than an unkind one. It may seem singular, but still it was only in accord with the weakness I have alluded to that he should have felt morbidly sensitive about Mrs. Neilsen coming to know of his disgrace. He did not so much mind his wife knowing, but he perfectly shuddered at the idea of the affair coming to the ears of Mrs. Neilsen, although she was a stranger to him, and he could not have been affected by anything she might have thought. To fully explain this peculiarity of Mr. Vecquerary's one would have to resort to a process of very subtle analysis, and bring all the laws of metaphysics to bear. Suffice it, therefore, to say that at the bottom of it was a certain vanity, and that vanity was one of his weaknesses.

When he arose on the following morning after his unpleasant experience of a police-court, and after having passed a very restless night, he, as was only natural, eagerly turned to the daily papers, and as he read the report of the case he went white and scarlet by turns. Bitter, indeed, were his reflections, and painful his feelings, and he could not help thinking:

'Whatever will Mrs. Neilsen think if she should see this? She will certainly come to the conclusion that, instead of the gentleman she took me to be, I am an impostor and a cad.'

If he had been asked to argue the matter out, he would probably have argued thus: 'Those who know me well know that I am neither an impostor nor a cad. But those who, like Mrs. Neilsen, only have a passing acquaintance with me, cannot help an erroneous conclusion.' It will be said, and said justly, that he need not have cared what strangers thought. But the fact remains that he did care—at least, he cared so far as Mrs. Neilsen was concerned. That is where his weakness and little vanity conspicuously displayed themselves.

His appetite was quite gone, and his breakfast went away almost untouched. He ought to have been back in Manchester days before this, but had been detained in London by the wretched police case. At first he thought of returning on this particular day. But he changed his plans; went forth to the telegraph-office, and apprised his people that business would detain him in London till the morrow, and then an hour or so later he jumped into a hansom and drove to the Quadrant, Regent's Park. It was a fatal step to take, and he must have been prompted thereto by his evil genius, while his good genius, for some inscrutable reason, remained dumb, and it may be—wept!

VII

THE FAITHFUL SLEUTH-HOUND

When Mrs. Neilsen read Vecquerary's name on the card that the servant handed to her, a little tremor of excitement thrilled her; and this displayed itself in her voice as she said to the servant, 'All right, Jane; I'll be down directly.' Then, when she was alone, she poured a quantity of eau-de-cologne on her handkerchief, and dabbed her forehead with it, as though she was under the impression that it was a sovereign remedy for disturbed nerves.

It was some minutes before she could proceed to finish her toilet, which she had only half completed when interrupted by the arrival of Mr. Vecquerary's card, and though she had told Jane that she would be 'down directly,' a full half-hour elapsed before she had put the finishing touches to her dressing and felt ready to go downstairs to see her visitor. It was evident that she had bestowed extra care in arraying herself, and she had dressed her pretty hair with scrupulous nicety, until it seemed as if not a single hair was out of place. With a final glance at herself in the wardrobe mirror she left the room, and when she entered the breakfast-room, where Mr. Vecquerary was seated, her heart was certainly beating faster than its normal rate, and there was heightened colour in her face. She was not altogether mistress of herself as she came into the presence of her visitor, who rose to greet her.

'Really, Mr. Vecquerary,' she stammered, 'I must apologize for having kept you so long, but I was engaged when the servant brought me your card.'

Of course, she did not say how she was engaged, and perhaps he did not even trouble to think. He feasted his eyes upon her as he took her soft, white hand, and for some moments felt like one under a spell. His attitude and his expression seemed to betray his thoughts, and they were: 'You are beautiful, and I am fascinated.'

'It is I who should apologize, Mrs. Neilsen, for taking the liberty to intrude myself upon you,' he began with a certain woebegoneness in his tone as he led her to a seat, artfully placing her with her face to the light, while he sat with his back to it, and he thus had her in full view; 'but the fact is, I—I have a sort of special object in coming here.'

'Indeed!' this with a pretty archness, as though she had not the remotest idea of the object that had induced him to call.

'Yes, though I don't know, I am sure, whether you will think my small matters justify this intrusion.'

'Don't say intrusion, Mr. Vecquerary,' she remarked sweetly, and then her face coloured as she felt that she ought not to have said that. It gave him courage, however, and he continued:

'It is very kind of you to say I don't intrude. That consoles me for a good deal. Since I had the pleasure of seeing you last I have had a very bitter experience.'

'I am sorry to hear that.'

There was genuine sympathy in her tone; but she was practising a little deceit, because, although she knew full well why he had come and to what he was referring, she affected to be ignorant of it.

'Yes, and I am sure that you will be surprised to hear that, for the first time in my life, I have figured in a police-court.'

'Really, you don't say so!' Here Mrs. Neilsen dropped her eyes, as though the little hypocrisy she was guilty of prevented her from looking him in the face.

His manner was that of eager earnestness as he braced himself for the recital.

'I am sorry to say, Mrs. Neilsen, that the cause of my disgrace was your own charming self.'

'Oh, Mr. Vecquerary, whatever do you mean?'

'Pray do not misunderstand me. Of course, you are entirely blameless. But you will remember the fellow who travelled up from Manchester with us, and who intruded himself upon you?'

'Yes; let me see, what is his name?'

'Hipcraft.'

'Ah, yes, I remember.'

'Well, in the smoking-room of my hotel, he dared to speak disrespectfully of you, and losing my temper I knocked him down.'

Mrs. Neilsen's face was scarlet and her eyes full of passionate fire as she ejaculated warmly:

'The wretch! What could he possibly say against me?'

'Nothing, I assure you, my dear Mrs. Neilsen; and in common honesty I should remark that what he did say was, perhaps, not very serious, and might have been best treated with contemptuous silence. But—but, I felt so deeply interested in you that, though you were all but a stranger to me, I felt impelled to champion you, and entirely losing my temper, I inflicted on the blackguard an undue amount of chastisement, and so have brought myself into trouble.'

'Oh, I am so sorry, Mr. Vecquerary. But how very good of you to take my part!'

'Are you really sorry?' he asked, leaning a little forward.

'Yes, indeed—indeed I am.' She spoke with genuine earnestness, and it almost seemed as if tears were gathering in her eyes.

Yielding to his weaker nature, and carried away by her manner and her beauty, he put forth his hand and laid it on hers, saying the while—

'To have your sympathy repays me for what I have gone through; and I would thrash the dog again tomorrow if he dared to utter a disparaging word against you in my presence.'

She withdrew her hand from his touch, and there was a warm glow in her cheeks.

'Oh, do let me beseech of you, Mr. Vecquerary, not to run any risk on my account; and for heaven's sake do not let my name be mixed up in any affair of the kind.'

'Pray don't agitate yourself, Mrs. Neilsen,' he answered, as he resumed his position, with some suspicion in his mind that he had been guilty of a liberty in touching her hand. 'I pledge you my honour as a gentleman,' he continued, 'that, so far as I am concerned, your name shall not escape my lips in any way that might tend to give you annoyance. But, tell me, are you cross became I championed you?'

'I think you showed the true spirit of a gentleman,' she replied with some fervour, 'but it pains me to know that you have suffered for your chivalry.'

'I care nothing for that,' he exclaimed, growing enthusiastic. I could not have suffered in a better cause. But do you guess now why I have come here?'

She hesitated before answering. Then gave utterance to a tiny white lie:

'I cannot exactly say that I do.'

'I will be candid, then. The affair has got into the papers, unfortunately, and as it appears there, I am made to look very black indeed, while the fellow Hipcraft is painted as a snaring saint. I could not bear the thought that you should receive your impressions from the newspaper report, should, unhappily, it chance to fall under your notice'—she did not tell him that she had already read the report—'I therefore resolved to come and ask you to hear my version of the shameful story. I hope I shall not seem guilty of anything like egotism if I venture to remark that I am generally considered to be a gentleman, and I humbly try to justify my reputation.'

'A reputation that, I am convinced, is fully deserved,' she remarked with earnestness.

'Thank you. I am truly desirous of earning your good opinion.'

'And, believe me, Mr. Vecquerary, you have it.'

'I cannot tell you,' he said, and seemingly struggling with his feelings, 'how it cheers me up to be assured from your own pretty lips that I stand well with you.' Mr. Vecquerary was perfectly conscious that in saying this he was saying that which he ought not to say, and he saw, too, for his eyes were fixed upon her in admiration, that his words brought the blushes to her face. But in the presence of this charming woman he did forget himself, and felt as if he could sacrifice all and everything for her sake.

Mrs. Neilsen seemed to understand the embarrassing position which her words and his own had placed them both in, and she hastened to try and undo what had been done.

'You see, Mr. Vecquerary, after all, we judge people in this world by their acts and deeds. And so I must judge you. You were exceedingly courteous and kind to me and my niece when as two unprotected women we travelled up from Manchester, and now, as I gather from what you tell me, you have been brought into an unpleasant position because an unmanly wretch spoke lightly of me. Therefore, although we shall probably never see each other again, I shall always remember you with gratitude and respect.'

He looked at her with some astonishment, for these words—'although we shall probably never see each other again'—stung him. He interpreted them as a delicate hint that she did not want to see him again, and his spirits drooped once more. With an impulse that he could not resist, he rose to his feet, and naturally she did the same. His handsome face was clouded with a sorrowful expression that was quite foreign to it, and standing before her and looking at her, although she did not meet his gaze, he spoke thus:

'Perhaps, as you say, Mrs. Neilsen, we shall never meet again. But this I can say honestly, I shall never forget you while I have power to think.'

She cast her eyes upwards at these words and met his, which had a pleading look in them. Her face was no longer red but pale, and it was evident from her heaving breast that she was agitated.

'You really flatter me, Mr. Vecquerary. What have I done to have made such an impression? I did not think that a poor little insignificant woman like myself had the power to attract the notice of anyone, much less a man like you.'

'You do yourself an injustice,' he said quickly. 'Nay, you are quite well aware that you are not a poor little insignificant woman.' He spoke with real sympathy, and almost involuntarily he put out his hand and took hers. For a moment or two she allowed it to remain in his. Then she withdrew it. It was manifest that he wanted to say something else. There was an awkward pause. He leaned towards her, and she played nervously with her chatelaine. Then in a lowered tone, a tone that was meant to be tender, he added—

'Before I go, Mrs. Neilsen, I must repeat that you have made a deep impression upon me. You are so charming that I—'

She glanced at him, as it seemed to him, in anger, and once more the colour leapt to her cheeks.

'Do you forget, sir,' she said, 'that when you first called upon me you expressed a hope that you might make my husband's acquaintance, and I told you he was abroad?'

Again she turned from him, and her emotion was unmistakable. Had he failed to notice the rebuke in her words, he would have been obtuse indeed. But he was only too conscious that she had rebuked him.

'Pray forgive me,' he said. 'I apologize for having forgotten myself. But, Mrs. Neilsen, I am a man of the world, and I flatter myself I can read signs—some sins, at any rate; and, unless I am singularly mistaken, you have some hidden sorrow. There is some unhappiness between you and your husband; and although I am almost an utter stranger to you, I would crave as an honourable man to be allowed to offer you my sympathy, to ask that I may try to prove myself worthy of your confidence, and to claim the privilege of tendering you the sympathy of an honest man for an honest woman.'

Mr. Vecquerary spoke with genuine sincerity, and at this moment with every regard for honour and truth. His nature was essentially sympathetic, and believing she had a sorrow, he was desirous of befriending her if she needed a friend. But just then he failed to see that he was treading on dangerous ground, and that her beauty had inflamed him. His words, winged with tender sympathy, as they were, found their way to her heart; and though she struggled hard to control herself, the struggle was ineffectual, and she gave way to tears.

'Now I have made you cry,' he cried, reproaching himself.

She laid her hand on his arm as an act signifying gratitude, and in tones of thankfulness she said, in a voice so sweet and low, albeit sad:

'I am very foolish to let you see my weakness. But my life has had some very dark shadows in it. You touch me, indeed, when you so nobly offer to befriend me: but you must not forget that the world does not tolerate a man in your position befriending a woman in mine.'

'What do you mean, Mrs. Neilsen?' he asked eagerly.

'My meaning is surely clear. You are a man, and should understand me.'

He turned from her with a sigh.

'Yes,' he said, 'I do understand you. Society erects barriers, and engraves thereon "Thus far and no farther." It is well that it should be so. And yet society cannot kill the natural sentiment of men and women's hearts. For me to seek to know your story from mere curiosity would be unpardonable impertinence; for me to seek to know it out of the excess of the real sympathy you have aroused within me will at least beget me your tolerance. We have met, and your image will abide with me. We part—I won't say forever, because I shall cherish a hope that Fate will be kind to me, and some day bring us together again. And so, not adieu, but au revoir.'

With a supreme effort she managed to say calmly:

'I do so thank you, Mr. Vecquerary, for your kindness. Au revoir.'

He noted that she repeated his words, au revoir. He raised her hand with the grace of a courtier to his lips, and kissed it, and without another word left the room. Then, when the door had closed, she sank down on the floor, and, bowing her head on a chair, she sobbed as if her heart had broken. And he, all unconscious of her grief, and with his head in a whirl, caught up his hat and umbrella from the rack in the hall, and letting himself out at the street door, hurried down the steps. Had he been less absorbed, he might have noticed a shabby-looking man who was slouching about on the opposite side. But he did not. In the next street was a cab rank. He walked there rapidly, hired a hansom, and drove off.

Then the shabby man went off also, and being more humble and more dependent than Mr. Vecquerary, he contented himself with a seat in a 'bus that was going citywards. This shabby man was not a pleasant creature to look at by any means. He was unmistakably a human ghoul. His face was cadaverous and pasty; his eyes were small and cunning; his habitual expression was one of greed, cruelty, cynicism, and craft; his clothes fitted him ill, and his shoes were down at

heels. His whole appearance, in fact, proclaimed with dumb eloquence that he found life a tremendous struggle; and yet he clung to life because he had not the courage to die.

The bus in which this shabby man was riding went along the Holborn Viaduct; and at the top of the Old Bailey the shabby man alighted, and proceeded on foot down the Old Bailey, and entered a building on the portal of which appeared the legend, 'Mr. Richard Hipcraft, solicitor.' This gentleman carried on his business under the very shadow of the grim, grey pile of Newgate, and almost immediately opposite the equally grim, black iron door, which in times past has so frequently opened to let some manacled wretch forth to be strangled there in the street while the bell of St. Sepulchre boomed 'death' in his ears. Such a scene as that is now happily a thing of the past, and the iron door is shut forever. In this region, where malefactors have so often looked their last on earth, and the yelling and execrations of foul and brutal mobs have rent the air, Mr. Hipcraft had for years carried on his business. The neighbourhood and the man seemed suited. His chambers were low-ceilinged, ill-lighted rooms, that reeked with the mould of ages. Up the rickety, greasy, dark stairway the shabby individual mounted, and tapped on a door in the dark landing.

'Come in,' called out someone; and the shabby individual entered into the den. Two or three dusty, mouldy clerks were perched on high stools.

'Is the guv'nor in?' queried the shabby one, with a sniffle.

'Yes,' growled one of the mouldy clerks.

So the shabby one tapped on an inner door, and a voice sung out, 'Come in,' and the tapper entered, and stood in the presence of Mr. Richard Hipcraft, whose arm was still in a sling, and whose head was still bandaged.

'Ah, Slark, my faithful sleuth-hound,' exclaimed the lawyer, as he saw who his visitor was, 'what news?'

'I followed him,' said Slark.

'Yes!'

'He went to her.'

'Yes.'

'And he was there nearly two hours.'

'Aha!' cried Mr. Hipcraft joyfully. 'I'm as good as a wizard. I knew he would go. I shall have him as sure as Fate. Now look here, Slark, shadow him, do you hear, till he leaves London. And mark you this, Slark; you must find out the past history of Mrs. Neilsen.'

'I'll do so if possible.'

'If possible, Slark! Nothing is impossible in that way to you, my good follow. Where is Vecquerary now?'

'He went off in a cab.'

'Alone?'

'Yes.'

'Get on his track again, and shadow him. Do you understand?'

'Yes.'

'Very well. You may go now. Come in tomorrow.'

The sleuth-hound retired. Then Mr. Hipcraft smiled—a nasty smile, that revealed his teeth, until he looked like a snarling hyena, and he muttered reflectively:

'He's a weak fool, that Vecquerary. He'll be snared to a certainty, and then he shall know what it is to have made an enemy of me.'

VIII

ERRORS, LIKE STRAWS, UPON THE SURFACE FLOW!

It has been hinted that Mr. Vecquerary's domestic life was not entirely free from friction. This friction, however, never reached a stage when it might have been looked upon as serious. To their friends the young couple seemed to be united by the bonds of truest affection, but Mrs. Vecquerary, who was at least five years her husband's junior, considered that she had a grievance, although, be it said to her credit, she did not shout forth this grievance from the housetop. She regarded it rather as a little private skeleton, that occasionally as an especial privilege she allowed some of her very, very intimate acquaintances to get a glimpse of. Her grievance was that she considered her husband spent too much of his time away from home. He left his home with almost, unvarying punctuality at ten o'clock in the morning, and was driven to his place of business in the city. He had a very neat little one-horse brougham for his own use; and his coachman was the nattiest of whips. Mrs. Vecquerary used a charming little pony phaeton, drawn by as perfect a pair of roan-coloured ponies as could be seen in Manchester. She and her children and their nursery governess used this conveyance a good deal, for the lady was fond of going out. And she rarely saw her husband after he left in the morning until seven in the evening—the dinner hour. And with the exception of one evening—Friday, when there was a formal dinner party, he left home again about half-past eight, and did not return until very late as a rule.

Indeed, it not infrequently happened that he came back in the small hours 'ayont the twal.' Now, his excuse for this was—an excuse that his wife generously admitted was not without some amount of validity—that he had so many engagements to keep. He was a popular man. He was an active and hard-working Freemason; he was a member of two of the best clubs in Cottonopolis. He was chairman of the Board of Directors of a working-man's society, and this Board held its meetings always at night. He was also a member of a crack whist club, which met once a week; and he took a great interest in a swell amateur theatrical society. Then again, as he was a cheery companion, could recite well, sing a capital song, and tell a good story, he was much sought after, and his engagements were numerous, for he moved amongst what was considered select circles. It must in common honesty be stated that Mr. Vecquerary was rather sensitive about taking his wife into these circles, as he considered that she lacked those necessary educational qualities which would have enabled her to do him credit. And so, while he denied her nothing that was calculated to add to her comfort and happiness at home, and imposed no restrictions as to the acquaintances she should make, feeling sure that she would not disgrace him in that respect, he liked to feel that he was a free lance in regard to the disposal of his time. And it was in this matter Mrs. Vecquerary found her grievance. She was in the habit of telling him that she might as well be without a husband as she got so very little of his society. He went to church with her on Sunday morning, and on an average, perhaps, of once a month he drove her and the children out after luncheon on Sunday. If he didn't go out on Sunday evening gentlemen friends dropped in, and their time was spent in the smoking-room.

This, in outline, is a sketch of Vecquerary's daily routine, and it will thus be seen that his wife's grievance was not entirely a groundless one. But there was another cause of the friction. The lady was essentially of a jealous disposition, and though she had no data to justify anything like actual suspicion, she did sometimes express her opinion to him that he found more pleasure in the company of other ladies than he did in that of his wife.

The Vecquerarys' residence was situated at Old Trafford, then one of the pleasantest of Manchester suburbs. The constant widening circle of bricks and mortar was as yet a considerable distance from this rural retreat, where many of Manchester's aristocracy had their dwellings. Old Trafford is close to the River Irwell, and at that time, if the wonderful undertaking of the Manchester Ship Canal was dreamed of at all, it was regarded as a very Utopian dream by all but enthusiasts. Vecquerary's house was known as 'The Cedars.' It was a mere fanciful name, however, for there were no cedars there. It was a pretentious house, standing in a considerable area of well laid-out grounds; and commanding from its back windows a very extensive panorama. On the one hand were the tall chimneys and dun pall of smoke which characterised Salford, but on the other the river glinted silvery in the sunlight, when there was any; and a very diversified landscape made up the picture.

It will be said that Mr. Vecquerary ought to have been a very happy man, for there was no reasonable thing that fortune had not given him. And he was happy, and might have continued so, had he not on that dark November day had as his travelling companions to London Mr. Hipcraft and Mrs. Neilsen and her niece. The day after Mr. Vecquerary had visited Mrs. Neilsen, and had been shadowed by Slark, who was a creature of Hipcraft's, he returned to Manchester, but he was no longer the same man that he was when he went away. Firstly, the disgrace he felt at having figured in a police-court affected him in a very marked manner. It was the first really dark shadow that had ever come into his life, and so morbidly sensitive did it make him that he actually fancied everyone was looking at him, and that whispers ran amongst the people, 'Ah, there is Vecquerary. That is the man who was brought up at Bow Street for an assault, and was fined ten pounds.' Secondly, although he did try to drive Mrs. Neilsen from his thoughts, he could not succeed. Her sweet face and gentle manner had fascinated him, and the hint of some Clark story in connection with her life had aroused his sympathies. When he left her and said au revoir it certainly was in his mind that he would see her again, although his inward monitor told him that he had no right to see her again. He tried to answer this admonition by arguing that he had a right, because it was the duty of every man to try and assuage the grief of his fellows. And so, by such false doctrine as in this case, men try to cheat themselves into a belief that they are doing right when they know perfectly well they are doing wrong.

There was one hope that Mr. Vecquerary cherished, and it was that he might be able to keep the knowledge of the disagreeable little London episode from coming to his wife. He did not reach Manchester until the evening, and as he went direct to his warehouse, where he was detained some little time, he did not arrive home until pretty late. Although it struck him that his wife failed to receive him with the same warmth and cordiality that she usually displayed after his return from a journey, she gave no indication that she knew anything about his London experience, and so his hopes rose. But these hopes were doomed to a sudden blight the next morning, when she said to him immediately after breakfast:

'Josiah, before you go out I must say something to you, for I am pained and distressed in a way that I have never been before.'

He guessed what was coming, and he felt like a man who is suddenly detected in an act of guilt. Irritated out of his usual suavity of manner, he exclaimed somewhat roughly:

'Well, what is it? You must be quick, for I am in a hurry; I have a great deal to do today.'

His wife looked at him sternly; and said, with a somewhat scornful curling of her lip:

'Perhaps if it were a certain lady in London who was talking to you you would not be in such a hurry.'

'What do you mean?'

'What do I mean! Surely, Josiah, you don't take me altogether for a fool. Two days ago, for the first time since our marriage, I blushed for you when I read in the newspapers of your disgraceful conduct in London.'

His countenance fell, and his hopes entirely died out; but, as he had not yet brought himself to that frame of mind when he might have admitted that he was entirely to blame, he felt that he stood in the position of an ill-used and misjudged man, and that being so, the last person in the world to cast a stone at him should be the wife of his bosom.

'Well, Emily,' he said, with a certain acidity of tone and a decisiveness of expression, 'if you are going to make unpleasantness on the strength of a shamefully one-sided report in a newspaper, it is a pity.'

'I am only going to ask you a plain question, Josiah,' she replied with dignity.

'Well, fire away,' he said irascibly; 'my time is up.'

'Oh, pray don't let me detain you,' she remarked with biting irony. 'My question will keep; but when you have more time to give to your wife I shall certainly require an explanation if you wish me to remain under your roof.'

'Well, what is your question?' he said in a somewhat milder tone.

'Who is the lady who seems to have been the cause of your quarrel—your disgraceful brawl in a public-house?'

This unfortunate remark stung Vecquerary as scarcely anything else could have done.

'You forget yourself, madam,' he retorted angrily. 'There was no disgraceful brawl in a public-house, as you are pleased to phrase it. But let me say that your phraseology is disgusting and insulting.'

'Indeed!'

'Yes. The "brawl," as you term it, took place in the smoking-room of a first-class hotel, which is not a public-house in the contemptuous sense in which you use the expression.'

'You are very choice about terms,' she replied. 'It was a brawl, nevertheless, although it took place in a first-class hotel. But my question remains unanswered. I want to know who the la—who the woman is who caused you to sink to the level of a pothouse brawler.'

Vecquerary's face became deep crimson, and for the first time since he had known her he flew into a passion with his wife and the mother of his children.

'You are a—you are a fool,' he exclaimed, checking himself, and using a milder epithet than he intended doing.

'I thank you.'

'I repeat it. You are a fool, or you would not have jumped to a conclusion on such flimsy evidence.'

'My evidence is the report in the newspapers,' she answered quietly.

'And I tell you, madam, the report is an infernal lie.'

'So it may be, sir, but it is on that report the public will judge you.'

'Let the public judge as they like. What the deuce do I care!'

'Perhaps you don't care, for a man who stoops to disgrace himself as you have done must needs be callous about himself, but I must remind you that I, at least, have some pride—'

'You!' he broke in with a scornful sneer. 'And pray what were you before I raised you to your present position?'

With calm, womanly dignity Mrs. Vecquerary replied to this:

'I was a poor and honest girl, sir, in your father's employ, and with a strong regard for truth and virtue. You deemed me good enough to make me your wife, and I have been an honest and faithful wife, and a good mother to your children. Therefore I am at least worthy of your respect. Are you answered?'

Never before did Mr. Vecquerary feel so contemptible, so mean, as he felt now. But his generous nature asserted itself as his wife rebuked him.

'Emily, forgive my hasty remark,' he cried, with very obvious distress. 'My remark was shameful, I confess it. I did, indeed, forget myself.'

'You did, indeed,' she returned caustically, for she could not suddenly forget that he had grossly insulted her.

'Do you forgive me?' he asked pleadingly.

She provoked him again by her reply to this.

'You have not yet told me who the woman is.'

'The lady, say,' he remarked correctively.

'Well, then, the lady, since you are a stickler for terms. So far, then, the report is correct when it says a lady was the cause of the quarrel?'

'Yes. But the lady was all but an utter stranger to me.'

'Why, then, did you deem it your duty to champion her in such a violent manner?' asked Mrs. Vecquerary quickly.

'Because the lady was a fellow-passenger with me from Manchester, as was also Hipcraft. I saw her then for the first time. In the smoking-room of the hotel the blackguard Hipcraft spoke disrespectfully of her, and insulted me.'

'The magistrate spoke of your conduct as blackguardly,' said Mrs. Vecquerary, causing her husband to wince. 'But why, pray, should you have so ill-used a man for speaking lightly of a woman—I beg your pardon, a lady—whom you had only seen once?'

'It is a man's duty to champion any woman who is grossly insulted,' he exclaimed.

'Is it, indeed? It strikes me, then, if you set yourself up as the chief and practical exponent of that doctrine, you will have no time for anything else, and, with the exception of Sundays and holidays, you will probably figure in a police-court every day in the year.'

'You had better keep your sarcasm to yourself. Now, have you done?'

'No, not quite. I want the name and address of the lady on whose behalf you have been acting the part of the gallant knight in the story.'

'You shall have both.' He suddenly checked himself and changed his mind, and added hotly: 'No, you shall not, for the good and sufficient reason that you have no right to demand them.'

'Very well, then. That being your opinion, I shall cease to be your wife except in name; for, though I was only a warehouse girl when you stooped to marry me, I have a high regard for my honour and dignity as Mrs. Vecquerary, and you shall not outrage them with impunity.'

She spoke with that true dignity that an honest woman who knows that she is being wronged can use with such crushing effect. And, having given emphatic expression to her feelings, Mrs. Vecquerary left the room, leaving her husband standing there bewildered, with the reflection that he had been thoroughly worsted in this, the first serious passage of arms with his wife. But he was in no mood then to acknowledge his defeat. His temper was up, and he left the house without going to the nursery to kiss his children, as was his unfailing wont.

Having begun the day badly, everything seemed to go wrong with him, and even his brother and partner deemed it his duty to give him a lecture. It can readily be understood how Mr. Vecquerary remained in a state of nervous effervescence the whole day, and when he returned to his home after midnight he was jaded and out of sorts. He was, therefore, ill prepared for the surprise that awaited him.

On going to the bedroom he was astonished to find that his wife was not in bed. This was strange, but it was soon explained by a letter which was addressed to him, and placed conspicuously on the dressing-table. With palpitating heart he tore open the envelope, and this is what he read:

'As I decline to remain your wife without your affection, and as you fail to treat me even with that respect which I as your wife have a right to look for, I feel that I am best consulting my own dignity and the future welfare of my children by no longer living under your roof. I return, therefore, to my mother's house, taking the children with me, and there I shall stay until you have learned that a wife's feelings and a wife's honour cannot be outraged with impunity. I am aware that I am taking a very serious step, but I am also aware that your conduct has been serious, not to say disgraceful. There is more in this London business than I wot of, and until you have cleared the mystery away, and given me an assurance that no one else shall usurp my place in your heart, our paths will run in different directions.'

Mr. Vecquerary was fairly staggered by the step his wife had taken. He had never before given her credit for so much spirit and determination. But her letter had an effect opposite to that she intended, and instead of softening him it hardened him. Crushing the letter in his hand with a certain fierceness, he muttered:

'So, madam, you set your back up against me, do you? Well, let it be so. You will come to your senses before I sue to you, I'll bet.'

IX

'WAS IT AN UNKIND FATE?'

Of course there will be diverse opinions as to whether Mrs. Vecquerary was justified in the course she took. She herself had spoken of it as 'a serious step,' and, indeed, it must ever be a serious step for a wife to leave her husband's protection. But in this instance it cannot but be admitted that the lady had received strong provocation; and being almost morbidly sensitive, as well as jealous, she felt that no other course was open to her. It was a hasty step, however, and her own mother thought so, and advised her to return, but Mrs. Vecquerary's frame of mind was indicated clearly, when, with passionate weeping, she exclaimed in reply:

'No, mother; I will not return until I am convinced that he is not carrying on an intrigue with this wretched woman in London, on whose account he has disgraced himself.'

On his part, Vecquerary, not being conscious of any serious guilt, considered that his wife had taken an extreme measure that nothing he had done or was likely to do could justify. And, in the arrogant sense of his own importance and authority, he resolved to read her a lesson. So he ordered his household in accordance with the change that had come about, and for many days he came and went and gave his wife no sign that he repented and wanted her back; and yet, as a truth, his heart was wrung at being parted from her and his children. But he considered that she was being punished, and was learning a lesson in sackcloth and ashes. So, though he spited himself, he maintained his stubbornness, and was miserable and unhappy accordingly.

And during these dark days Mr. Vecquerary, though all unconscious of it himself, was the subject of great attention on the part of Mr. Hipcraft. That gentleman, having a legal mind, felt that a man could not know too much about his enemy; and, therefore, he regarded it as part of his legal duty to learn Mr. Vecquerary's history, and, in order to better carry this out, he enlisted the services of Ephraim Slark, who for several years had been one of the most faithful curs in the lawyer's employ.

Mr. Hipcraft had long made it an unswerving rule for the conduct of his business that in every case in which he was engaged he should come to the fray armed with some particulars of the past history of his opponents. He was, therefore, often able to spring a mine upon these arrayed against him, and thus shatter their case to atoms. It was a knowledge of this characteristic on his part that made him feared as an antagonist.

In carrying out his peculiar system of legal warfare, which in plain words meant the blackening as much as possible the characters of those who were pitted against him, he found the services of Slark invaluable. Slark was a pure specimen of the genius sneak. Some wonderful instinct, guided by peculiar craft and cunning, enabled him to ferret out all sorts of buried secrets in connection with the lives of the people in whom his employer was interested. In his movements Slark was as noiseless as a tiger that, scenting prey, steals through the jungle on its track. When in pursuit of his prey, Slark had the appearance of being a dreamy, half-witted fellow. But woe betide anyone who was misled by that appearance. A basking crocodile on the banks of a tropical river could not prove more dangerous to an incautious traveller who ventured to sit on its head under the notion that it was a fallen tree. Thus Mr. Slark proved to be dangerous to those who were deceived by his seeming innocent exterior.

A day or two after Mr. Vecquerary's departure from London, Slark, the sleuth-hound, received a commission. His commission was this. He was to go down to Manchester and learn as much as he could about Vecquerary, for, as Hipcraft thought, though he did not say it, 'It is well to know something about him, for the fellow will commit himself with the woman Neilsen as sure as eggs, and that done, he shall find that he cannot hide his light under a bushel.'

It thus came to pass that the shabby man might have been seen prowling about certain parts of Manchester. But he began to think that for once his mission would be fruitless, for he found that the Vecquerarys stood in high repute, and 'Mr. Josiah' was regarded as a man of unblemished honour. But by-and-by Slark tracked his victim to Old Trafford; and whether the shabby spy possessed the knowledge of fern-seed, and was thus enabled to gain admission to households in a condition of invisibility or not, is scarcely worth discussing. But this much is certain, he was enabled to report to his master that Mr. Vecquerary since his return from London had had a serious difference with his wife, who, with the two children, was then living under her mother's roof.

'Ah, my friend Vecquerary!' exclaimed Hipcraft as he heard this, and rubbing his hands after the manner of a man who is well pleased with some good work done, 'That little item of intelligence goes into my black-book! And should it ever happen that I can again get my legal talons upon you, this knowledge gained may be of great service. It is at least one black spot on your white escutcheon.'

To be in ignorance of danger is to be without fear, and Vecquerary, having no knowledge that he was being shadowed, was not troubled about it, and some two weeks later he went to a Manchester jeweller, to whom he was well known, and bought an exquisite little necklet of real pearls, for which he paid a very considerable sum. The New Year had just come in, and so it may be thought that Vecquerary's intention was to present this pretty trinket as a peace-offering to his wife. But anyone who thinks so is mistaken. For without any indication of who the donor was he despatched it to London, addressed to Mrs. Neilsen. Yes, there was an indication—one that Mr. Vecquerary overlooked. The little case that held the necklet had stamped on the silk lining of the lid the name and address of the Manchester jeweller, and, of course, when Mrs. Neilsen received the present she was puzzled at first to guess who had sent it. She had friends in Manchester. But she did not think any of them were rich enough to buy such a thing as this; but, even if they were, there was not one surely who would have sent it anonymously. Then suddenly it flashed upon her that the giver was none other than Vecquerary, and she was troubled thereat. For some days she kept the trinket locked up in a drawer, where she had so many other secrets of her life. But at last she felt that she could keep this one as a secret no longer, and so one day she brought it out, and, dangling it before Muriel's eyes, said:

'What do you think of this, Muriel?'

With a rapturous, ecstatic expression of delight, the girl exclaimed:

'Oh, auntie, that is lovely'—of course she used the barbarism 'lovely' because she was a woman—'it's exquisite. Wherever did you get it?'

Muriel took the necklet. She examined it from every possible point of view; she tried it on and admired herself in the glass, and told her aunt that it just suited her complexion.

'But do tell me, auntie, who gave it to you?'

'Guess.'

'Oh, how can I possibly guess?'

'Well, it has come from somebody who lives in Manchester.'

'I know! Mr. Vecquerary!'

'Yes. Well, I expect it comes from him, although there wasn't a line with it.'

Muriel remained thoughtful for some moments. Then she said:

'Auntie, that man is desperately in love with you.'

'Tut, child, what nonsense you talk!'

'It is not nonsense, aunt. A man does not send a lady a present of that kind unless he is smitten with her.'

'Well, whether he is smitten or not, I don't intend to see him again, for I have given orders to the servants to tell him I am not at home should he call. And as for the necklet, I think I shall send it back.'

'Why, aunt, you would surely never do such a thing as that. Let's see how it looks on you.' And suiting the action to the words, she clasped it round her aunt's neck. 'Well, it just looks magnificent. Pearls, you know, always do suit you.'

Mrs. Neilsen glanced at herself in the glass, and smiled prettily as she said:

'Well, I must say it looks very nice.'

'Nice! Nice is not the word for it.'

'But still I don't think I ought to keep it,' urged the lady.

Muriel looked quite hurt, for she failed to see the incident in the same light in which her aunt saw it.

'I am sure you would be very silly to send it back,' she said. 'If Mr. Vecquerary chooses to give you such a thing as that, why should you not keep it?'

'Ah, dear,' sighed Mrs. Neilsen, kissing her niece's white forehead, 'there are reasons why I should not. But under the circumstances, seeing that Vecquerary has not declared himself the giver, I think I will keep it.'

'And wear it?' asked her niece in a tone of delight.

'Yes.'

And so for a time the matter dropped, and Mr. Vecquerary's name was no more mentioned.

A fortnight later Mrs. Neilsen, in the company of her niece and some friends, went to the Crystal Palace to see the pantomime. Mrs. Neilsen looked even more charming than usual, for she wore a bonnet of grey velvet trimmed with red, and a magnificent cloak edged with real blue fox fur. She was an artist in her dressing, and always displayed the greatest taste, both as regards colour and design. By request of her niece she had clasped her snowy throat with the pearl necklet, though it was only displayed when her cloak was opened at the neck.

Almost faultless in figure and face, and dressed with the greatest possible taste, Mrs. Neilsen attracted much attention. Women looked at her enviously, if critically, and men longingly. But she seemed to carry herself with an utter absence of self-consciousness, and though men's and women's eyes followed her movements she gave no sign that she knew she was being noticed.

The only gentleman in the company was a young man who was making advances to Muriel, and about whom something will have to be said in a little while, for he was destined to play no mean part in the strange story that we are gradually unfolding. After the performance in the theatre this gentleman took the ladies to one of the refreshment-rooms to give them a cup of tea before going home. They were a merry little party, for there were four ladies in all, and they seemed to thoroughly enjoy themselves. Presently two gentlemen entered the room. One was a handsome fellow, wearing an overcoat trimmed at the collar and cuffs. with fur, while his hands were clad in perfect-fitting kid gloves of canary colour. This gentleman seemed to be suddenly attracted by the laughter of Mrs. Neilsen's party, and, looking towards them, he gave a visible start.

'Excuse me a minute,' he said to his friend. 'Here are some people I know.' And going to the table where the ladies sat he raised his hat, put out his hand, and said: 'How do you do, Mrs. Neilsen?'

That lady turned quickly, with a little nervous tremor thrilling through her body, and beheld Mr. Vecquerary, and as she saw who the speaker was the colour fled from her face.

Was it an unkind fate that had thus brought this man and woman together again?

X

DRIFTING ON THE SILENT TIDE TOWARDS THE MAELSTROM

By Vecquerary's unlooked-for appearance, at such an inopportune moment, Mrs. Neilsen was quite thrown off her balance; and she showed by her manner that she was confused and agitated. Muriel was not slow to notice this, and she came to her aunt's rescue. She rose from her seat, put out her hand, saying the while:

'How do you do, Mr. Vecquerary?'

His eyes had been so filled with Mrs. Neilsen and the necklet she wore—for her cloak was thrown back, and her fair, white throat exposed, with his gift thereon—that for the moment he had failed to see that Muriel was one of the party.

'Ah, how do you do, Miss Woolsey?' he exclaimed heartily; and so they greeted each other. Then Muriel introduced him to the other ladies, and lastly to the gentleman, Mr. Oriel Verecourt.

This gentleman was, perhaps, four-and-twenty; a somewhat showy young man, but, still, with a manly bearing and dignity withal. He had a frank expression of face, and a fearless look in his eyes that begot confidence. His high-curling moustache did not hide the fact that he had a mouth of such perfectly even white teeth as to lead to a belief at first that they were artificial. But such was not the case. They were all his own, and were really something to be proud of. He was a well set-up, smart, handsome young fellow; and Muriel, or any other sensible girl, might well feel attracted towards him. But it was not only his physical attributes that were attractive, for he gave robust evidence of the fact that he did not belong to the 'la-de-da' school of young men, but had stuff in him that would enable him to accomplish almost anything he undertook. His grip of the hand was hearty, and his laugh was hearty—two good signs; and any man with half an eye would have said at once: 'That's a fine young fellow. There's go in him.' And so there was go in him. His father, who was dead, had been an East India Company's officer, and Oriel had wanted to walk in his footsteps. But the father objected, and got him into the diplomatic service. He soon gave evidence of the 'go' in him, and had been rapidly advanced; and in the fulness of time he expected to receive a valuable foreign appointment. In fact, he believed, and sometimes to his intimates jokingly expressed his belief, that he was 'an ambassador in embryo.'

He and Muriel had been acquainted about six months. They had met the previous summer on board the yacht of a mutual friend, who was taking a happy party on a cruise round Ireland, He had been very attentive to her during the trip, and when parting asked if he might be allowed to call upon her. She told him that he could call and see her aunt. This he did. Mrs. Neilsen was much struck with him, and gave him to understand that he would be welcome if he came again. For something like four months he called on an average once a week, and he had occasionally accompanied Mrs. Neilsen and her niece to places of entertainment. But though he seemed to delight in Muriel's company, he never breathed a syllable of love during the whole of the four months. After that period his visits became more frequent, and once he invited Mrs. Neilsen and Muriel down to see his mother and sister. They lived at Kew, and were people who prided themselves on their high respectability and good lineage. Miss Verecourt took to Muriel, and told Oriel that she thought she was a very nice girl. Perhaps he took his cue from this, for a fortnight later he said to Muriel:

'Miss Woolsey, my sister likes you very much, and my sister's brother likes you very much also.'

For the moment she did not quite catch his meaning, and exclaimed:

'Your sister's brother! To whom do you refer?'

'I am my sister's brother,' he answered, with a laugh.

Of course Muriel was a little confused, and thought that she had been very obtuse. But she told him that she felt very much flattered, and that she was always happy to know that her friends liked her. This was a little bit of that pardonable hypocrisy which a woman is entitled to use, and knows so well how to use to advantage when she has reason to believe a man is going to make a declaration.

'But I wish to be something more than your friend, Miss Muriel,' said Mr. Verecourt.

'I—I do not quite gather your meaning,' faltered pretty Muriel, still dissembling.

'I want to be your lover,' boldly exclaimed Mr. Verecourt, catching her hand, which she allowed him to retain. 'I am, in fact, your lover now, because I love you; but I want you to acknowledge me in that character.'

It was a somewhat unhackneyed way of declaring his love, and it pleased her. So she answered, of course, with downcast eyes and half-averted face—for that is the orthodox attitude into which all young ladies fall under such circumstances:

'You flatter me very much by deeming me worthy of your attention.'

'You estimate yourself too lightly,' was his response.

And so, after more bandying of passages of this kind, she confessed that she loved him. So they kissed each other, and 'auntie' was pleased to say subsequently that she approved of the love-making. The young people were thus made very happy; but up to the time that we find them at the Palace, Mr. Verecourt had not asked Muriel if she would be his wife.

By the time Mr. Vecquerary, Muriel, and Verecourt had said their say, Mrs. Neilsen was herself again; that is, she had so far recovered her presence of mind as to seem quite at ease. She questioned Vecquerary as to when he had come up, and how long he was going to stay; and he noticed that she gradually drew her cloak together, which he took to mean that she did not wish him to see that she was wearing the necklet. In fact, the expression of her eyes clearly indicated that that was her motive. He answered her questions; then she said:

'But I am keeping you from your friend. Pray don't let me detain you any longer.'

He took that remark to mean that she wanted to get rid of him, and he felt hurt, though why he should have felt hurt he could hardly have explained. Anyway, he was determined not to go.

'Oh, my friend is all right. But may I introduce him? He is a very good fellow.'

Mrs. Neilsen gave a half-reluctant consent; so Vecquerary brought forward his friend, and presented him as Mr. Philip Goldstein, of the firm of Goldstein and Henry, stockbrokers in the city of London.

Mr. Goldstein was a fine fellow, very gentlemanly and very jovial, so he soon won his way into the good graces of the ladies.

After some pleasant chat and a few harmless jokes, Vecquerary said:

'I think as we have met so opportunely we must dine together. I therefore move that we adjourn for dinner.'

'Oh, no,' exclaimed Mrs. Neilsen, again showing that agitation she had displayed when Vecquerary came up and spoke to her. 'Muriel and I must really get home.'

Muriel, who was fond of society and being out, gave her aunt away, as the saying is—of course, innocently and ingenuously enough—by saying quickly:

'Why, auntie dear, there is no occasion for us to hurry.'

'Hear, hear,' cried Mr. Vecquerary, with a jubilant chuckle.

Mrs. Neilsen reddened, but felt powerless, and as the other two gentlemen heartily supported the motion, and as the other ladies expressed no dissent, Mrs. Neilsen could not hold out, and Mr. Vecquerary carried his point, so a move was made for the dining-room.

While the gentlemen were discussing the menu the ladies retired to the toilet-room to straighten their hair and wash their hands. When they came back Mrs. Neilsen was carrying her heavy fur cloak on her arm, and Vecquerary gallantly hastened to relieve her of it. Then he noticed that the necklet was no longer round her neck. She had removed it, thereby betraying to him that she suspected or knew him to be the donor. Moved by the impulse of the moment he said sotto voce:

'I noted that you had a necklet on just now. You have not lost it, have you?'

He saw the colour mount to the very roots of her hair, and her confusion made him sorry that he had uttered the remark. Her only answer was the monosyllable:

'No.'

If she had had the slightest doubt before that he was the sender of the trinket, the doubt now was entirely removed. And a certain frigidity in her manner of uttering that 'No' made him feel rather uneasy, and he feared that she was angry. However, the subject was not referred to again then, and the dinner, which was admirable, put them in the best of humour, while the wine, which was of the best, tended to promote 'the feast of reason and the flow of soul.' They seemed indeed to be a singularly happy party to whom life was as a choice flower garden, full of sweet sights and odours. Alas! how often does the outward laughter but mock the aching heart! Two of the little company at least had their familiar skeleton which sat at the feast with them.

The dinner ended, the ladies rose, saying that it was time to be going, and as the hour for the closing of the Palace was drawing nigh, no opposition was offered by the gentlemen. So they filed out of the room in a little procession, and by some skilful and artful manoeuvring on his part Mr. Vecquerary managed to bring up the rear with Mrs. Neilsen. When they got down on to the platform they found it very crowded, and they had lost sight of their friends. Mrs. Neilsen was agitated, but Vecquerary said:

'Pray do not feel any concern. It's doubtful anyway if we could all have found seats together in one carriage. Our friends will wait for us at Ludgate Hill. Come, there are two seats here; let us get in.'

They had been moving as hurriedly as the pressure of the crowd would permit, and she had peered anxiously into every carriage they passed. But he in his heart hoped she would not find her friends then; nor did she, and yielding to his persuasion she got into the compartment he indicated, and he took his seat beside her.

As the train steamed slowly on its way citywards—slowly because it was a foggy night, and there were several other trains in front—he found opportunity to talk to her, so that what he said should not be overheard.

'I am so glad a lucky chance has given me this pleasure,' he said.

Why did he say 'lucky?' Did he really believe that the luck was good? It is highly probable he did not think anything at all about it. He found his pleasure in the immediate present, and this pretty woman blinded him, so that he could see nothing ahead—nothing of the dark shadows that must gather about him if he allowed himself to be lured by his charmer, who charmed not of her own free will, and who would have preferred to have avoided him.

She was at a loss how to answer him, and what she did say was this:

'It is strange we should meet so unexpectedly at the Palace; isn't it?'

'Yes.'

'Do you often go to the Palace?'

'No; but Goldstein and I have been doing business today, and by way of a little relaxation—and pour passer le temps—he suggested we should run out to the Palace. He must have been a sort of good angel to me.'

'Why?'

'Because his suggestion has given me the pleasure of your company.'

'But you must not think my company is a pleasure to you. Indeed, you must not see me any more.'

She spoke in very evident distress, and with no less evident earnestness.

'Can you be so cruel as to condemn me to misery?' he asked.

'But why should you want to see me?'

'Why? Because I—' He checked himself before the word that would have made him feel guilty even in his own eyesight had slipped from his lips. 'Because you talk so sensibly, and because I feel so deeply interested in you,' he added.

'It is very kind of you to say that; but you really know so little about me.'

'True; but I know this: I know that you have had some unhappiness, and you have awakened my sympathy.'

His words touched those springs of emotion that are always so near the surface in women who have suffered, and she had no words to reply. She could only gaze out with dimmed eyes through the blurred window-pane to the impenetrable darkness beyond, dreaming mayhap that that darkness prefigured the years that lay before her.

He knew intuitively that he had pained her by his somewhat thoughtless remark, and laying his hand on hers, that rested in her lap, he whispered into her ear:

'Poor little woman. How I wish that I could blot out of your memory every pang you have ever known.'

A woman who has had a sorrow yearns ever for sympathy, and to a man who satisfies that yearning she shows even against her will that she regards him with gratitude. To earn such a woman's gratitude is going a long way towards earning her love; and when a woman truly loves a man she's but as potter's clay in his hands.

Mr. Vecquerary's words threw Mrs. Neilsen off her guard, and in her gratitude she twined her fingers about his hand, and expressed the gratitude she felt by a silent pressure.

He knew then that from that moment the barriers of conventionality were swept away, and that she regarded him as her friend.

When they reached the city they rejoined their friends. The other ladies were escorted to their destinations; and as it happened that one lived at Kensington, where Mr. Goldstein also resided, that gentleman became her escort, and Mr. Verecourt and Mr. Vecquerary saw Muriel and her aunt home. While Muriel and her lover were taking leave of each other Vecquerary was enabled to have a few words with Mrs. Neilsen.

'May I come and see you tomorrow?' he asked.

'If you really desire to do so,' was her answer.

'You know I desire it,' he said. Then they shook hands and parted. As he wended his way back to his hotel his mind was busy with many thoughts. He knew that Mrs. Neilsen had, all unwittingly, as far as she was concerned, been the cause of his disgrace in London, of his separation from his wife and children; and yet he felt drawn towards her. She had won his sympathy without seeking it, and he wanted to make himself believe that the part he desired to play towards her was that of a good Samaritan, though a tiny voice that he could not stifle whispered to him to be careful, for he was playing with his fate.

XI

MRS. NEILSEN'S STORY

If he had ever studied Addison he might at that moment, when he was struggling with his better nature, have fittingly repeated the words:

> 'If we hope for what we are not likely to possess, we act and think in vain, and make life a greater dream and shadow than it really is.'

From a life of very substantial reality, and in which there was less than the average fret and wear, Mr. Vecquerary seemed to have passed into a dream and shadow. The one person of his dream was Mrs. Neilsen, and the shadow that environed him, and was deepening, had begun on that luckless night when he quarrelled with Mr. Hipcraft in the smoking-room of the Golden Star Hotel. If Vecquerary had not had a decided flaw of weakness in his character he would have risen equal to the position in which he now found himself, and he would have said in effect:

'I have been foolish; I have made an error. I must atone for my foolishness; I must repair the error. Only one woman in the world has any real claim upon me; that woman is the mother of my children—my wife. In honouring her I honour myself, and lay the foundations for an honourable future for my children. Between that woman and me a breach has occurred, but it is my bounden duty to repair it, and take her to my heart again with the old love, the old faith.'

He ought, in fact, to have kept before him, like a text for the ordering of his life, Goethe's beautiful lines:

'Like the star
That shines afar,
Without haste
And without rest;
Let each man wheel, with steady sway,
Round the task that rules the day,
And do his best.'

The truth is, however, he believed himself an injured man. He believed his wife was decidedly in the wrong, and that she had failed in that deferential respect for him which she ought to have had, and he believed, further, that in offering Mrs. Neilsen his sympathy, he was doing that which as a man and a gentleman he had a right to do. It was fatal obtuseness, though he could not see it; and thus on the morrow, when he had completed his business in the city, he once more wended his way to Mrs. Neilsen's residence. There was one thing that struck him as soon as ever she came into the room where he was waiting; and he would have been obtuse, indeed, had he not seen it; her face wore an unusual look of anxiety and trouble. He greeted her warmly, but it did occur to him that in her manner there was a certain reserve.

'I hope nothing is wrong,' he said, as he gazed into her clouded face.

'There is something wrong, Mr. Vecquerary,' she answered with that lady-like dignity she seemed so able to assume as occasion might require. 'After you left me last night I was exceedingly troubled, and could not help feeling that you had been very wicked in separating me from my friends as you did, though I blame myself for having allowed it.'

'Surely, Mrs. Neilsen, you are hyper-sensitive,' he remarked, with an attempt at a laugh.

'Perhaps I am,' she returned, 'but I value my good name beyond price.'

'Really, my dear lady, you do not suppose that I wish to jeopardize that good name,' said Mr. Vecquerary, with an air that was meant to be one of lofty virtue.

But her answer staggered him; brought him down from his height; knocked him off his perch, as it were.

'Have you forgotten, sir, that I told you I was a married woman?'

That is what she said, but he saw instantly its point. He did more, he felt it; for it stabbed him. Nevertheless, he tried to justify himself.

'You did tell me that, Mrs. Neilsen, but I am not so lacking in perception as not to see that there is something wrong, that there is a great sorrow in your young life, and I have hoped and dared to think it might be my privilege to offer you consolation; and perhaps even be the means of effecting a reconciliation.'

She broke into tears at these words, and yet her indignation—not altogether with him—gave her strength and fire.

'Never!' she exclaimed, with great nervous energy. 'Reconciliation is absolutely, absolutely impossible.'

'Why? Do tell me. Do make me your confidant. I will be a true friend to you.'

'You seem so kind, so generous and noble, that I feel as if I could not say no to your request. But do not press me. Respect my weakness and my sorrow. Leave me now, never to return; and believe me when I say that you will revive to some extent my dying faith in man, and I shall say that there is one honourable and true man at least in the world.'

Had he allowed the request and the words of this poor lady to weigh with him as he should have done, he would have respected the wish and have gone. But she estimated him at too high a value. He was not quite the man she thought he was.

'No,' he made answer, with great decisiveness. 'I will not leave you so long as I feel I may be of service.'

'Oh, yes, you must, indeed,' she pleaded, 'and you know you did very wrong to send me that necklet. I am going to give it to you back—'

'If you do,' he interrupted, 'I'll throw it in the fire, or scrunch it under my heel. No, Mrs. Neilsen, you misjudge me'—she did, indeed, but not quite in the sense that he meant—'I want to be your true and honourable friend.'

'God knows,' she moaned bitterly, 'I need a true and honourable friend.'

And, overcome by her feelings, she sobbed and covered her face with her handkerchief. A man under such circumstances as these would have needed to have been made of much sterner stuff, much less impressionable clay than Mr. Vecquerary was. At the sight of that pretty woman in tears his resolutions, if he had made any, were scattered to the winds; his wife and children were forgotten, and he proved himself to be but a very ordinary mortal. He moved his chair nearer to her until he was able to put his strong hands round her white delicate wrists, and gently uncovering her face he said, as he looked into her tear-blinded eyes:

'Poor dear little woman! My heart bleeds for you. I'll be your friend in spite of the world. And though it damns my immortal soul to say it, I love you.'

She gave a shudder, and uttered a little cry, and though she did make some feeble attempt to resist him, he drew her to him, and her fair head rested on his shoulder. After a time she said in broken tones:

'You have taken me captive, and made me your slave.'

'And the slave shall rule the master,' he answered, thinking, no doubt, that it was a very pretty and very apt reply.

She was a woman, and he had conquered her, and now that the barrier of reserve was cleared away she felt more free to talk to him. But she said this:

'You must not say you love me. I belong to another; and yet I hate that other, though the law has fettered me to him.'

'Tell me, do tell me, Sabena—I am going to call you Sabena now—all about this man.'

'He is a villain,' she exclaimed, with an emphasis of passion which corroborated her statement about hating him. 'And yet—my God! What a blind, mad fool I was!—I thought once that I loved him.'

'Ah! women do sometimes make mistakes,' remarked Vecquerary.

'Heaven knows they do,' Mrs. Neilsen returned, in a tone of despair.

'How long is it since you were married?'

'Seven years. Seven long years, and those years have taken all my youth away, and made me old before my time.'

'Tut!' exclaimed Vecquerary, with a laugh of derision. 'You are still young, and still beautiful enough to bring men to your feet.'

She appeared to take no notice of this flattery, but continued, with the air of a person whose whole thoughts were concentrated on her subject:

When I first met this man—this wretch, whom I have been compelled to acknowledge as my husband—I was as happy a girl as you could have met anywhere. I was then living with my people near York. My father was a country gentleman of considerable means, and both he and my mother were members of good old country families. They were very honourable and very proud, and particularly anxious that their children should occupy good social positions.'

'Were you the only child?'

'No. I am the youngest of three girls. And I have a brother, my junior, who is a lieutenant in the navy, and is with his ship in the Pacific.'

'Are your sisters living?'

'Yes.'

'And your parents?'

'My father is, but not my mother.'

Mrs. Neilsen's feelings overcame her again at this point, and she sobbed.

'Come, come,' said Vecquerary, tenderly and persuasively, 'don't give way like that.'

'I know it's stupid, but I cannot help it,' she said between her sobs. 'I am so unhappy; for all my people have cast me off. They couldn't have treated me worse if I had been the greatest of criminals.'

'Then, I suppose, you married against their wishes?'

'Yes.'

'Is Neilsen your right name, may I ask?'

'No. It was a name I took after my husband left me, for I did not want anyone to know where I was.'

'Will you tell me what your real name is?'

'It's Tortolini'—this after some hesitation.

'That's Italian, is it not?'

'Yes, my husband is an Italian.'

'How did you first become acquainted with him, then?'

'It was during the time I was in London on a visit to some friends. I had been to a party, and was introduced to him. From that day he never let me rest, and I suppose I must have become infatuated with him. Some months later he went down into Yorkshire to see my people; but they did not take to him, and subsequently my father forbade me to hold any further communication with him. On my asking "Why?" he said he was an adventurer. In spite of this I could not give him up. I thought my parents were stupidly prejudiced against him. It was my father's wish that I should marry my cousin, who was a captain in the army and heir to a large fortune. But I did not like him, and resolved at all hazards to have Tortolini. I was married to him secretly, and for six months kept the secret, living with my parents all the time. At last Tortolini got impatient and came to my father's house to claim me. There was a terrible scene. I shall never forget it as long as I live. I thought my father and mother would have gone mad. My father swore I should never darken his door again. I came up to London with my husband, and soon found that he was truly what my father had described him—an adventurer. He had one absorbing passion in life—gambling. He thought that I had money, or should be able to get it, and finding himself disappointed he became a devil. He sold my jewellery, my clothes; everything, in fact, that he could possibly convert into money. He treated me shamefully, and seemed to take a fiendish delight in telling me that he hated me. Oh, I was so miserable, so unhappy, for all my friends and relatives had cast me off. My husband's conduct became so outrageous at last, he subjected me to such degradation and cruelty, that I left him. He managed, however, to find me out, and said that though he hated me no one else should have me. He was, or professed to be, mad with jealousy, though I can solemnly declare, in the sight of heaven, I never gave him the slightest cause for it.'

'Then how did you get away from him at last?'

'He had contracted so many debts through his gambling propensities that he had to fly from the country. He told me that he was going to Italy to get some money, and would come back to me in a few months. But he left me in a state of absolute destitution, and, not knowing what to do, I went to an aunt of mine, who lived in London. She was a somewhat eccentric old woman, who had been a spinster all her life, but had adopted a child of whom she was passionately fond. My aunt wrote to my parents, but they were more indignant than ever, and said that I was rightly served. This annoyed my aunt, who showed me every kindness, and I stayed with her for three years, when she was seized with sudden illness. As her case was hopeless from the first she appointed me the guardian of her adopted child, who had always been taught to look upon me as her aunt. She provided for the girl handsomely, and she also left me a small fortune, to be strictly settled on me for life and to revert to her adopted daughter in the case of my predeceasing her.'

'Then I gather that the adopted daughter is Miss Woolsey?'

'Yes, that is so. After aunt's death I took the name of Neilsen, and Muriel and I have been inseparable. She is a dear girl, and has given me something to live for.'

'And have you never seen your husband since he left you?'

'Never. But I know that he has been in London, and has tried repeatedly to find me out; though so far he has not succeeded. I must tell you that Muriel knows nothing of my unhappy married life. She thinks that I am a widow, and I have been strong enough to keep my dark secret all to myself.'

'In future I will share it with you,' said Vecquerary, taking her hand and peering into her beautiful face, that was now so full of trouble and care. 'From this moment you shall not be able to say that you are friendless. I will champion you through evil and good report; come what may, I will be your friend.'

'How good you are!' she murmured sweetly. Then with an expression of the most painful solicitude, and in a pleading, earnest tone, she added, 'But, oh, Mr. Vecquerary, do not compromise my good name. Not for the world would I give my husband and my relatives the slightest justification for speaking evil of me, and you know how quick people are to say evil things about a woman situated as I am.'

'Yes, I know. But you must have no fear. Besides, you are your own mistress. You are not bound to study all the little nonentities who like to concern themselves more about other folks' business than they do about their own.'

This was a fallacious argument, and he knew it to be fallacious. And yet he did think, and did believe, that he was truly playing the part of a good Samaritan; but he did not pause to inquire whether the circumstances warranted him in assuming that rôle. What was clear was this: he had probed Mrs. Neilsen; he had dragged her sorrow to light; he had found out her weakness, found that she was yearning for sympathy; he had tendered it, and she had accepted, and now her future might be said to be in his keeping. It is well, perhaps, that the future is always veiled from mortal eyes; but in this case it would have been better if Vecquerary could have seen what lay before him. How much sorrow, how much suffering, how much agony of mind he might have avoided!

XII

TRULY, HUMAN NATURE IS A RIDDLE AND A MYSTERY!

For four months following that eventful afternoon when Mrs. Neilsen took Vecquerary into her confidence, and told him the cruel story of her married life, he spent far more of his time in London than he did in Manchester, and he was a constant visitor at the lady's house. To such an extent had he become infatuated that the continued absence of his wife and children gave him no concern. Mrs. Vecquerary had told him that until he knew how to treat her she would not return, and she kept her word; for he had made no advances towards a reconciliation, and she was stubborn. But the whole fact of the matter was, he did not want her to return; for while she kept away he was a free lance, and felt that he could do as he liked. During those four months a very strong friendship sprang up between Vecquerary and Oriel Verecourt, and they became very much attached to each other. As the saying is, Verecourt swore by him. He believed him to be a 'splendid fellow,' a man who was 'as clear as glass,' and one 'who was worth knowing.' Now, it is something in Vecquerary's favour that he was enabled to earn such high encomiums from a shrewd man like Verecourt, who did not readily take to people. He, like Muriel, was under the belief that Mrs. Neilsen was a widow, and that Vecquerary wished to make her his wife. One day Muriel said to her aunt:

'Auntie, dear, when does the wedding take place?'

'What wedding?' asked Mrs. Neilsen, as she turned a little pale.

'Why, yours; for of course you are going to become Mrs. Vecquerary.' The thoughtless girl laughed merrily, and was surprised to see that her aunt was very pale, and greatly agitated, and this led her to add, 'Why, aunt, whatever is the matter with you? Surely the discussion of your prospective marriage cannot be distasteful!'

'Muriel,' said Mrs. Neilsen sternly, 'never again under any circumstances mention such a thing as that. You have no business to come to any such conclusion. Between me and Mr. Vecquerary there is nothing but the purest and most disinterested of friendship, and marriage, as far as we are concerned, has not only never been thought of, but is absolutely impossible.'

Muriel's dark brown eyes opened to their fullest possible extent, and on her beautiful face was a concentrated expression of surprise.

'Absolutely impossible!' echoed the girl, as though she thought that her ears must have deceived her.

'Yes, absolutely impossible,' repeated Mrs. Neilsen, with greater emphasis and still more decisiveness. 'I admire Mr. Vecquerary, as a woman may admire a man who has shown her sympathy and kindness, and who is not commonplace, but brave, generous, and noble. So far the connection extends and no farther; and I repeat that you must never again speak of my probable marriage with Vecquerary.'

This little speech, it need scarcely be said, did not tend to lessen Muriel's surprise, though it did silence her for a time. But that evening she told her lover about it, and added this comment:

'Poor auntie must think I am very dull if I am going to take that in. Why, Vecquerary just worships the very ground she walks on; and I am as certain as I am of anything that she dotes upon him. Why should she want to make such a mystery about it, then? Surely it's not such a dreadful thing for a woman to marry a second time.'

Mr. Verecourt was puzzled as much as Muriel, for he had had the same impression that she had in regard to the connection between Vecquerary and Mrs. Neilsen. It is true his friend had never mentioned the subject of marriage to him. But there was nothing in that, for men do not talk of these things as women do.

Muriel's thoughtless, though perfectly excusable remarks, were the cause of much annoyance to Ms. Neilsen, so that she was led to speak to Vecquerary on the subject.

'The fact is, Josiah,' she said—she called him Josiah when they were alone, by his very special desire—'you must not come to the house so often; and you must act in a more circumspect way towards me, or we shall be talked about. It really is dreadful. I declare the very thought of my being the subject of scandal makes me quite ill.'

Vecquerary bit his lips with chagrin. He knew how upright and honourable she was, and that her honour and uprightness were being jeopardized by him. Still, he was so weak that he was powerless to resist her magnetic influence, and he answered, not altogether with absolute sincerity:

'Sabena, I cannot keep away from you. By heaven, I think I shall blow my brains out if we are to be separated!'

'Oh, Josiah!' she exclaimed with a shudder, 'Don't talk like that. I vow that if I thought you were so weak-minded as to have any serious notions of that kind my whole opinion of you would change.'

'Well, perhaps it's not the right thing to say,' he returned, feeling a little ashamed of himself; 'but I do absolutely feel that life without you would not be worth living.'

There was a certain earnestness in his pleading tone and manner that touched her deeply, so that a tremulous quiver passed through her lips. There was a rift in her breath, and tears gathered in her eyes. He noticed these signs, and he knew perfectly well why they arose; he knew that she, in her secret heart, loved him, but remembering how she was fettered, she felt the hopelessness of the love she bore. Yielding to an impulse that he ought to have checked, he threw his arms around her neck and kissed her sweet face, now so pitiful in its expression of bitter sorrow. And while he thus embraced her the door opened and Muriel appeared. Surprised and startled by the little love-scene that she had so unexpectedly intruded upon, she withdrew hastily before she had been observed. As she went upstairs to her own room she smiled curiously, and thought:

'Well, really, aunt must take me for a fool if she supposes she can blind me to the truth. Why, she is as madly in love with the fellow as ever she can be. Why, then, should she not marry him?'

Poor girl! She saw things only as they appeared. Her unsophisticated mind did not dream of deception, and that Mr. Vecquerary had a wife and children in Manchester. Nor had it ever flashed across her mind that her aunt, instead of being a widow, was a wife. No wonder, therefore, that she was more and more puzzled. No wonder that she was impressed with the idea that her aunt was treating her too much as a child in not making her more of a confidante.

When Mrs. Neilsen had recovered herself, she said in a distressful way:

'Oh, Josiah, you must leave me; you must go away and never come any more.'

'Why?'

'Because it's wrong for you to be here. You know that while he lives I can never be your wife.'

Vecquerary turned away towards the window to hide his face, which too clearly betrayed his feelings at that moment. Her words made him feel guilty, because even if the mysterious he was dead, Mrs. Vecquerary stood in the way. He was all-conscious, too, that he could make no answer to her, for he was too much under her spell to confess his error, and tell her the truth as regarded his own position, but still it was necessary to say something, and this is what he said:

'Well, dearest, we must wait, in the hope that Fate or chance will remove the barriers that are between us, and make us one. You know the old saying: All things come to those who wait.'

'Not always,' she answered sadly, and with a sigh. 'Proverbs usually do no more than express a problematic truth. A woman whose hopes have been blighted, and whose heart has been crushed in her youth, has little to hope for and little to expect in this world.'

'Tut, tut, you mustn't talk like that,' he said, trying to encourage her. 'I will never believe your heart is crushed, and you may depend upon it the future will compensate you for the bitterness of the past.'

'Ah, I am afraid not!' she sighed sceptically.

She cheered up after a time, and a little later Mr. Verecourt arrived. Then Muriel was sent for, and the four engaged in whist, and spent a pleasant evening.

A stranger entering then would never have thought that the handsome woman with the fair hair, which lay about her well-shaped head like bands of red gold, and whose voice rang clear and musical with laughter, had a 'crushed heart;' or that the equally handsome man, with the clear, frank blue eyes, was playing the part of a traitor to himself, to his good name, and to those whom be was pledged to honour and respect.

Truly, human nature is a riddle and a mystery!

XIII

SOWING THE WHIRLWIND

'Well, Slark, anything new?' asked Mr. Hipcraft in a preoccupied way, as that individual entered his sanctum one morning, with the noiseless tread of a cat.

'Not very much. I've been keeping my eye on Vecquerary lately.'

'Oh yes,' exclaimed Hipcraft, displaying awakening interest, and looking up from his desk. For some weeks he had been very busy in connection with two notorious forgers who were committed for trial. They were wealthy enough to engage quite an array of legal talent; and Hipcraft had been deputed by the leading counsel to gather up every scrap of evidence that would tell in favour of his clients, and to find as many flaws as possible in the prosecution. As it was just the sort of work he revelled in he had become very absorbed, and Vecquerary had been put out of his head. But his faithful creature had kept the trail with the persistence of the bloodhound.

'Well, and what about Vecquerary?' asked the lawyer.

'He's constantly at her house now.'

'Aha,' cried Hipcraft exultingly, and showing his yellow teeth as usual when he grinned with satisfaction.

'I knew the fool would fall into her trap. And what have you learned about her, Slark?'

'Little or nothing.'

'Little or nothing!' echoed his employer, elevating his shaggy eyebrows. 'That is not like my clever shadower.'

'The fact is, there is very little to be learned about her. She seems to be a very respectable woman.'

Mr. Hipcraft broke forth into a very unpleasant laugh—a laugh that was calculated to make one shudder on account of its cold-blooded cynicism. Did he think there were no respectable women in the world?

'A very respectable woman!' he repeated, with a horrid sneer. 'Well, well, things must be corning to a pretty pass when even the lynx-eyed Slark can be deceived.'

Without a muscle of his face moving, and in his cold, unemotional tones, Slark replied to this irony:

'No, I am not deceived. Mrs. Neilsen bears a high reputation in the neighbourhood, and I have not been able to learn anything against her.'

'Bah!' growled the lawyer, with a snap of his teeth like an angry animal. 'Respectable, forsooth! She is a dangerous devil, is that woman, and all the more dangerous because she is good-looking.' Then he added, as if to himself: 'She does not like me, and I don't like her.'

He dismissed his factotum, not exactly with a blessing, after he had discussed other business matters with him; and when Slark had left the room, Mr. Hipcraft seemed to be ill at ease, and troubled in his mind. He got up and walked to the window, chewing the end of a quill pen, and with his left hand thrust deep into his trousers-pocket. He stared abstractedly through the dust-coated pane to the grim prison, where the forgers he was working for were incarcerated pending their trial. But it was not of them he was thinking, as was made obvious by his muttered reflections.

'If she had given me a shadow of encouragement, I would have made up to her, and have married her. But I was not such an ass as not to be able to see that she snubbed me. Well, so much the worse for her, that's all. People who turn me into an enemy make an enemy of the wrong man.'

In thus expressing himself Mr. Hipcraft rendered it clear that he was absolutely a prey to the green-eyed monster; and yet that was most remarkable, for he had only called upon the lady once; that was when he went to return her scent-bottle. There is no doubt, however, that he had been very greatly struck by her when travelling up from Manchester. The strong probabilities are also that he had formed a wrong opinion about her; and when he called, and was treated with such cold and studied courtesy, he was surprised and annoyed. Mrs. Neilsen made it plain that she did not by any means consider herself flattered by his calling. But he could have had no serious intention then of making up to her, as he termed it, for he did not know at that time but what she was living with her husband; and his jealousy must have come about afterwards, when he learned that Vecquerary was being well received where he himself had been very decidedly snubbed. After all, vanity was probably at the bottom of this jealousy, for a man does not like to see another man succeed where he fails.

Mr. Hipcraft turned from the window full of a new-born intent, for he sat down hurriedly at his desk, and struck his bell.

'Has Slark gone?' he demanded of the clerk who came in obedience to the summons.

'He has just this minute gone out, sir, but he can't have got far.'

'Run after him, and bring him back.'

In a few minutes the shadower returned.

'Slark, I think you said that Mrs. Vecquerary was living apart from her husband?'

'Yes.'

'She is living with her mother?'

'Yes.'

'What is the mother's address?'

'Mrs. Turner, 25, Rood Street, Cheetham Hill, Manchester.' Slark read this address out from his note-book.

'That is all right, You can go.'

When he was alone again, Mr. Hipcraft laid a sheet of paper before him without any heading, and, dipping his pen in the ink, he busied himself for some little time with writing. Having finished, he read over what he had written; and evidently he thought it good, for his sallow face was wrinkled with that unpleasant smile of his—a smile that, being put into words, meant: 'Ah! Ah! Hipcraft, clever fellow, you've scored again.' Once more he struck his bell. Then to the clerk:

'Copy this letter into my private letter-book.'

'Yes, sir.'

Of course the clerk glanced over the letter as he took it away to copy, and this is what he read:

'Dear Madam,

'It is always exceedingly painful for any conscientious person to feel impelled to make a breach between man and wife, or widen one already made. But a sense of moral duty often necessitates our doing what in itself is repugnant to our feelings. That is my case in venturing to address you on a subject that is not less delicate than it is painful. Yet in the interest of yourself, your children, and even your husband, who is the sinner, I feel that you should no longer be kept in darkness and hoodwinked as you have been hoodwinked for a long time. I know your husband, but I regret to say that my acquaintance with him has not been of a nature to beget my esteem. I also know something of his domestic affairs; and my grief for your unhappy position is so keen that I cannot longer keep reticent, as I am sure that you are not aware to what an extent your husband has wronged and is still wronging you.

Some time ago he formed the acquaintance of a person—a female—in London, who seems to have exercised such a fascination over him, that he has become dead to every sense of moral right, as well as to the honour and good name of his family. With this woman—whose name is Sabena Neilsen, and whose address is 28, The Quadrant, Regent's Park—he has carried on a disgraceful intrigue, and much of his time is spent with her. Mrs. Neilsen poses, I believe, as a married woman; but whether she has any legitimate right to call herself a wife may be open to doubt. If she is, her guilt is the heavier; but whether or no, the result, as far as you are concerned, is the same. She has estranged his affections from you, and has made him completely forgetful alike of you, his children, and his own honour. Painful as this revelation must be to you—if it is a revelation—it is better that you should at once know the truth; for you may yet be able to cure your unfortunate husband of his madness, and save him from future shame and misery. Nay, I cannot help thinking that he may still be amenable to reason—the reasoning of his lawful wife—and that he will thus be brought to see the error of his ways, and by unwavering devotion in the future to you and his children, he may make atonement for his sin. That this may be the case is the earnest prayer of one who, while preferring to remain anonymous, may safely subscribe himself

'Your Well-Wisher.

'P.S.—Although I write anonymously, you can easily prove the entire truth of my statements.'

As the clerk finished reading, he muttered:

'Umph! The guv'nor's got his knife into somebody. Then, turning to a fellow clerk, he asked: 'I say, what was the name of that fellow that the old man had the row with? You know, he had him up before the Bow Street beak.'

'Do you mean Vecquerary?'

'Ah, yes; that's the name.'

'What do you want to know for?' asked clerk number two.

'Oh, nothing; just the satisfaction of my thoughts,' and clerk number one, being the confidential clerk, locked up the letter-book in the safe where it was kept, and then he carried the letter to his master. And that genial gentleman read it over again, without a single blush of shame mantling his cheek; on the contrary, he was evidently well pleased with himself; and having folded the letter up and put it into an envelope, he addressed it with his own hand and instructed the clerk to send the office-boy to post it at once. And the good Mr. Hipcraft dismissed Mrs. Neilsen and Mr. Vecquerary and Mrs. Vecquerary from his mind for the time being, and busied himself with the case of the swell forgers who were languishing in the gloomy prison across the road.

XIV

THE STORM BREAKS

One morning Mr. Vecquerary had finished his breakfast at his residence, Old Trafford, Manchester, and having read his correspondence, was glancing over the morning papers, preparatory to starting for the city, his brougham being already at the door. It was a bright, frosty morning, and the sun shone in a comparatively clear blue sky. The robins chirped merrily, and a few other birds trilled lustily in the branches of the trees, as if singing a jubilant pan of praise for the first breath of spring The sun's rays made nature glad, and seemed to beget cheerfulness in the heart of Mr. Vecquerary, for, as he tossed his paper on one side, sprang to his feet and shook his trousers down over his boots, he whistled blithely; and while he whistled, the door of his breakfast-room was suddenly thrown open, and a lady stood in the doorway—a lady stern, angry-looking, flushed with excitement—and that lady was Mr. Vecquerary's wife. In an instant Mr. Vecquerary's whistle was stopped—frozen, as it were, on his lips. His eyes indicated his wordless amazement; and the whole expression of his face told of a certain inward shrinking—that shrinking which comes from a knowledge that all is not well; of danger near; of a something going to happen.

'Emily, you here!' exclaimed Mr. Vecquerary, in a hollow, despairing sort of voice.

'Yes, I am here,' she answered with an intensity of bitterness that warned him of the coming storm. 'I suppose,' she added, you would rather have seen Satan himself than me?'

Such a remark as this could only have emanated from a woman who was smarting under a sense of outrage and cruel wrong.

'Well, really, madam, you seem to have a very good opinion of me,' he said cynically. 'If a man prefers rather to see the devil than his own wife she must have made herself peculiarly obnoxious to him.'

'Yes, unhappily for me, I am your wife, but you shall find that I am neither your slave nor your puppet.'

'Well, perhaps you will be good enough to come in and shut the door. I do not care about my servants' ears being filled with my domestic differences.'

'Oh, so you are ashamed of your servants knowing of your disgraceful conduct, are you?' sneered the lady vindictively. 'Well, it is something that you are capable of shame. I thought you had got past it.'

Mrs. Vecquerary advanced a step or two, but she did not close the door, and her husband crossed the room and did it himself.

'Pray don't give yourself so much trouble for nothing,' exclaimed the irate lady. 'Your misdeeds shall not be hidden, I assure you. Not only shall your servants, from the highest to the lowest, know of them, but Manchester shall ring with them.'

Mr. Vecquerary was growing very angry.

'Now, look here,' he said; 'what do you mean, and what have you come for?'

'I mean that I will thoroughly expose you; and I have come here to let you know that I am still your lawful wife.'

'In order to do that,' he retorted bitterly, I don't know that it is necessary that you should make a fool of yourself.'

'I have been a fool too long,' she cried with an outburst of passion, 'and I am going to let you see that I do not intend to be a fool any longer.'

'Very well then, fire away. I am glad to hear that you are coming to your senses.'

'You may find, my fine fellow, that I have more good sense than you give me credit for.'

'Now, look here, Emily,' said Vecquerary, with stern determination, 'I'm not going to waste time in wrangling and jangling with you. I have too much to do.'

'Indeed I suppose you wouldn't consider it a waste of time if I, instead of being your outraged wife, were a certain woman from London.'

'What do you mean?' he asked angrily, while the blood leaped into his face.

'You know what I mean, you deceitful wretch.'

'If you choose to talk in riddles, you will have to talk to yourself, for I am going,' he said.

'Stay. I have not quite done yet. Who is this wretched creature in London; this shameless thing, who has seduced you from the honourable allegiance you owe to your wife and children?'

'No wretched creature or shameless thing has exercised any such influence over me,' he answered scornfully.

'It is false, sir—a lie—a disgraceful lie,' shouted Mrs. Vecquerary, raising her voice to a high pitch of heated anger. 'You have been intriguing with a Mrs. Sabena Neilsen, of 28, The Quadrant, Regent's Park. Ah! you see, I am not quite so ignorant of the matter as you thought I was.'

Mr. Vecquerary's face was glowing red, and his eyes had taken on an altogether unnatural brilliancy. He was manifestly uneasy, and there was a certain nervous twitching about his mouth that was quite unusual with him; and, moreover, like most people who suddenly find themselves in a predicament of this kind, he did not seem to know how to bestow his hands.

First he thrust them into his trousers pockets, and rattled his loose money, then he drew them out and clasped them first in front of him, and then behind him, then he ran his fingers through his hair, and finally, he dived his hands again into his pockets. These various movements were infallible signs of the nervous agitation that he was suffering from.

'Let me tell you this, madam,' he began with set teeth. 'There has been no intriguing between me and Mrs. Sabena Neilsen.'

'You wicked, deceitful scoundrel!' cried his wife, almost foaming with rage. 'How can you possibly look me in the face and give utterance to such an abominable and scandalous falsehood? I suppose that this shamefaced creature, this Sabena Neilsen, is the woman for whose sake you committed such a cowardly assault on the lawyer, and got yourself forever disgraced by being exposed in a public police-court.'

Mr. Vecquerary's hair almost bristled as his wife thus poured out her vials of wrath on his head. It was evident that jealousy had stung her into an entire forgetfulness of her usual self-possession and quiet dignity. Jealousy had deprived her of the power to reason or to listen to reason. To give vent to her feelings, as well as her passion would allow her, and to let her husband know what she thought of him—that seemed to be her one ruling idea at that moment.

'Well, I tell you what it is, Emily,' said her husband, making a powerful effort to control himself, and to speak as if he were not disturbed. 'It seems to me that at the present moment you have lost your senses, and you are making a perfectly unjust accusation against me. It is true I am acquainted with a lady in London by the name of Neilsen; but I deny that I have intrigued with her—'

This inflamed Mrs. Vecquerary again, and she exclaimed:

'God forgive you for your utter disregard for the truth! But I tell you I am no longer to be hoodwinked. I have documentary evidence of your guilt, and I will make Manchester ring with your baseness.'

'Very well, do whatever you like, woman,' he snapped despairingly, and moving towards the door. But Mrs. Vecquerary caught his arm, holding him by the coat-sleeve:

'Oh, you are not going yet. I haven't quite done,' she hissed. 'I have something more to say.'

Unable longer to endure the scene, he swung his arm round to free it from her grasp, and in doing so, he unfortunately, and quite by accident, struck her a blow on the forehead. This was the culminating point in the unhappy difference between the husband and wife. Mrs. Vecquerary, who had already reached a white heat of excitement, now became hysterical, and she gave utterance to a shrill scream. The servants, who had been attracted into the passage by the altercation, here flung open the door, as that scream seemed to indicate that murder, or something near it, was being done.

'I am glad you have come,' cried Mrs. Vecquerary, who was deadly pale, save for her forehead, where there was a flaming red patch. 'I call upon you all to witness,' she went on, 'that my husband has struck me. Look at the marks of his cowardly blow,' and the excited woman pointed to the place on her forehead where there were only too evident signs of a blow having been struck.

Poor Mr. Vecquerary—for really he was to be pitied—was almost beside himself with shame, grief, and mortification. He found himself suddenly hurled from his pedestal of pride, and, so to speak, grovelling in the dust before his menials. In this instance all the appearances were against him. It was well known in his household that there had been a temporary breach between himself and his wife; and now the primâ-facie evidence was that he had really beaten her. But let it be written that, whatever his faults, he was far too brave a man to lay his hand on any woman save in the way of kindness, let alone his wife. But he rose somewhat to the occasion now. He was conscious that he must make an effort to clear himself from the unwarranted accusation, and addressing his wife in a tone that was half appeal, half command, he said:

'Emily, whatever your feelings are, be just at least. Unsay those cruel words. You know perfectly well that I did not strike you intentionally.'

'You did, you did,' she returned, and no doubt she was at that moment under the impression that she was strictly accurate in her assertion.

'It is absolutely false,' said Vecquerary sternly, and still addressing her and not the servants, 'absolutely and cruelly false. I wished to leave the room, when you seized me by the arm, and in wrenching myself free from you I unfortunately struck you, but it was a pure accident. In common fairness corroborate that in presence of the servants who have dared to take the liberty to intrude on our privacy.'

This made the servants feel ashamed of themselves, and they shrank back into the passage. But Mrs. Vecquerary's excited state prevented her from seeing that she had placed herself in a false and foolish position. Usually so full of good, sound common sense, she was now little better than a madwoman, and she defiantly repeated her assertion that her husband had purposely struck her. Unable longer to endure the painful scene, Mr. Vecquerary did what scorned to him then, in his distress of mind, the most dignified thing he could do—he walked away; he put on his coat and hat, and went out to his brougham, that stood at the door. But the cab which had brought Mrs. Vecquerary also stood there; and the foolish wife followed her husband and exclaimed:

'Don't think you will escape the results of your villainy in that way.' Then, turning to her cabman, she said: 'Cabman, this man is my husband, he has assaulted me. Look at my forehead. I call you as a witness that I bear the marks of his blow.'

It was altogether a pitiable and distressing scene; miserable exhibition, on the part of the unhappy lady, of loss of self-respect and self-control. Mr. Vecquerary could not trust himself to make any answer to her renewed accusation. It seemed as if the very blood was bubbling in his veins, and every nerve in his body was vibrating like a roughly struck harp-string; so he stepped into his brougham, and told his coachman to drive to the city. Mrs. Vecquerary intended to follow him, and gave the cabman instructions to that effect; but now that Mr. Vecquerary had gone the servants' tongues were freed, and the chambermaid, who had been a favourite and privileged servant with Mrs. Vecquerary, took the excited lady in hand. She talked soothingly and kindly to her, and sensibly pointed out that no possible good could come of any renewal of the quarrel in her husband's place of business. Mrs. Vecquerary yielded. And as the reaction from her tremendous excitement set in, she became absolutely prostrate, and was compelled to take some restorative and to lie down.

In the meantime, Mr. Vecquerary, full of the most gloomy thoughts and feelings, drove down to his warehouse; but it can be readily believed that after such a scene as that with his wife he was not in a fit condition to give any attention to his business. His brother Alfred noticed that something was wrong, and asked him what had put him out.

'I can't tell you now,' he answered. 'I have been terribly annoyed, and am fretted and harassed almost to death. But don't worry me with questions, there's a dear fellow, and you will have to do without me today; in fact, for several days.'

'That is unfortunate,' said Alfred, and much struck by his brother's agitated manner and pale face. 'You know how busy we are; and you have been away so much lately that we are getting quite in a muddle.'

'I cannot help it. For a few days you must do the best you can. After that I will stick to business.'

Alfred felt that it was undesirable to enter into any discussion then. Something had gone wrong with his brother, that was plain, but he would have to wait to know what it was, for Josiah was not inclined to satisfy his curiosity. So Alfred wisely held his peace. Presently Mr. Vecquerary called the warehouse porter and told him to fetch a cab and put his portmanteau in. He always kept a portmanteau at the warehouse, with a few spare things in readiness for hurried and unexpected journeys.

'Are you going out of town?' asked Alfred.

'Yes.'

'Where are you going to?'

'Oh, really, Alfred, there is no reason why I should tell you. Don't worry me with questions now. You see how irritated and nervous I am.'

'Well, I only asked so that I might know where to send your letters.'

'I don't want any letters. I want to get away from everything and everybody, even myself, for the next few days.'

Alfred was greatly distressed. He had never seen Josiah in such a strange mood before, and much he marvelled what it all meant. A few minutes later Mr. Vecquerary got into the cab, and told the cabman to drive to London Road Station, and arrived there, he took a ticket by the mid-day express for London. He had some project in his head, and he was also carrying his fate in his hands, while the shadows that hung about him were deepening.

XV

THE MAN IN THE BOX AT THE THEATRE

On reaching London Vecquerary drove straight to the Golden Star Hotel, which he still patronised, and singularly enough, as he alighted from the cab, who should be standing at the door of the hotel but Mr. Hipcraft. The lawyer was complacently smoking a cigar, and talking to a friend. Vecquerary bore in his face unmistakable tracts of an anxious mind. He was unusually pale; and so great had been the effects of the stormy interview with his wife that he was still agitated and confused. Hipcraft noticed this. He could not fail to notice it, and he thought to himself, 'Aha, the letter has done its work.'

Vecquerary—so absorbed was he—did not observe his enemy until he almost rubbed shoulders. Then he instinctively drew back, as he would have done from something very obnoxious. The lawyer smiled, and said tauntingly:

'Hello, how do you do, Vecquerary? You are not looking as well as usual. Something gone wrong, eh? Well, life's not all skittles and beer, even to a prosperous Manchester man. By the way, say something nice for me to Mrs. Neilsen. You will be seeing her, of course.'

Vecquerary had passed on, but at these words he turned with an angry flash in his eyes.

'You despicable cur!' he hissed savagely, 'I pounded you once when you insulted me. Take care, or I may horsewhip you the next time.'

'That is a distinct threat,' retorted Hipcraft coolly, 'and I call my friend here as a witness. The law grants protection to a threatened man. You shall hear again about this, Mr. Vecquerary.'

Vecquerary dare not trust himself to make any answer. His fingers were just itching to thrash the contemptible scoundrel who so far had got the better of him; but he wisely controlled himself, and without another word went to his room.

It can be easily conceived that this little incident did not tend to soothe his already greatly ruffled feelings. But by an effort he dismissed the objectionable Mr. Hipcraft from his mind, and allowed his thoughts to dwell upon Mrs. Neilsen. He had come up to London on purpose to see her—and, as he thought, and so far had determined, to see her for the last time. He could not, and did not attempt to, disguise from himself that it would be a tremendous wrench to break of the connection, but the terrible scene with his wife had opened his eyes and showed him the gulf that yawned in his path. To avoid that gulf he must turn from the course he had been pursuing.

The few short months that had elapsed since that luckless day when he first met the fair-haired little woman, as he travelled up from Manchester, had worked a marked change in his life, and now the culminating point seemed to have been reached with that interview with Mrs. Vecquerary. What was done could not be undone; but he could at least place himself in such a position for the future that his reputation from that day would be unassailable.

And so, full of these thoughts, he had journeyed to London, fully intending to tell Mrs. Neilsen what he ought to have told her at first—namely, that he was a husband and a father, and that henceforth he and she must see each other no more. His accidental meeting with Hipcraft on the steps of the hotel rather tended to add strength to the resolution, because he saw how he was laying himself and Mrs. Neilsen open to insult as long as the connection was continued.

Man's proposals, however, are very frequently influenced and determined by circumstances totally undreamt of and it proved so in Mr. Vecquerary's ease. When he arrived at Mrs. Neilsen's residence it was nearly seven, and within five or six minutes of his being announced the lady entered the room. She was dressed for going out, but instead of a bonnet she wore an exceedingly pretty opera cloak of white and gold, the hood being over her head, and adding picturesqueness to her sweet face. She seemed to be in unusually good spirits, and her face was dimpled with smiles.

'Well, Josiah, this is unexpected,' she exclaimed. 'I never thought of seeing you tonight. But how glum and miserable you look. Are you not well?'

'Oh, yes, I'm well enough in health; but—but have been greatly annoyed. However, I won't tell you now what has gone wrong, for I see you are going out.'

'Yes, we are all going to sec the pantomime at Drury Lane. We've got a box. Of course, you will come with us. There will be plenty of room, and we want another gentleman.'

'Who is going?'

'Muriel and Verecourt, of course, and Mrs. Shenstone. You remember you met Mrs. Shenstone at the Palace the night that you and your friend Goldstein were there, and we dined with you.'

'Oh, yes, I remember her,' answered Vecquerary somewhat absent-mindedly.

'How queer you are tonight, Josiah,' remarked Mrs. Neilsen, with the most ravishing little pout, as she noticed his abstracted air. 'Why, you are not yourself at all,' and she put her small, gloved hand on his shoulders, and looked up into his face with an expression of tender solicitude. Then the strong man became weak again.

Her light touch took his strength away as effectually as if she had bewitched him. His resolution vanished; he was oblivious of everything and everybody save her, and, throwing his arms round her, he strained her to his breast; and as he did so he noted that the pearl necklet he had given her was clasped about her neck.

'One moment of rapturous bliss is worth a world of pain,' he must have thought; and he resolved to put off telling her what had happened until some other time.

'I am all right now, Sabena,' he said. 'I live again in your presence—'

'Hush! You mustn't say that. That is the language of a lover, and you are not my lover—'

'Yes—'

'No, Josiah; *my friend*, but not my lover,' she returned, with decision of tone. 'It is hard, but it may not be. Perhaps those who are good and true will obtain in another world what is denied them in this.'

He was unable to make reply, because at that moment the door opened, and Muriel and Mrs. Shenstone entered. Muriel, who did not know he was in the house, was, of course, amazed.

'Well, this *is* a surprise. Has auntie told you we are going to the theatre?'

'Yes, and I am going with you.'

'Oh! I am so glad. You know Mrs. Shenstone, don't you?'

'Yes. I have had the pleasure of meeting the lady before,' and he shook Mrs. Shenstone's hand. She was a pretty woman, with dark eyes and hair, and a clear olive complexion. They were a trio, in fact, of charming women, and how very strong and very self-denying, indeed, Mr. Vecquerary would have had to be, had he decided not to make one of the merry party. Even good St. Anthony himself must have fallen under such circumstances, and have proved himself mere mortal clay.

'How are you going to the theatre?' he asked.

'We have ordered a brougham from a neighbouring livery-stable,' answered Mrs. Neilsen. 'It should be here by this. Mr. Verecourt is to meet us at the theatre. He had an engagement beforehand which prevented him coming here.'

In a few minutes the brougham was heard at the door.

Then the ladies drew their cloaks about them, and went down the steps, preceded by Vecquerary, who handed them into the carriage. He took his seat beside Mrs. Neilsen, and a casual observer would have envied him sitting there amidst the lace and frills of the three pretty women, who seemed to exhale perfume from their dainty dress. About thirty yards away a hansom cab was drawn up by the side of the pavement, and seated in the cab was Mr. Hipcraft, who had suddenly taken it into his head to follow Mr. Vecquerary from the hotel, with a view to prove whether he was right in supposing that Vecquerary's intention was to visit Mrs. Neilsen. And, having proved himself right, he chuckled as usual, and metaphorically patting himself on the head, he thought, 'What a clever devil you are, Hipcraft! I declare you've got the power of prescience.'

Having so far satisfied his curiosity, the cunning lawyer was going to drive away again when he noticed the brougham stop at the door, and naturally his curiosity was aroused to a very high pitch, and that curiosity turned to amazement, mingled with a sense of envy and jealousy, as he saw his enemy leading three ladies down the steps.

'Cabby, follow that brougham,' said Mr. Hipcraft, and of course the cabby did until it stopped at the door of Drury Lane Theatre. Then Hipcraft dismissed the cab and went into the theatre, and was just in time to see the people he was shadowing joined in the vestibule by Mr. Verecourt, whom, however, he did not know. He watched them go upstairs, and inquired of an attendant what part of the house they were going to, and was informed that the party had a private box.

As Mr. Hipcraft had learned all he could learn just then, and as he did not care about spending the evening at the theatre, he went back to the hotel to play billiards, and he warmly congratulated himself on being an exceedingly smart fellow.

The gloom that had shrouded Vecquerary's brow when he went to Mrs. Neilsen's house gave way to cheerfulness as he found himself sitting next to Mrs. Neilsen in the box. He forgot his troubles for the time, although he must have been conscious that he was only staving of the inevitable for a brief space. But the ladies and Verecourt were so lively, they seemed to so thoroughly enjoy themselves, that he would not have been the man he was had he not been infected with the laughter and lightness of heart which characterized his companions.

The theatre was crammed with a brilliant audience, and the music, the lights, the gay dresses, the flowers, the perfume, the dazzling scenes on the stage, made up a tout ensemble that to a person not absolutely blasé was as exhilarating as a draught of champagne. As far as Vecquerary was concerned, however, he did not seem to have eyes for anyone or anything but Mrs. Neilsen. He could not help thinking that she looked more charming than ever. Even a plain woman becomes passable when elegantly dressed; while a pretty woman is simply ravishing. But Mrs. Neilsen wore her clothes with a grace and ease that is frequently absent in women even of the better class. Moreover, she never gave one the idea that she was conscious of either being well dressed or fascinating. Some women are like peacocks. They strut and shake their feathers, and in every movement of their bodies seem to say: 'Behold me, am I not bewitching?' Mrs. Neilsen was not of that class. She was gifted with a natural modesty, and was utterly without obtrusiveness; and this could not fail to make her all the more charming.

In a box immediately opposite that occupied by Mrs. Neilsen's party were two men and a lady. One of the men was rather a handsome man, or rather, he had been so; but it was too obvious that he was a roué. Dissipation and recklessness were written in his face. He was dark to swarthiness, and his hair was absolutely black. He wore a heavy moustache, waxed and curled at the ends, but the rest of his face was clean shaved. His eyes were small, glittering, and dark, his nose thin and sharp. He was in evening dress, which fitted him well; and though he was rather a small man, he seemed to have a superbly knit figure. For a long time his attention had been concentrated on Mrs. Neilsen's box. His companions seemed to be absorbed in the performance; but the stage had no interest for him. Keeping well back, he watched the opposite box through a lorgnette, until it is certain that, had people not been so engaged with the performance, his conduct would scarcely have passed unnoticed, and he would have been voted excessively rude. At last, during the dénouement of the transformation scene, when the house was resplendent with light, which brought out every detail and pierced even the habitual shadows of the boxes, Mrs. Neilsen's eyes happened to wander to where the dark man stood in the opposite box, and she saw him. He must have realized that he was observed, for he drew suddenly back. Mrs. Neilsen gave a little involuntary cry as if from a spasm of pain, and with a nervous paroxysm she seized Mr. Vecquerary's arm. He alone heard that cry, for the others were bending over to get a better view of the dazzling scene on the stage, and were completely absorbed with what was going on.

'Sabena,' he whispered, 'whatever is the matter? Are you ill?'

'Oh, it's nothing,' she faltered, evidently in great distress, and pushing her chair right back into the deepest recess of the box until the man opposite could no longer see her. But he had disappeared in the shadows, and she could not see him. 'A sudden faintness has come upon me,' she added.

Vecquerary noticed how deathly pale she was, and felt quite alarmed.

'Let me take you out,' he said. 'The heat has affected you.'

'Yes, I think I will go out,' she answered. Then, bending forward, she whispered to her niece: 'Muriel, dear, I have come over quite faint, and am going out. Pray don't disturb yourself. It is nothing serious. The heat of the theatre has affected me, that is all.'

Muriel was rather alarmed, and wanted to accompany her aunt, who, however, would not hear of it: and so Mrs. Neilsen and Vecquerary went out into the passage together. She took his arm, and leaned on him.

'I am so sorry you are not well,' he said, with genuine sympathy. 'Can I get you anything? Will you have a glass of wine?'

'Yes, please. Get me a glass of sherry.'

There was a cushioned form in the passage, and on this she sat while he went to the refreshment-room for the sherry. A minute or so later the dark man, who had been watching her from his box, came along the passage, and approached her evidently with the intention of speaking. But the moment she caught sight of him she uttered a cry, and slipped from the form in a dead faint. The dark man paused for a single brief instant, then, changing his purpose, he hurried back again and disappeared. An attendant, who was standing on the landing leading to the stairs and just outside of the passage, heard the cry and rushed in to find Mrs. Neilsen on the floor. In a few moments Vecquerary returned with the sherry, and was greatly distressed to find Mrs. Neilsen unconscious. Other attendants were summoned, and means were taken to restore the lady; and these means were happily successful. As she expressed a wish to go home, Vecquerary informed her niece and the others, who decided not to remain any longer, and they all drove home together in the brougham.

Vecquerary displayed the greatest anxiety about Mrs. Neilsen, who seemed truly grateful; and, as she was still much agitated and upset, she stated her determination to go to bed, and she requested that, after her guests had partaken of supper, he would see Mrs. Shenstone home, which he consented to do, and as he wished Mrs. Neilsen good night, he said tenderly:

'I do hope you will be better soon. I shall come and see you in the morning.'

XVI

MR. VECQUERARY AND MRS. NEILSEN PART FOREVER

The next morning Mr. Vecquerary intended to go round to Regent's Park soon after breakfast to ascertain how Mrs. Neilsen was; but before he left his hotel the porter brought him a letter from her. She had evidently written it the night previous, after his departure, and had sent it to a pillar-box. He opened the letter in some trepidation, and this is what he read:

'You are a gentleman and a man of honour, and in the name of honour I ask—nay, demand—that you will not come here again. Remember, I am a defenceless woman, and it will be cowardly if you do not respect my wishes. But you are no coward, and, therefore, will do as I wish. We must, in fact, never meet again. I shall ever remember you with feelings of the warmest regard. You have brought some sunshine into my embittered life, and given me many happy hours since that memorable day when I was your fellow-passenger from Manchester. But all sweet dreams come abruptly to an end. My acquaintance with you has been a dream. It is over now, and I am a lonely woman again. But as I sit in the shadows that environ my life, I shall enjoy a certain bitter pleasure in recalling all the little incidents of the dream. You will be to me as the hero of a fairy tale is to a child. I shall think of you as possessing all the virtues and goodness and bravery that characterize a noble and dauntless man. In a little while I shall have become only a memory to you, and any blank that my severance from you may make in your heart will soon be filled by another and worthier person. As for myself, I must steadily keep my course until, in God's good time, I shall be released:

"From old heartache, and weariness and pain,
Sorrows that sigh, and hopes that soar in vain."

And now, dear friend—for friend I shall ever deem you—farewell. Do not fail to respect my wishes, as you value my good name and your own. Once again farewell.

Sabena.'

By the time Vecquerary had finished reading this pathetic letter his head was in a whirl, and his heart seemed swelling up with a wordless grief. His first impulse was to go off to Regent's Park at once, and try to solve the mystery. But he checked this, for had she not said, 'It will be cowardly if you do not respect my wishes?' In the face of that he could not go. His misery was now complete. He had come up from Manchester, feeling wretched and crushed. Then for a brief space he had had a spell of ecstasy, but it was only like a lurid gleam of sunshine that suddenly flashes out from a wrack-hidden sky, and then speedily fading leaves all darker than before. His domestic troubles seemed now to him to be painfully accentuated; and wrong as it was, and irrational, too, he experienced a sense of disgust with his wife; for had she not exposed him before his domestics? Had she not dragged him through the mud, as it were? And for a time, at least, his reputation was soiled and besmirched. His wounded pride smarted at the recollection of this as it had never smarted before.

It is impossible at times for us, for all of us, to avoid instituting comparisons between something we possess and something we should like to possess, and the comparison in such cases is always unfavourable to our possessions. So did Vecquerary now in his bitterness of heart place his wife and Mrs. Neilsen side by side before his mental gaze; and to him then, Mrs. Neilsen seemed immeasurably superior. But between him and her was an unbreakable barrier.

The Peri who sat at the gate of Paradise, with sorrowful eyes yearning for entrance to that forbidden region, was not more disconsolate than was Mr. Vecquerary, as he realized now that in a paroxysm of delirium he had been yearning for the impossible. Had he been all that Mrs. Neilsen deemed him to be, he would have roused himself to the occasion. He would have admitted his folly; he would have said, 'The man who yearns for the stars is a fool.' Then he would have gone to his wife, have freely confessed himself in the wrong, and sued for a reconciliation, and all might have been well. But he was not quite that man. His human frailties were in keeping with those of most men, and so his disappointment and grief got the better of his judgment. His temperament was essentially a nervous and excitable one, and such temperaments invariably seek to counteract their excitement by other excitement. Thus did this unfortunate man. He went into the city, where, as a Manchester merchant, representing a flourishing firm, he was well known. And gathering about him half a dozen bons camarades—convivial souls—he invited them to dine with him.

As far as he was concerned, the dinner was only an excuse for a frequent—too frequent—appeal to the chalice in which Lethe of a kind lurks. To drink delirium is, for a time at least, to deaden pangs. 'Tis true the remedy is more deadly than the disease; but men who suffer from the world's thorns are seldom good metaphysicians and know less of philosophy. They do not take as their motto, *Vincit qui se vincit*. So it came to pass that Mr. Vecquerary found a temporary oblivion. But he also found that the evening's enjoyment would not stand the morning's reflections. With a still greater sense of chagrin, mortification, and humiliation, he made all sorts of absurd resolutions. He would realize his share in the business. The breach between himself and his wife should never be closed. He would go abroad—to America, Australia, China, Central Africa; anywhere, in fact, so that he found distraction. His life was blighted, and the sooner it was ended the better. Such were his foolish thoughts; but, reader, blame him not too strongly, for hast thou not at some period of thy career had some such experience? We are all more or less spoilt children; and when we cry to wander unchecked in the gardens of the Hesperides, and find them closed to us, do we not fume and pout, and deem ourselves badly treated? Human nature is inherently weak, and he that can overcome that weakness is a man indeed!

For three days more did Mr. Vecquerary struggle with himself. Let it be clearly understood what is meant by this. He wanted to wrench himself away from the power that ever seemed tugging him towards Mrs. Neilsen's residence. But oh, it was so hard! The nectar had been tasted, and there was a passionate crying out for more. He tried to stifle the cry, but could not. Never to feel the pressure of her soft hand again; never again to hear her sweet musical voice, to see her beautiful face, almost Madonna-like in its shade of pensiveness, was a something he could not comprehend, could not grasp; a something that had a sort of stupefying effect. Of course this was infatuation. But what of that! Infatuation is ever hard to conquer. Certainly during these troubled days Mr. Vecquerary, the long-headed, shrewd Manchester man, was completely changed; and he felt disposed to sacrifice everything, even his hopes in this world and the world to come, for Mrs. Neilsen's sake. At length he himself yielded to himself. The struggle had worn him out, and he felt that, though Destruction yawned in his path, he must go to her again, to hear from her own lips the last farewell uttered. This decision arrived at, he was soon bowling along in a hansom to 28, The Quadrant, Regent's Park. But arrived there he was doomed to disappointment again.

'Mrs. Neilsen and Miss Muriel, sir, are out of town,' said the servant who opened the door to him.

'Out of town!'

'Yes, sir. They went away the day before yesterday.'

'Where have they gone to?' he asked with something like a sigh of despair.

'To Hastings, sir.'

'Have you their address?'

'Yes, sir, it's the Cliff Hotel.'

Mr. Vecquerary had nothing more to ask, and very little more to say. But still desperate and yielding to himself, when he got back to his hotel he procured a time-table, and found out the time that the next train went to Hastings, and when it did go he was a passenger by it.

He had at first thought of putting up at the Cliff Hotel; but he could not close his eyes to the fact that that would be a gross outrage on propriety. So he selected another house, and then sent by hand the following note to Mrs. Neilsen, with a request that she would return her reply by the same messenger:

> 'I have come here to see you for the last time. You must see me, if only for five minutes. Appoint a rendezvous, or something desperate will happen.—J.V.'

Poor Mrs. Neilsen was thunderstruck on receiving this note. It took her breath away, and tore open the wound again from which she had suffered. But she could not resist his passionate appeal. So she wrote:

'I will meet you at nine o'clock tonight on the beach, close to the pier. But remember, after that we part forever.'

It was a cold, blustering night, with a wintry wind lashing the sea into a sullen roar. The sky was filled with masses of broken clouds, and through the rifts the moon occasionally cast down rays of light, and threw a weird gleam over the tumbling sea. Such few pedestrians as were out were well clothed, for the bitter wind had the sting of the icy north in it. The shore and the pier, however, were deserted, for there was little to tempt ordinary people from the comforts of the fireside. But one veiled lady made her way towards the pier as the clocks of the town were striking nine. The lady was Mrs. Neilsen, and she was punctual to her tryst. When she arrived at the rendezvous she was joined almost immediately by a gentleman, clad in a heavy top-coat, trimmed with fur. The gentleman was Mr. Vecquerary.

'Josiah,' she said reproachfully—she still called him Josiah—'you ought not to have followed me. It is too cruel of you, after what I said in my letter.'

'Sabena, what does this mystery mean? Why have your feelings towards me so suddenly changed?'

'Do not probe me with questions. If you bear for me the friendship that you have always professed since unhappily we first became acquainted, go away and respect my wishes.'

'No. I will not leave you until you have told me why you have so suddenly changed. There is some mystery, and I am determined to solve it.'

He tried to draw her arm through his, but she resisted him, and there was a little struggle.

'You are unkind; you are cruel, to treat me like this,' she sobbed; 'and unless you respect my wishes I shall think you are not a gentleman.'

Vecquerary was astonished at this repulse—this rebuff.

'It is you who are unkind and cruel,' he exclaimed.

'Very well,' she returned, a little excitedly, 'you must think so. I cannot help it.'

'So be it,' he sighed. 'I have been living in a fool's paradise; but my dream is over, and now I care not what happens. The world is wide, and somewhere I may find forgetfulness.'

'Don't talk such nonsense,' she said, with an unmistakable reprimand in her tone. 'I am surprised that you should speak in such a way. Let us bow to the impossible, and not quarrel with our destiny.'

'I think I should quarrel with anything and anybody who stood between me and you,' he answered. 'But, since you will it, we will part. You must kiss me before I go.'

'No, I cannot.'

'Sabena, you must. One farewell kiss. It is all I ask.'

He tried to put his arm round her neck, but she struggled with him, and pushed him away. He was greatly excited. He walked a few paces from her, and then there was a sudden report and a flash of fire. With scarcely two seconds' interval they were followed by another report and flash. Mrs. Neilsen staggered. Vecquerary gave one wild leap and caught her in his arms.

'My God, you are shot!' he cried in agony.

As she sank against him, her life-blood pouring over his clothes, she faintly murmured, as the welling blood in her throat half strangled her:

'Oh, Josiah, why—why—have you done this? God forgive you!'

She slipped from his hands on to the sands, and the wind caught up her dying gasp, and bore it out over the sea to where the shadows were like a pall.

'Sabena, Sabena, speak to me,' he cried, with the madness of a terrible despair wrenching his heart and searing his brain. But his words fell on deaf ears; the dear lips would speak no more, for death had sealed them.

XVII

'THE ALARM BELL THAT WITH BRAZEN CLAMOURING PROCLAIMED SOME DIRE EVENT'

It is well known, not only in the medical profession, but to laymen, that a sudden mental shock produces a sort of paralysis of mind and nerves. That is to say, the nerves for the time are stunned out of feeling, and the mind is inert, much the same as when a naturally heavy sleeper is suddenly aroused from sound slumber; for a little while he is confused, bewildered. The brain does not follow with sufficient rapidity, so to speak, the quick transition from sleep to wakefulness.

These remarks are àpropos to Mr. Vecquerary's condition, as he saw with starting eyes poor Mrs. Neilsen sink down at his feet dead. He fell upon his knees and began to wildly chafe one of her hands, rather as if he were moved by some cunning mechanism than as if he were obeying the dictates of intelligence.

The grim tragedy on that wind-swept beach had not been without a witness, though that witness could only have seen the action of the whole thing worked out indistinctly in silhouette. The witness was the watchman on the pier. He had first of all observed the lady approach. His attention had been attracted to her, because it seemed somewhat strange for a lady to come to such a spot on such a night. The next thing the old man saw—for he was an old man—was that the lady had been joined by a gentleman. That seemed to argue that the meeting was nothing more than a lover's assignation; and, as later on was to be proved, the watchman on the pier would have taken no further notice had his interest not been aroused by a seeming struggle between the two, and by hearing heated words. He was thereby induced—actuated, no doubt, by the curiosity which is more or less strong in all human beings—to walk along the pier until he was almost over the spot where the man and woman stood. He could not see the figures on the beach in detail. The night was too dark for that, though he made out that the gentleman wore a large coat. Presently he saw the figures separate for a brief space. Then came a report and a flash, succeeded by another report and flash. The rest was like some disease-begotten dream to the old man. He was conscious that a tragedy had been enacted, that the man had shot the woman, who was dying or dead. The watchman confessed that, owing to the startling suddenness with which this knowledge came upon him, he was deprived of his usual presence of mind; for how long he could not tell.

Under such dread circumstances moments are gauged by a different measurement to that which applies in an ordinary case. But when something like his normal condition was regained he blew a shrill whistle that he always carried for emergencies, and rushing to the end of the pier he clanged the alarm-bell, that with brazen clamour proclaimed some dire event, though its tongue could not spell out M-U-R-D-E-R, and yet murder had been done.

The shrill blast of the whistle and the clanging bell galvanized Vecqueray into activity, and his first lucid thought was that of self-preservation; and though the bell, the shrieking wind, and the roaring sea seemed to be uttering a maranatha in unison, he turned and fled from that damned spot.

In a few minutes the unusual summons brought men from various parts. It might have meant fire, but no indication of fire was to be seen; and wreck was suggested—a fishing smack had probably crashed into the seaward end of the pier, driven by the fierce wind and angry waves. But when these men—fishermen, sailors, loafers—swarmed over the locked gates on to the pier, they met the affrighted old man coming towards them, his white hair streaming in the wind; and in answer to the united chorus of 'What is it? What's up, Dick? What's amiss now?' he raised his hands despairingly, and cried:

'My God, there's been murder done!'

'Where? Where? Where?'

'Down there, on th' sands. I saw it mysel'. A chap has shot a woman.'

With a thunder of heavily-booted feet, the crowd of men clattered along the wooden pier. Some swarmed over the railings, and clambered like monkeys down on to the sands by the iron supports; others went the proper way. And they found a woman lying there. One and all drew back with an instinctive dread, and not one touched her; but there was a confused murmur of many voices—voices of sympathy that mingled with the voices of the sea and the wind.

A policeman was soon on the spot, and his lantern revealed a ghastly sight. The once beautiful face of poor Mrs. Neilsen was now awful in its stony whiteness—a whiteness that was accentuated by the red blood that still flowed from a wound in the temple. Following the policeman came a doctor, fetched from a house near by. He stooped down, felt the pulse, put his hand on the region of the heart, touched her face, and then uttered the ominous words 'She's quite dead.' After a pause: 'Show your light here, policeman.' The light from the lantern was turned full on to the face, and a groan of pity broke from the throng, and the half-closed eyes of the dead woman seemed to appeal with pathetic and mute eloquence for vengeance on the cruel slayer who had cut her off so suddenly in her youth and beauty. Into the hole in the temple the doctor inserted his index finger, and then he muttered grimly: 'Umph! she's been shot.' The next thing the doctor did was to note in his pocket book the exact position of the body. Then, by aid of the lantern light, a search was made round about and, five or six yards from where the body lay, a revolver was picked up and taken charge of by the policeman.

A messenger had already been started off post-haste to the station for a stretcher, which now arrived, and on this the corpse was borne to the station, followed by the doctor, who, on his arrival, proceeded to make a more minute examination, aided by the police surgeon, who had been hastily summoned. That examination revealed the fact that the poor lady had been shot twice, and each wound was a mortal one The first bullet had struck the right temple, injuring the brain and lodging in the anterior portion of the skull. The second had entered the left breast, passed through the upper lobe of the lung, and lodged near the spinal column, from whence it was to be extracted later on. Both doctors expressed an opinion that, after receiving the wounds, the unfortunate lady might possibly have lived ten minutes, but probably did not live five.

When the body was searched for evidence of identity by the police authorities, it was soon made manifest who the victim was; and in her purse was found this note:

'I have come here to see you for the last time. You must see me, if only for five minutes. Appoint a rendezvous, or something desperate will happen.—

'J.V.'

The letter bore no date and no address, save 'Hastings.' Who was 'J.V.'? mentally asked each man who read that, for was it not the clearest possible piece of presumptive evidence that the writer of those lines had murdered the lady? Although there was no voice there to speak and reveal how the deed had been done, those whose duty it was to investigate the affair seemed to grasp the whole situation, and to learn the story by putting this and that together. The story, according to them, was common enough, and yet not without its romance. The victim was a young, good-looking woman; and her delicate white hands, small feet, and the quality of her clothing proved that she did not belong to the lower strata of society. She had had a lover in J. V.! She had quarrelled with him. His passionate appeal had induced her to meet him once again. They had failed to reconcile their differences, and the man had murdered her. This was the version according to the knowing ones; and it was but an oft-repeated incident in the history of human kind. But its repetition did not reduce it from the degree of murder—murder cold-blooded, cowardly, and cruel, and murder demanded that the law should avenge it, so the hounds were slipped to get upon the track of the slayer.

It was after eleven o'clock when a policeman entered the Cliff Hotel to make some inquiries about Mrs. Neilsen. Muriel had been in terrible distress of mind about her aunt. When Mrs. Neilsen was going out Muriel wanted to go with her, but her aunt said:

'No, dear, you cannot go. Amuse yourself till I come back. I shall not be away more than half an hour at the very outside.'

Mrs. Neilsen had not considered it prudent to mention that Vecquerary had followed her to Hastings, so that the girl knew nothing about the assignation. When an hour had passed Muriel began to think it was strange her aunt had not returned. In another half-hour she grew uneasy, and when two hours had elapsed she was in a state of great agitation. And as chance would have it she was with the landlady in a little parlour off the entrance-hall when the policeman entered. The landlady had been trying to soothe her by telling her that all was right. But Muriel had frightened herself into a condition of nervous feverishness, when the mind was capable of conceiving the most gloomy notions. She could not bring herself to think that her aunt would have remained away so long if something dreadful had not happened, and, as it proved, she was right. The policeman who had been entrusted with the delicate duty of making inquiries at the hotel was not the most fitting person who could have been chosen for the task. Addressing himself to the porter in the hall, he asked:

'Had you a Mrs. Neilsen staying here?'

Muriel, catching sound of the familiar name, rushed out of the room, and, seeing the policeman's uniform, a dread foreboding chilled her to the heart.

'Where is Mrs. Neilsen?' she asked, with a catching in the breath, such as is common in sudden fear.

'Well, miss,' answered the stupidly thoughtless policeman, 'she has been found dead on the beach, and it's supposed she's been murdered.'

Then there rang through the hotel a piercing scream of pitiable human agony, as Muriel reeled like one that had been stricken a cruel blow, as in fact she had. Her grief was terrible—so terrible that words could hardly describe it. All attempts to pacify her seemed unavailing; and no less so were the efforts that were made to obtain from her particulars about Mrs. Neilsen such as were requisite for the purposes of justice. Such alarming symptoms of hysteria did she display that a medical man was sent for, and he at once had her removed to bed, and he was emphatic in his injunctions that she was not to be asked questions about her aunt, for any augmentation of the dangerous excitement she was suffering from might be productive of brain-fever.

So far as the people of the hotel were able to give any information, Mrs. Neilsen and the young lady, 'Miss Muriel Woolsey,' were from London, and were aunt and niece. They had come down for a week or a fortnight, as the elder lady was not very well.

Of course, the police could not do much that night. They absolutely had no clue to the murderer beyond the vague one of the note asking for an assignation, and signed 'J. V.' The watchman of the pier could give no description of the man who had met the lady on the beach, beyond that he wore a big coat. The revolver that had been picked up near the body was found to be one of Smith and Wesson's, of Springfield, Mass., United States of America. It was loaded in four chambers, and the other two had been recently discharged. The bullet lodged in the back of the victim's head was quite easily cut out, as it was very near the surface, and it was found to correspond exactly with the bore of the revolver. It was, therefore, pretty conclusive evidence that the revolver was the weapon that had slain the poor lady, but whose was the hand that had pulled the trigger?

Such, then, was the extent of the information that was wired up to London by an enterprising newspaper reporter ever on the *qui vive* for 'copy.' But it was, in newspaper parlance, 'good copy,' and well merited the respective headings that were given to it by the various papers—'Strange Affair at Hastings,' 'Murder of a Lady at Hastings,' 'Lady Shot on the Beach at Hastings,' 'Dreadful Tragedy.'

XVIII

HATE

Mr. Richard Hipcraft was not, as a rule, a particularly early riser, because he was not a particularly early goer to bed. On the night that pretty Mrs. Neilsen was lying dead on the beach at Hastings, Mr. Hipcraft was supping with a select party of friends at the Holborn Restaurant in London. A merry party they were, and the wine they drank set loose the tongue of wit. When the lawyer retired to rest that night the small hours were well advanced, and when he arose, after a somewhat disturbed night, it was past the hour of ten. He was then, as his housekeeper was in the habit of describing him on such occasions, 'as grumpy as a bear with a sore head.' He complained of his coffee being cold, his toast being insufficiently buttered, his bacon being rusty, and his egg being ancient. He wound up with declaring that he was exceedingly feverish and unwell, owing to the 'beastly weather,' and he ordered the housekeeper to go round to Dr. Turner and ask him to call in as soon as possible.

'I know what is the matter with the old fool,' remarked the housekeeper to the small slavey who helped her in the kitchen. 'He did not come home till three o'clock. I heard him a-fumbling away with the latch-key for nearly half an hour afore he could open the door. But, says I to myself, says I, I ain't a-going to get out of my warm bed to let the old fool in. He just ought to be ashamed of hisself a-going on as he does. He ain't a young man now, though he tries to make folks believe he is, and if he don't mind what he's a-doing of he'll be getting a fit of happleplexy, or a-dropping down dead with ingestions in the stummick, the same as my poor old mother a-died on, and I wonder what he'll say then.'

The slavey looked seared and said:

'Lor, missus, what a hawful thing if master was for to go to do the like of that. Ingestions in the stummick must be hawful when they kills a person as sudding as that.'

All unconscious that he was the subject of his amiable domestics' criticism, Mr. Hipcraft pushed his breakfast away almost untasted; then he wheeled the couch up towards the cheerful fire, and with an extra cushion for his head, he adjusted his spectacles, opened out his Daily Telegraph, and lay back on the couch to read the news at his ease. The first thing that he turned to was the police column. The items about the police-courts necessarily had special interest for him. Presently he sat bolt upright, as if an electric current had passed through him. His face wore an expression of absorbed and eager interest, and he was evidently excited. The heading, 'Lady Shot on the Beach at Hastings,' had attracted him, and when he learned by the paper that the lady who had been murdered was Mrs. Neilsen, his excitement increased tenfold. The last lines of the half-column devoted to the sensational item of news said:

'Up to the hour of telegraphing, our correspondent says that the police had not succeeded in getting any clue to the perpetrator of this dastardly crime. But it is hoped that the note found in the lady's purse, and bearing the initials "J. V.," may be the means of unravelling the mystery and bringing the criminal to justice, for it is certain that a savage and brutal murder has been committed.'

Mr. Hipcraft flung the paper from him. His sallow face was now a study in its expression of fierce joy.

'Aha! Aha! My friend Vecquerary. So you've done it at last, have you? You couldn't shake her off, and you've shot her, and it's my privilege to be the Nemesis to hand you over to the bloodhounds of the law. Poor Mrs. Neilsen! Well, I'm sorry for her. She was a pretty woman, but weak.'

In his excitement he rang his bell violently, and when the old housekeeper hobbled in, he exclaimed:

'You needn't go to Dr. Turner's now. Bring me my shoes quick, and brush my hat, and get my gloves and coat ready.'

'I'm blessed if ever I seed anythink like it in all my born days!' mumbled the housekeeper, when she got out of her master's hearing. 'The old fool's evidently a-got the jumps. That's what's the matter with him.'

Ten minutes later Hipcraft was hurrying as fast as he could go to Great Scotland Yard. Arrived there, he sent in his card to the chief of the Criminal Investigation Department.

'And look here,' said he to the messenger, ask Mr. Blank to see me immediately, for my business is of the most urgent character.'

Hipcraft's name was well known at Scotland Yard, and his message procured him a speedy interview with the chief he sought.

'Has any arrest been made yet in connection with the Hastings tragedy?' he asked, with feverish eagerness, and fearful lest he should be balked in the inexpressible satisfaction he would feel in handing Vecquerary over as the murderer. Fate itself had given him a weapon wherewith to strike his enemy, and to be forestalled in the blow would be unbearable. He therefore hung, as the saying is, on Mr. Blank's answer.

'Up to nine o'clock,' said that gentleman, 'when we received a message from Hastings, no arrest had been made.'

Mr. Hipcraft could not suppress a chuckle of delight as he said:

'Then I can put you on the track. The J. V. stands for Josiah Vecquerary, of Vecquerary and Sons, Manchester. Vecquerary has carried on an intrigue with Mrs. Neilsen for some time. He is a married man with a family; and, in my mind, there is no doubt that he lured the poor lady to Hastings on purpose to murder her. I know he was in London, because I met him four or five days ago at the Golden Star Hotel, where he always stays when in London.'

These particulars were written down, as was also Mrs. Neilsen's London address, supplied by Hipcraft. Then with a sense of keen delight the lawyer took himself off, and hailing a cab, he drove to his office in the City.

Not long after Mr. Hipcraft had left the great criminal establishment, a detective called at the Golden Star Hotel, and learned that Mr. Vecquerary had gone away hurriedly the day previous without saying where he was going, which was very unusual for him. He had only taken a small hand-bag with him, as he said he would be back in a couple of days.

'Had anything strange been noticed about him?'

'Well, he seemed to have been depressed, as though he had something on his mind.'

A little later the wires were flashing to Hastings the name of the suspected man, and to the police at Manchester instructions to keep an eye on Vecquerary's place of residence and business, with other detailed instructions, all in cipher—which it would not be policy to publish here. For Scotland Yard does not like to have its mode of working in great criminal cases blazoned forth to the world for the mere gratification of curiosity, however natural it may be. Suffice it to say, the instructions were calculated to make Vecquerary's entry into Manchester, supposing he returned there, next to impossible without the police knowing. And should he already be there, his chance of leaving again would be reduced to an almost infinitesimal margin. In fact, if these instructions were strictly obeyed, as they were almost sure to be, the suspected man could neither telegraph nor write to his friends in Manchester without running the risk of having his communication intercepted.

Every hour of the day that was big with Vecquerary's fate increased the hue-and-cry, and the wires carried instructions to every seaport in the kingdom. A mid-day paper, which fattened on sensational news, gave a whole column to 'The Tragedy at Hastings,' and it was able to add:

'We understand that Mr. Richard Hipcraft, the well-known Old Bailey lawyer, had an interview this morning with Mr. Blank, head of the Criminal Investigation Department at Scotland Yard, and was able to supply him with valuable information, which renders it highly probable that before many hours have elapsed the suspected murderer will have been captured.'

Mr. Hipcraft read this. He read it with every manifestation of delight. He rubbed his thin hands; he grinned; he chuckled. He thrust his hands deep in his pockets and rattled his money and keys, as he stared through the dusty panes of his office window to the black and time-stained prison opposite, and no doubt he was thinking to himself:

'Ah, I should be much more satisfied if I knew that the fellow had been safely caged, and was locked up in the strongest cell over the way there. I always thought Vecquerary was a dangerous and murderous character. I believe he would have murdered me if he had got the chance.'

It was not a pleasant disposition to thus be able to find satisfaction in the sin and downfall of a fellow-man. But then Mr. Hipcraft's disposition was certainly far from pleasant. It was too revengeful, too cynical.

In the course of the afternoon Slark called, and was at once shown into his employer's room.

'Of course, you've heard the news, Slark?'

'You mean the murder of Mrs. Neilsen?'

'Yes,'

'Oh yes; I read the account this morning in the papers.'

'And what is your opinion?'

'Well, I think there is not a doubt that Vecquerary has murdered her.'

'There is not the shadow of a shade of doubt,' exclaimed Hipcraft gloatingly. But I should like to get to the bottom of the mystery. He was at Drury Lane Theatre with her a few nights ago. Now, look here, you take up the scent from there. Find out why she went to Hastings. The note found in her purse would seem to indicate that they had quarrelled. She went to Hastings to escape him. He followed, lured her to the beach and shot her. That, on the face of it, seems to be the whole story, and no man with half a grain of common-sense in his composition can doubt for a moment that Vecquerary's the murderer. It's a queer business altogether. But I'm not surprised. Vecquerary's just the man for a crime of that sort. He is as dangerous when aroused as an African savage.'

'Do you wish me, then, to interest myself in the case?' asked Slark.

'Yes. I want you to learn everything you possibly can about Vecquerary's movements for me. We know enough about him already to forge a powerful chain of circumstantial evidence. But there mustn't be a single weak link. The case against the fellow should be overwhelmingly strong. Trace his footsteps from the time he left Drury Lane with her, to the time he lured her on to the beach at Hastings and shot her. It can be done, and you are the man to do it.'

Slark made a slight inclination of the head by way of a bow, and he rubbed his greasy and napless hat as though he was a little confused—being a modest man—by his master's praise, and in a few minutes he took his departure to carry out that master's instructions.

XIX

DESPAIR

Let us follow the footsteps of Mr. Vecquerary from the moment when he fled from the scene of the terrible crime on the beach. The stormy night was in his favour, as so few people were abroad that his flight was not witnessed. He hurried along like a man whose mind was incapable of taking note of his surroundings, or where he was going to. A horrible, deadly fear had frozen his blood, and caused him to totter as if he had been seized with palsy. His destination was his lodgings—a small private hotel in the west end of the town. He had deemed it politic, in visiting Hastings specially to see Mrs. Neilsen, not to be there in his own name, and so he had given that of Walter Pennington.

He reached the hotel and passed to his room without being seen by anyone about the place. He turned the key in the door and threw himself across the bed and groaned with the agony he was suffering. At last the numbed brain seemed overcome with a sort of coma—no uncommon occurrence in cases of this kind—and for some two or three hours Vecquerary was oblivious of everything.

When he awoke it was the dead of night. The room was in total darkness. The house was silent as the grave. It took him some time to realize his position. Then he groped in the darkness for the matches, found them, and lit the gas. His face was of an ashen pallor; there were dark rims under the eyes, and he had a drawn, scared, bewildered look. And he was bewildered; he passed his hand over his brow as he leaned heavily against the mantelpiece.

'My God,' he moaned, in his distress, 'what does it all mean? What have I done? Am I mad, or am I the victim of some hideous delusion?'

He started, shuddered, looked nervously towards the door; covered his face with his hands, and acted like one who was suffering from cerebral excitement, the result of over-stimulation from alcohol. But it was not alcohol in his case; it was the effect of a tremendous nervous shock, acting on a nervous and excitable temperament. He next darted at his handbag and, with trembling fingers, opened it, and diving his hand in he found what he wanted. That was a flask of brandy. The flask held at least a quarter of a pint, and putting the bottle to his lips, he drained it of its contents at one draught. It was a powerful dose, and nearly choked him, but he recovered his breath, drank a little water, and then, divesting himself of his clothes—for he had not yet undressed—he got into bed, leaving the gas still burning.

The large dose of brandy acted like a narcotic, and he sank into a deep heavy sleep. It was after ten when he awoke. He was hollow-eyed and haggard. His lips were parched and cracked, his tongue was dried up. He drew aside the curtains from the window, and looked out on to the tumbling sea, and the grey, neutral sky. All wore an aspect of sadness and melancholy that accorded with his own frame of mind.

Slowly he dressed himself; pausing occasionally to stare blankly at nothing. As soon as he was ready—it was then eleven o'clock—he went downstairs. A smirking waiter was standing in the passage, and with an oily smile wished him good morning, and asked him if he would take breakfast.

'I don't want anything,' Vecquerary answered shortly. What time does the next train go to London?'

'Ten past one, sir.'

'Nothing before that?'

'No, sir. Are you going away today?'

'Yes. I shall go by that train.'

The strangeness in the visitor's manner could not fail to strike the waiter, but he said nothing more, and Vecquerary went out. He glanced about him nervously, and his face unmistakably indicated that he felt as if he was being hunted. He passed a shop door at which was a placard of a local newspaper, and in big, heavy type were the following lines:

'EXTRAORDINARY AFFAIR.
A LADY SHOT DEAD ON THE BEACH LAST NIGHT.'

He read the announcement, and walked on, but turned in a few minutes, and going into the shop, bought a paper. Thrusting it into his pocket, he went hurriedly down to the beach, where, opening out the paper, he read the long account that was given of the murder. The report wound up by saying: 'Up to the hour of our going to press the police have not succeeded in getting any clue to the perpetrator of this horrible crime. If he is still in the town, however, it is next to impossible for him to escape, and we hope to be able to announce his arrest in a later edition.' Vecquerary thrust the paper into his pocket again, and paced up and down the beach, stopping now and again to gaze out across the sepia-coloured sea, as if he was wondering whether there was any place far away beyond those tumbling waters where he could find rest, peace, and forgetfulness of the past. And then, with a sudden paroxysm of mental anguish, he pressed his hand to his head and moaned:

'Oh, my God, my God, I shall go mad! Can it be possible that Sabena is dead? She who was so beautiful, so good, so true! What is the hideous mystery? Can it be that I am really insane?'

He pulled out the paper again from his pocket and glanced over the report. There was no mistake in that, unless he was the victim of some remarkable delusion, and the paper he held was not a paper at all, and the report he thought he read was simply evolved from a diseased imagination. But, alas! the evidence of the truth of it all admitted of no doubt, and Mr. Vecquerary knew that the dear woman who had fascinated him was lying cold and dead, and he was a hunted man. Well might he have exclaimed then:

'He who throws the dice of destiny, though with a sportive and unthinking hand, must bide the issue, be it life or death.'

Truly he had thrown the dice of destiny, and what the issue would be he could not tell. In his then frame of mind—in his dire distress and mental anguish, that was like the torture of the damned—he could not think, save in a confused way. The events of the last few days seemed to revolve before him as a kaleidoscopic horror. He had been dreaming. Mrs. Neilsen had been a dream to him, but he was awake now; he had awakened to madness. In his distress he had but one clear idea—that was flight, flight if possible even from himself. In a little while he went back to his hotel, and was conscious of slinking, as it were, up to his room. It still wanted half an hour to the time of starting of the train. He rang the bell for the waiter, and told him to bring the bill and a glass of brandy. The waiter retired to execute the order, but before he could do so someone knocked on Vecquerary's door. He called out, 'Come in.' The door opened, and a detective officer and a stalwart policeman entered.

'Mr. Walter Pennington, I believe,' said the officer.

Vecquerary staggered back to a chest of drawers, and fell against it, supporting himself on his elbow. He was no longer Vecquerary of old, but a crushed, horrified, despairing man; and when he spoke his voice was hollow, blank, utterly without resonance: if one could imagine the dead speaking, it was such a voice as might be peculiar to a dead man.

'No,' he answered, 'I am not Walter Pennington.'

'I am aware of that,' replied the officer. 'You are Vecquerary.'

'Yes. I am Josiah Vecquerary, from Manchester.'

'Then, Josiah Vecquerary, I arrest you on a charge of murder.'

XX

LOVE

Oriel Verecourt was on his way to business from his home at Kew, when on opening his morning paper in the train he read of the murder of Mrs. Neilsen at Hastings. That very morning's post had brought him a long, loving letter from Muriel, written, of course, the day before, in which she reiterated for the thousandth time how precious he was to her. And as he thought then that Muriel was better than any other woman in the world, her letter filled him with joy unspeakable. The gushing sentiment and avowals of love between lovers may be very commonplace, and seem even foolish to us, whose fires of life burn low, and when we have only phantom memories to remind of our halcyon days; but to lovers love is ever new and sweet, and sentiment is its very essence. Love without sentiment would be like a plum-pudding without the plums in it. Oriel was very much in love with Muriel, and that love coloured and sweetened his life, and gave it the zest of romance. Now, as he read that terrible and startling item of news, he seemed for a moment to almost turn to stone; for quite apart from the relationship between the lady and Muriel, he had come to regard Mrs. Neilsen with very strong affection. Few people, in fact, knew her without coming to like her, for she had a sweetness of disposition and a womanly winsomeness that could hardly fail to endear her to her acquaintances.

When Mr. Verecourt read the account of the murder, and that a letter had been found in the dead lady's purse bearing the initials J. V., he came to the conclusion, as Mr. Hipcraft did, that the initials could stand for no other person than Josiah Vecquerary. It was a terrible thought, and one that caused a peculiar shrinking feeling of horror, mingled with a sense of indignation and anger.

As soon as he reached London Verecourt telegraphed to Muriel to say that he would go to Hastings in the course of the day. He was obliged, first of all, to present himself at his office, and urgent matters detained him there until after two o'clock, in spite of his anxiety and distress. But as soon as ever he could get clear he drove down to the station to catch the afternoon train, and as he went the newspaper boys were yelling out, 'Arrest of the supposed assassin of Mrs. Neilsen!' He bought a paper, and found a bare telegraphic statement that 'Josiah Vecquerary, the man who is supposed to have shot Mrs. Neilsen on the beach last night, has just been arrested in a hotel in the town.'

This was the second act in the tragic drama, and Verecourt would have been a strange man if his thoughts had not turned to the course that the third act might probably take. He did not know that Vecquerary had a wife and two children; but he did know that he occupied a good social position, and seemed to be a man who was endowed with some of the most prominent qualities of a true gentleman. That being so, the assumption was that he was not likely to yield to the fierce passions of human nature as readily as a man whose moral faculties had not been so well disciplined, and he must, therefore, have been led into the commission of this cruel and horrible crime by a sudden accession of fury that amounted to absolute madness.

This was the charitable reflection of Mr. Verecourt as he travelled to Hastings in a train that, though an express, seemed to him to jolt along with painful slowness.

As soon as he reached Hastings he jumped into a cab and drove to the Cliff Hotel. He was told that he could not see Miss Woolsey, for though she was a little calmer the doctor had left strict orders that she was not to be disturbed, and a nurse had been sent to take care of her. Under these circumstances Verecourt had no alternative but to call on the medical man, state in what relationship he stood to Muriel, and crave his permission to let him see her. The doctor was clearly of opinion that the presence of the girl's lover, so far from having an irritating effect, was calculated to soothe and comfort her, and so he said he would walk round to the hotel with him.

'Of course you were acquainted with the unfortunate Mrs. Neilsen?' he asked.

'Oh yes, I knew her very well.'

'I think, then, it is a matter of duty and necessity for you to go with me first to identify the body. The identity of the poor woman is almost beyond doubt; but still some legal confirmation is required.'

Verecourt felt it to be a duty, and so he went, painful as it was.

Poor Mrs. Neilsen! The suddenness of her death had left her features free from any expression of pain or anguish. But it was possible to imagine that her white face wore a pleading look—a look that seemed to say her last thought in life had been, 'Why have I, who am so young, so beautiful, so womanly, been mortally hurt in this way?'

Who shall say that some such thought as that did not flash through the brain in that supreme moment when the world was fading before the poor eyes as the shadow of death rapidly deepened? To say that Verecourt was affected would be mere commonplaceness. The marble face, with the ghastly wound in the temple, the half-open eyes, and the beautiful hair gathered like an aureole about the white forehead, would have affected a cynic and a stoic. And Verecourt was the exact opposite of a cynic; and though he might have exhibited stoicism under the infliction of personal pain to himself, he could not do so in the presence of this dead woman whom he had regarded with such warm affection. It was no weakness, therefore, nor mere sentiment, that caused tears to gather in his eyes.

When his identification of the dead lady had been officially recorded, and he had been questioned as to her relatives and friends, he was shown the things that had been found on her person, including the letter, which he could not hesitate to say was in Vecquerary's handwriting; for he had in the course of the acquaintance received several letters from Vecquerary, and knew his handwriting well. From Mrs. Neilsen's neck a pearl necklet had been taken, and Verecourt identified that as having been a gift to her from Vecquerary. He knew Vecquerary had given it, because Muriel had told him so.

As the doctor and Verecourt left the station the latter was very thoughtful and very sad. Presently he asked his companion:

'Do you think the man who has just been arrested—that is, Vecquerary—really killed Mrs. Neilsen?'

The doctor's face wore an expression that seemed capable of interpretation as 'What a very senseless and stupid question!' and he answered thus:

'Why, my dear sir, I do not think there can be a reasonable doubt about it. Of course he killed her. The circumstantial evidence even at this early stage is complete.'

'I confess,' remarked Verecourt, after a long pause, 'that I find the greatest possible difficulty in bringing myself to believe that Vecquerary did this. He has always struck me as a man who had such firm control over himself, who was so generous, so kind, that he would not hurt a worm, much less commit murder.'

'Ah, my dear sir!' exclaimed the doctor didactically, 'the human brain is a very complex piece of mechanism, and the line between sanity and insanity is more or less narrow. It is often difficult to say where the one ends and the other begins.'

'Then you think Vecquerary must have been insane when he did this deed?' asked Verecourt quickly.

'Well—there are degrees of insanity. A man in a sudden burst of fury may not have control of himself, and in that state commit murder. But the law would, I take it, nevertheless hold him guilty. In the case, of course, of a known lunatic it would be different. But a sane man, who in a passion of wrath—which may or may not be admitted to be madness—commits a crime, will certainly not be held irresponsible by the law. The difference in degree between a murder committed deliberately and in cold blood and one committed in the heat of passion may be very great, but it does not relieve the criminal from responsibility legally.'

Verecourt did not care to pursue the argument further. He was forced to admit in his own mind that the doctor's logic was unanswerable from the strictly legal point of view; for the law in effect says a man should keep his passions in check. Nevertheless, Verecourt could not bring himself to believe that his friend was guilty of deliberate murder. This was his frame of mind as he came into the presence of Muriel.

The poor girl looked pale, anxious, and scared. But she was mistress of herself now, for the paroxysm of hysteria had passed away, though there was a corresponding prostration. Her eyes were red with weeping, and her voice hoarse with sobbing. In spite of the doctor's presence she threw her arms round her lover's neck as an outward expression of the relief she felt that somebody she knew was with her at last. She wept passionately as she found a sanctuary, as it were, in his embrace; restraint over her grief was impossible under such circumstances, and he allowed her to weep for some little time, and then he placed her in a chair.

'Oh, Oriel,' she moaned out at last, 'this is terrible! I think I shall go mad. Poor dear auntie! And only to think she should have been killed by Vecquerary. Oh, how I do hate him!'

She shuddered with a sense of horror and repugnance, and clung to her lover's arm as if for protection.

Her knowledge that Vecquerary was suspected of the crime had only been gained a little while previously. All the day she had sobbed and moaned, and almost incessantly cried out, 'Oh, who can have done this? Is no one suspected? Have they not arrested anyone?'

At last the nurse, who had heard the people in the hotel say that Vecquerary had been arrested, told her charge, thinking to pacify her.

'Of course you know that Vecquerary has been caught?' Muriel asked of Oriel.

'Yes, I have heard of it,' he answered.

As the doctor felt that his presence was embarrassing now, he withdrew, and motioned to the nurse to follow him.

When the young couple were alone Muriel's grief found vent in a fresh outburst of weeping, and for a little time even her lover's influence seemed powerless to restore the balance of self-control. But presently she grew calmer, and though Oriel would have preferred that she kept silent or talked of something else, she insisted on discussing the tragedy, and she was singularly bitter when she spoke of Vecquerary.

'Had there been any quarrel between them?' asked Oriel.

'I don't know that there had been any actual quarrel, but ever since the night we were all at Drury Lane, auntie seemed to have become very strange, as though she had something on her mind. I know that the same night that we came from the theatre aunt wrote to Vecquerary, telling him that he mustn't come again. And her reason for visiting Hastings was to get rid of him, for she was afraid that, in spite of her letter, he would call.'

This was news to Oriel, and it certainly did seem to point very conclusively to Vecquerary as the criminal. And yet, when Verecourt reviewed his friend's acts and deeds—when he summed him up as he had known him during their short acquaintance—he could not bring himself to think that Vecquerary had deliberately murdered Mrs. Neilsen. He must either have gone mad when he did the deed, or he shot her by accident. This was a charitable view to take, but Oriel could not feel the bitterness of resentment that Muriel displayed, and though he did not tell her that he would do so, he resolved to endeavour to have an interview with the prisoner next day.

XXI

EPHRAIM SLARK, THE CHRISTIAN!

In pursuance of this resolve, Mr. Verecourt, having remained in Hastings all night, set to work early the next morning to obtain the necessary permission to see the accused man, and with the aid and influence of the doctor he was successful. He was perfectly startled at the change that had taken place in Vecquerary's appearance. He seemed to have become ten years older. His face had a blanched, haggard, woe-begone appearance. He burst into tears, and was shaken with a passion of grief as Oriel spoke to him.

'Thank God,' he said in hollow tones, 'that you have come. You will save me from madness; for I can declare to you solemnly, and in the name of the Almighty, that I am guiltless of this awful crime. I loved Mrs. Neilsen too well to kill her. She was killed in my presence, but who fired the shot I know not. It is all a mystery to me. I seem, in fact, as if I had gone through some horrible dream. I have very little recollection of what I did after I realized that the dear woman was dead. From then to the time they arrested me there is a sort of blank in my mind. I can recall nothing definitely. The suddenness of the awful deed, stunned me, I suppose. But my head is clear enough now, and I see that everything must point to me as the criminal. But, in God's name, I assert again I am not.

I have been guilty of much folly, but that folly did not prompt me to slay the woman I have adored. Verecourt, we have been friends, and may I hope that you are yet my friend? If you are, move heaven and earth to clear up this awful mystery. I am rich, and you need spare no expense; only prove me guiltless, for guiltless I am. Communicate with my friends in Manchester. I have relatives there. My brother is my partner; and I have also a wife and two children.'

This last piece of information startled Verecourt, for it was unexpected news to him, and its effect was to shake somewhat his faith in Vecquerary.

'If he could practise deception in one thing,' he thought, 'he would do it in another.'

But the prisoner renewed his passionate appeal and his solemn asseverations of innocence, so that Verecourt was in a conflict between doubt and belief.

The interview came to an end, and having promised to procure the best legal advice in the town, Mr. Verecourt took his leave with that conflict still raging in his mind. That day the inquest was opened, and the evidence that had been got together seemed to point conclusively to the prisoner's guilt. The letter that Mrs. Neilsen had written to him, beginning, 'You are a gentleman and a man of honour,' was produced, having been found in his pocket-book; and his short note to her was also read, in which he told her she must appoint a rendezvous or something desperate would happen.

That seemed on the face of it to be a black and damning piece of evidence. Then her answer to him, which was also found in his pocket-book, was read:

'I will meet you at nine o'clock tonight on the beach, close by the pier. But, remember, after that we part forever.'

This again appeared strongly corroborative of the prisoner's guilt; for what it seemed to point to was that the man and woman had been guilty of an intrigue; she was desirous for some reason or other of breaking it off, and at his pressing solicitation had given him a final interview, but told him that after that they must part forever. Although no human ears heard what passed between the two on that fatal night, people asked each other, 'Can anyone doubt for a moment that the poor woman was inflexible in her determination not to see him again, and so the villain shot her?'

Another solid link in the chain of evidence was the revolver that had been picked up on the beach close to the body. It was of American make, and bore the name of the makers, Smith and Wesson, of Massachusetts. It was nickel-plated, with rifled barrel, and of a somewhat unusual bore, being 38° calibre. Engraved on a small medallion-shaped plate let into the stock of the pistol were the initials 'S. W.' The production of this weapon overwhelmed the accused with amazement, and he declared through his solicitor that he had never before set his eyes on it. As the evidence was not completed that day, the inquest was adjourned for two days, and when the court reassembled a man appeared and tendered himself as a witness. He gave his name as Ephraim Slark. Asked if he was a Jew, be answered no—he was a Christian, and at this assertion there must surely have been some of the listeners in the court who blushed for Christianity.

Asked what his business was, this Christian said he was 'a private inquiry agent in the service of Mr. Hipcraft, solicitor, of London.'

The evidence of Mr. Ephraim Slark, Christian, tended to very materially strengthen the links that were being forged around the accused. He was able to tell the coroner and jury that Vecquerary had carried on 'an intrigue' for some time with the deceased. This had been brought under the notice of Mrs. Vecquerary, the prisoner's wife, and had led to a very painful scene, indeed, during which he struck his wife. That very day he journeyed up to London from Manchester, and in the evening took Mrs. Neilsen to the theatre, when there was reason to believe they quarrelled; for they were seen alone in the vestibule of the theatre, and the lady went into a swoon. That night, after she returned home, Mrs. Neilsen wrote to him, and went out herself at two o'clock in the morning to put the letter into a pillar-box in the next street. The letter that she wrote had been read in court. The rest was clear. He had followed her down to Hastings and shot her. The Christian Mr. Slark had something else to add. The accused was a very violent-tempered man. Some months before he had committed a violent assault on Mr. Hipcraft, and had been summoned at Bow Street, where he had been heavily fined. The attack on his wife was also evidence of his violence; and on the very day that he took Mrs. Neilsen to the theatre he threatened to thrash Mr. Hipcraft, whom he casually met in the Golden Star Hotel.

When Slark retired it was generally felt in the court that he had woven a strand in the rope that was to hang Vecquerary.

Mr. Slark was succeeded by another witness, Mr. Alfred Vecquerary, a young, handsome, intelligent man, who, while compelled sorrowfully to confirm that part of the evidence which told of the quarrel between his brother and his wife, that quarrel being the result of a cowardly and anonymous letter, was able to state emphatically that his brother did not strike his wife. The blow was an accidental one. It was true that in the heat of passion Mrs. Vecquerary had accused her husband before his servants and a cabman, who had brought her to the house, of having struck her. She had since admitted that it was an accident, and she would have been present that day in the court but that the news of the awful charge against her unfortunate husband had prostrated her with dangerous illness. And Alfred added that, so far from his brother being passionate or violent, he had all his life been a gentle, considerate, generous man, to whose nature violence was foreign.

Alfred's quiet, gentlemanly demeanour and obvious candour won him many sympathizers, but it was felt his evidence was naturally biased and could not counteract that of Ephraim Slark.

Then, when it was proved that Vecquerary had come to Hastings in a false name, that beyond all question of possible doubt he was with Mrs. Neilsen on the beach when she was shot, it seemed like insulting the intelligence of the jury to expect them to return anything else than a verdict to the effect that, as proved by the medical evidence, the deceased had been shot twice. One bullet had penetrated the head, injuring the brain, and the other had entered the breast, torn the lung, and lodged in the spine. Either wound was sufficient to cause death; and they found that the person who fired the shots was the accused. And so, as the spring day sun was declining to the west, and reddening the waters of the sea, over which the chill wind blew with fitful moaning, that coroner's jury pronounced Josiah Vecquerary guilty of murder. And the prisoner, looking like a man who was shattered and stunned, was taken back to his prison cell to await his trial.

XXII

A STRANGE AND STARTLING THEORY

It was on that last day of the coroner's inquiry that Alfred Vecquerary and Oriel Verecourt met each other for the first time. Alfred bore a striking resemblance to his brother, although he had not his brother's physique; but he had the same mild expression, the same open frankness of face, the same clear blue eyes. It would convey but an inadequate notion of Alfred's state to say that he was distressed. He was, in fact, broken-hearted by the magnitude of the awful sorrow and shame that had come upon the family, whose escutcheon up to then had been without a blemish. It would, perhaps, have been expecting too much to suppose that even Alfred—of the same blood and bone though he was—should have been absolutely without belief in his brother's guilt. To follow the story line by line from that ill-starred day when Vecquerary met Mrs. Neilsen for the first tine while journeying from Manchester to London to the dark and fatal night when he met her for the last time on the Hastings sands seemed to leave no room for doubt that in a fit of despair, anger, or disappointment he had shot her. It was terrible—very terrible, to have to think this, but even one's affection and love cannot altogether blind one's eyes to common-sense and facts. Mr. Oriel Verecourt, possibly because he was not a relative, and more possibly still because he was gifted with a farseeing, logical, and analytical mind, could not bring himself to think that Josiah was guilty, and he gave expression to that view to Alfred.

'It is very kind and generous of you to say that,' answered Alfred, 'and it cheers me. My poor brother never mentioned your name to me. But it is testimony to Josiah's goodness that you should speak so well of him, and go so far as to express your belief in his innocence, when, alas, the case seems so irrefragable.'

'It seems so,' returned Verecourt deliberately and thoughtfully, like a man who had weighed the matter with the utmost care. 'And perhaps it is so,' he added. 'But I find it an utter and absolute impossibility to bring myself to think so. My knowledge of your brother has been limited to weeks; but there must have been something strangely fascinating in his nature to have won my strong regard, for as a matter of fact I do not readily take to people. But though your brother withheld from me the knowledge that he was a married man, and to that extent might be said to have deceived me, he gave me the impression of being a man of remarkable integrity—'

'So he was,' exclaimed Alfred with deep emotion.

'And I am sure of this, however much the world may condemn him for it,' went on Verecourt, 'he perfectly idolized Mrs. Neilsen, and he must have been mad indeed to have brought himself to a condition when he could take her life. When I visited him before the coroner's inquiry he vowed to me in the most solemn manner that he was innocent. I went through a mental struggle after that, and my belief in his innocence has triumphed.'

At these words Alfred seized the hand of his new-found friend and wrung it, but for some moments his emotion so overcame him that he could not speak. When at last he did so he exclaimed:

'If you, a comparative stranger, believe him innocent, why should I, his brother, think otherwise? There is some mystery in the affair, and you may depend upon it, Mr. Verecourt, that neither money nor trouble shall be spared to get at the bottom of it.'

'One thing is clear,' remarked Verecourt; 'your brother has a bitter and relentless foe in Hipcraft, who is a lawyer of a most objectionable stamp. And your brother said to me only a very short time ago that he believed Hipcraft bad enough for any crime under the sun, and that his hatred was so intense that he would, if he could, accuse his enemy of murder if he thought he could get him hanged.'

This statement caused Alfred to start, and a new light seemed to dawn upon him.

'Do you mean to say,' he cried, 'that you think this fellow Hipcraft shot Mrs. Neilsen?'

'I don't exactly say that,' answered Verecourt cautiously. But I can tell you this much: Mrs. Neilsen detested Hipcraft. He called upon her two or three times, and I am of opinion that on one occasion he must have grossly insulted her, for she spoke to me about him in the strongest terms; though, when I threatened to go and thrash him, she said she had taken an exaggerated view of his conduct, and she implored me to let the matter drop. Now, for argument-sake, knowing what passed between your brother and Hipcraft, and knowing, as we do now, from the evidence of Ephraim Slark today, that your brother's footsteps were dogged by this fellow and all his movements recorded, is it not probable that someone else was present at that meeting on the beach, and that that someone committed the crime?'

'What do you mean?' gasped Alfred breathlessly.

'Well, this is what I mean, but let me preface it by saying that we shall have to conceive a human being so hellishly constituted as to be capable of a fiendish atrocity. Granted that such a person is a possibility, we may suppose it equally possible that by some means Hipcraft was aware of Vecquerary's presence in Hastings. Now, suppose further that a tool of Hipcraft's was shadowing your brother, tracked him to the beach on that dreadful night, witnessed the meeting, and for no other reason than to ruin your brother, shot Mrs. Neilsen himself.'

The very audacity of this idea deprived Alfred of speech for some moments.

'You will see,' continued Verecourt, 'given the existence of such a creature as I have suggested, how everything was favourable to the rest.'

'Yes,' said Alfred, with a sort of moan. 'Such a thing might be; for there is absolutely no limit to human iniquity. But even supposing it was so, would it not be a hopeless task to try and prove it?'

'Oh dear, no. I don't think so. Human brain never conceived a plot yet that another human brain could not be found to unravel. Of course, my theory may be a wild and absurd one. But I do consider it of the highest importance that we should learn all we possibly can about Hipcraft and the fellow Slark: for if ever I looked on a Judas, I looked on one today when I watched Slark give his evidence. Now, it has come out that a serious quarrel took place between Mrs. Vecquerary and her husband, as the result of an anonymous letter the lady received. Who sent that letter? If Hipcraft did not not, I'll eat my hat. If he did, one need not do outrage to one's conscience to suppose that he could descend still further in the path of guilt—slay the woman who had repulsed him, and fix the crime on his enemy, whom he mortally hates and would ruin without the slightest compunction.'

This conversation caused a complete revolution in Alfred Vecquerary's views. It would be folly to deny that up to half an hour before then he had most certainly believed in his brother's guilt. But the extraordinary theory set up by Verecourt placed the affair in a totally different aspect, and that belief gave place to doubt. Urgent business compelled his return to Manchester without loss of time, but he resolved that neither time nor money should be spared to prove or disprove the theory. When Verecourt parted from Alfred he returned at once to the Cliff Hotel, where Muriel was anxiously awaiting his coming. When she heard the result of the coroner's inquiry she expressed satisfaction, and said that she hoped Vecquerary would meet with the penalty he deserved. Verecourt told her plainly that he did not share her views, and that he believed Vecquerary to be innocent. This made Muriel angry. She pointed out that the accused had deceived her aunt about his being a married man and, according to her logic, a man who would do such a thing as that was bad enough for anything.

As Oriel saw that it would be useless then to attempt to convert her to his views, he wisely kept his thoughts to himself, and he busied himself in arranging for the last sad ceremony in connection with all that was mortal of Mrs. Neilsen. Two days later the beautiful woman, whose short life had been so cruelly overshadowed and darkened, was laid to her final rest in the Hastings Cemetery. She was buried, of course, in her lawful name—Sabena Tortolini. And on the coffin Verecourt placed a magnificent and costly wreath of pure white exotic flowers, in the name of Josiah Vecquerary.

It was a sad and impressive scene. Thousands of people, either from curiosity or sympathy, followed the cortége, and an enormous crowd struggled about the grave for the sake of satisfying a morbid desire to gaze on the flower-covered coffin.

The funeral ceremony was a terrible ordeal to poor Muriel, and it is doubtful if she could have borne up had it not been for her lover's encouragement. When the painful duty was ended, Oriel took her back to London, and she felt that one act of her life had ended—ended in gloom and woe: while Verecourt, firm in his faith in his friend's innocence, resolved to lose no time in trying to place that innocence beyond doubt.

XXIII

ENTER A NEW CHARACTER

Three or four days after the close of the coroner's inquiry at Hastings into the circumstances of Mrs. Neilsen's death, Mr. Richard Hipcraft stood at his office window, staring at the prison of Newgate. It was a favourite attitude of his. It probably gave him inspiration. At any rate, he had a habit of occasionally getting up from his desk, going to the window, standing with his legs slightly apart, his left hand thrust deep into his pocket, his right holding a quill pen, the end of which he chewed. He always wrote with a quill pen, and he invariably chewed the end of it to pieces. Now, what his reflections were as he contemplated the pile opposite is not within the power of the writer of this narrative to say. Perhaps, and I only say perhaps, he moralized on human sorrow and sin; for Newgate was calculated to suggest such a theme. Or he might have taken pleasure in contemplating the prison with that warm regard which one necessarily has for a loved object, whether animate or inanimate. Certainly the dwellers in Newgate—that is, some of them—were profitable customers of his. Moreover, he had passed so many years of his life in its heavy shadow that he could not fail to regard it as an old acquaintance, at least, if not in the light of friendship.

Or maybe at these times of his meditations he wished, with a heartfelt wish that he could chain all his enemies together, and thrust them deep into Newgate dungeons. But had that wish been gratified the prison would have needed enlargement, for Mr. Hipcraft's enemies were very numerous. This was a painful fact, and it might have been due to the wooden-headed obtuseness of people generally, who failed or refused to see his virtues—if he had any. Or, what is more likely, he made enemies because he had allowed the rank and poisonous weed—hate—to grow up in his heart instead of cultivating the divine flowers of love and charity. But, whichever it was, it was a misfortune for Mr. Hipcraft, as it is for any man, to have enemies. Some philosopher of old said, 'Better a beggar with friends than a king with enemies.' But this axiom was not one that seemed to have recommended itself to Mr. Hipcraft's consideration. To be a good hater appeared to him to be a virtue; but possibly he forgot that he who hates must in turn be hated.

On this particular morning, as he stood in his accustomed pose, there was a vernal balminess in the air, while a blaze of sunshine relieved London's city of some of its sombreness. It even softened the harshness of Newgate, and the black, suggestive door, with the carved manacles above it. Close to this very door stood an old, grey-headed, bowed man, wearing thick boots and a countryman's long smock, while he bore in front of him a huge basket of pale primroses. He who was not utterly indifferent to commonplace pictures might have seen in this old, tottering man and his basket of early flowers a suggestiveness of the morning and evening of life. It may, however, be safely asserted that Mr. Hipcraft saw nothing picturesque in the primroses and the man in the smock-frock. Indeed, he would seem to have been so absorbed in his thoughts that it is doubtful if he saw anything. At any rate, he did not hear, for three knocks at his door elicited no response from him. So the clerk, who knocked, opened the door and spoke. Then Mr. Hipcraft wheeled on his heel, as on a pivot, and mumbled and muttered:

'Oh, ah yes, umph—what is it?'

'A gentleman wants to see you, sir.'

'Who is it?'

'Here is his card, sir.'

The card that the clerk handed to his master bore the inscription 'Calvin Velacott.' There was not even the usual prefix of 'Mr.,' and there was no address—nothing but the bare name.

'Who the devil is Calvin Velacott?' growled Mr. Hipcraft.

'I don't know, sir.'

'What does he want?'

'I don't know, sir.'

'Ask him what his business is, then.'

'I have already done so, and he won't state his business. He says it is of a private nature, and that he must see you.'

'Umph. Very well, show him in. Stay; what sort of a fellow is he?'

Well, sir, he ain't a gentleman. He looks like a begging-letter-writer or a mock parson.'

'Oh, ah! Well, show him in. He's a new client, I suppose.'

The clerk retired, and Mr. Hipcraft took his seat at his desk, and became deeply absorbed in the perusal of a formidable-looking blue document, so that when a minute later Calvin Velacott entered the room the lawyer did not see him—that is, he affected not to see him, and Calvin Velacott coughed to attract his attention.

'Oh, I beg your pardon!' exclaimed Mr. Hipcraft. 'You are Mr. Calvin Velacott, I presume?'

'Calvin Velacott,' answered the individual correctively, as though he thought the prefix of 'Mr.' quite unnecessary, showing thereby that he was humble and modest at least, even though he might be a 'begging-letter-writer or a mock parson.'

He was certainly a peculiar-looking individual. In stature he was below the middle height, but carried himself erect, and there was something in his carriage and bearing that suggested unusual muscular strength, although he was a little man. His cheeks and chin were clean-shaved, but he wore a moustache, though this could not hide the firm-set mouth that indicated, by its formation and lines, extraordinary determination. He had a large, straight nose, and a somewhat low, though square-cut forehead. He was a little bald, and wore blue glasses that entirely concealed his eyes.

He was dressed in a frock-coat that must have seen many summers and winters, while the seams were not without a certain suggestiveness of blacklead polish. His trousers, too, were frayed at the bottoms, and his shoes had patches on them; otherwise they were fairly good, and must have been recently cleaned, for they were not even dusty. The hat that Calvin Velacott carried in his hand was a billycock that had also seen its best days. In addition to his hat, he carried a very ordinary stick, that might have cost a shilling, and certainly not more than eighteenpence.

Anyone with pretensions to a knowledge of character, in looking at Calvin Velacott, would have thought, 'One doesn't see all that man,' meaning thereby that Calvin Velacott was a human riddle; and you might make fifty guesses as to what he was before you guessed rightly. He had been described by the clerk as looking like a begging-letter-writer or a mock parson; though it is difficult to know what are the precise characteristics of the begging-letter-writer and the mock parson. Certainly there was a slight suspicion of sanctimoniousness in Calvin Velacott's general appearance. On the other hand, he might have been a blackleg, a horse-stealer, a card-sharper, a crimp, a tout for some charitable institution, a broker's man—anything, in fact, according to one's imagination, for imagination goes a long way in such cases. And there was a certain silkiness in his voice, and a soupçon of cat-like stealth in his tread—that is, the stealth of the cat when it is after prey. But his voice was pleasant and insinuating, and his movement slow and calculating, such as one associates with particularly cautious people. Calvin Velacott was not an obtrusive man, and yet he was a man you would not have passed over in a crowd. Mr. Hipcraft prided himself on being a fair, if not a very good, judge of character from face and general style, but had he spoken honestly then he must have confessed that Calvin Velacott was a closed book to him. The imperturbable face, the deliberate manner of speaking, the soft voice, and the blue spectacles that concealed the eyes conveyed no more information to him than a tablet of Egyptian hieroglyphics would have done. This sense of being baffled, as it were, irritated Mr. Hipcraft, and he remarked, in a tone that was far from suave:

'I suppose you want my professional services?'

'Well—no—not exactly,' replied Calvin Velacott, pausing between each word.

This answer caused the lawyer to scrutinize his visitor a little more keenly, but without making any discovery.

'To what, then, am I to attribute this visit?' asked Hipcraft somewhat surlily.

'My business concerns you very closely,' was the answer; 'but if you'll allow me I'll take a chair.'

Velacott placed his hat and stick on the floor, drew a chair up, and sat down.

'Do you represent any of my clients?' asked Hipcraft, still showing by his manner that he considered himself to be at a disadvantage.

'I cannot say that I do. But, not to keep you longer in suspense, I am deeply interested in this murder case—I mean the murder of Mrs. Neilsen.'

At these words a slight flush showed itself in Hipcraft's sallow face, indicating that the subject was one the mere mention of which was capable of stirring his blood.

'Oh, indeed! You knew Mrs. Neilsen, then?'

'Well—I cannot say that I knew her. But I know Vecquerary.'

'Yes?'

This with quick eagerness.

'Of course there is no doubt—at any rate in the minds of some people—that he murdered the woman.'

'There isn't justification for the shadow of a doubt, and he'll be hanged to a certainty,' snarled Hipcraft.

'I hope he will,' replied Velacott. Then, after a pause, he added pointedly, 'That is, if he is really guilty; and I am particularly interested in proving him guilty—or innocent. Now, I believe, Mr. Hipcraft, you knew a great deal of Vecquerary—'

'Oh yes; and I know him to be a thorough-paced blackguard and bully. Of course, you are aware he brutally assaulted me, and that I had him before Jones at Bow Street for it.'

'I am aware of that; but what I was going to observe was, you know a good deal about his connection with Mrs. Neilsen?'

'Yes. He intrigued disgracefully with her.'

'Ah!'

'He spent a great deal of his time at her house.' 'Ah!'

'He dined at the Palace with her, certainly once, if not oftener, and he frequently accompanied her to the theatre.'

'Ah! You had him watched, then!'

Mr. Hipcraft displayed some confusion at this question, as if conscious that he had been a little too free in his admission. Velacott relieved him, however, by saying quickly:

'Oh! I merely asked the question out of curiosity. But I am not wrong in supposing that when his trial comes on you will be glad if the jury should convict?'

'If he is guilty. I don't see why I should be sorry.'

'Ah! Just so. If he is guilty. But, after all, the evidence may not be sufficient to convict him, although the coroner's jury have returned a verdict of wilful murder against him.'

'Why, good God! The evidence, while being circumstantial, is as clear as any case I have ever known in the whole course of my career.'

'It seems so,' answered Velacott. 'First'—here he held up his left hand, with the fingers spread wide out, and, as he enumerated his subjects, he touched, one after another, the outspread fingers with the index-finger of his right hand. 'First, it is clear that he formed an acquaintanceship with the unfortunate lady while journeying up from Manchester. Second, he improved on the acquaintance, and visited her frequently, and took her out. Third, his acquaintance with her was the cause of a serious quarrel between him and his wife, owing to an anonymous letter that was sent to her. Fourth, after that quarrel he came up to London immediately. Fifth, that very night he was at Drury Lane Theatre with her, and something passed between them that induced her to write and tell him that he must not see her again. Then, to escape him apparently, she went to Hastings. By the way, did you know she was in Hastings?'

'No, I had not the slightest idea.'

'Well, he followed her to Hastings. You didn't know that at the time, I suppose?'

'Certainly not.'

'Ah, well, he went after her. Wrote pleading for an interview, and saying that something dreadful would happen if she did not meet him. She did meet him, and the watchman on the pier saw them together, and has stated in evidence that they appeared to be quarrelling. The same man saw the flash, and heard the report of the pistol, and he saw—indistinctly, it is true—but still saw the lady sink down to the ground. Vecquerary fled, and by the side of the dead body of the victim—'

'His victim,' interrupted Mr. Hipcraft, with emphasis.

'Very well, his victim. By the side of her dead body a revolver was found with two barrels recently discharged. And, finally, the bullets in the lady's body corresponded with the calibre of the pistol.'

'I declare,' exclaimed Hipcraft, 'you've trammelled the circumstances up, link by link, with the clearness and conciseness of counsel for the prosecution.'

'Thank you. Now as to the motive for the murder.'

'Ah, there can be no vagueness about that,' said Hipcraft triumphantly, and oiling his hands after his manner.

'What is your theory with respect thereto?' asked Velacott.

'Why, that he wanted to force himself upon her again. She refused to continue the acquaintance, and he shot her.'

'Of course he must have gone to her with murder in his heart. Otherwise, why did he arm himself with a pistol?'

'Just so. In my mind, there is no doubt that the murder was deliberately planned in cold blood. He arranged that meeting on purpose to kill her.'

'It looks wonderfully like it,' remarked Calvin Velacott softly. But supposing—I say supposing—that a clever counsel should find a flaw in the chain, and the prisoner should escape on a mere doubt?'

'Oh, nonsense; it's impossible. Where the deuce is there a flaw?'

'Well, now, supposing—I say again, supposing—it should be suggested, and with a strong show of probability, that Mrs. Neilsen shot herself, and that Vecquerary, fearing he might be blamed for it, fled.'

'Tut, ridiculous! Absolutely ridiculous—too absurd, in fact, for a moment's consideration!'

'No, not quite so ridiculous and absurd as you seem to think. If Mrs. Neilsen could only be proved to have been in possession of the pistol—'

'Ah, if she could! But your "if" is a potent factor in the calculation.'

'I grant it. But there is yet another theory. If we could imagine that Vecquerary had a very bitter and relentless enemy, a man who hated him with the malignancy of—what shall we say?—a devil, would it be an outrage on common-sense to think that that enemy might have employed some unscrupulous knave to shadow Vecquerary, who having learned by some mysterious means or other that the ill-starred pair had an assignation, tracked them to the rendezvous, and there shot the woman from some place of concealment in order that Vecquerary might be ruined by being accused of the murder?'

Mr. Hipcraft broke into derisive laughter at this, and he exclaimed:

'Well, upon my word, I have never heard anything more absurd in my life. But what does this discussion point to? Who are you, and what is your interest in the matter?'

'My interest is money,' answered Calvin Velacott bluntly.

XXIV

MR. RICHARD HIPCRAFT HAS A SOMEWHAT UNFLATTERING OPINION OF HIMSELF

Mr. Hipcraft fixed his eyes on his strange visitor as he thus expressed himself. But his gaze was the gaze of one who was puzzled as well as annoyed, and unquestionably Hipcraft was puzzled, clever as he believed himself to be; and he was annoyed because he was puzzled. 'I wish,' he said tartly, 'you would be a little more explicit and a little less involved; as, in fact, you must be if you wish me to give you any more of my valuable time.'

Velacott smiled for the first time during the interview, but his smile was as much a riddle as he himself appeared to be, for it was difficult to say if it was a smile of derision, triumph, or pleasure.

'I am sorry, I am sure, that I have intruded on your valuable time.' There was just a touch of irony in this. 'But now we will come to the point. Now, I happen to know that you mortally hate and detest this man Vecquerary. Never mind how I got to know it, but I do know it.'

'Well?'

'And that being so, and as you in your own mind are convinced of his guilt, you would not like him to escape by a mere fluke.'

'Oh, there's no fear of him escaping. The evidence is such that it will convince the most wooden-headed jury that could possibly be got together.'

'It may—and it may not. At any rate, I can tell you for a certainty that the theory I have mentioned will be set up by the defence.'

'How do you know that?' asked Hipcraft very quickly.

'I have learned it because I am much interested in this case. But what I am coming to is this: if I could put into your hands—of course, in the strictest confidence, and with a solemn engagement from you that you would not disclose the source of your information—a certain document, or letter, placing Vecquerary's guilt absolutely beyond cavil, what would you give me?'

The lines on Mr. Hipcraft's face softened with that unpleasant grin of his which did duty for a smile whenever he felt pleased with himself. It seemed to him now that the mask had fallen off his visitor, and he was no longer the slightest little bit of a riddle, but stood revealed a shallow trickster, a blackmailer, a humbug. But Mr. Hipcraft was far too clever—in his own estimation—to make an enemy of a possible tool, and he asked pointedly:

'Have you got such a document?'

'That is the Scotch way of answering a question, by asking another, and it is a most objectionable way. It almost invariably argues a suspicious mind. My question requires a different answer from that.'

Hipcraft was not quite pleased with this little reprimand. It wounded somewhat his *amour propre*, and he said with a certain piquancy of tone:

'I should want to have very good evidence that you possessed such a letter before I began to bargain with you.'

'Excuse me,' said Velacott, as he reached across the desk, took a sheet of paper from the paper-box, a pen from the inkstand, and deliberately wrote the following:

'I, Calvin Velacott, hereby undertake to supply Richard Hipcraft, Esq., solicitor, with documentary evidence of the kind he requires on condition that he gives me twenty pounds.'

'There, will that convince you?'

Hipcraft read what had been written; then turned up his nose scornfully.

'I don't see that that is of much use.'

'It is of no use except, perhaps, to convince you that I have what you want.'

'I don't know that it does even that.'

'Very well,' said Velacott, with a display for the first time of irritability. 'We can't trade;' and he put the paper in his pocket. He rose, picked up his hat and stick, and, with a brusque 'I'll say good-day to you,' turned towards the door.

'Stay,' came from Hipcraft.

Velacott turned, and on his face was an expression that seemed to say plainly: 'I thought, old man, you would take the bait.'

'Well, are you prepared to make an offer?' he asked.

'Is that your sole object in coming here?' queried the lawyer.

'Surely my object is plain enough,' was the somewhat equivocal answer.

This answer would not perhaps have misled Hipcraft if he had not had Vecquerary on the brain. But as it was, he scrutinized his visitor keenly from his head to his shoes, and he wished to himself that those blue spectacles had been away, for the most telling feature—the eyes—were hidden; and the eyes are capable of betraying much.

'Well, I'll undertake to give you the twenty pounds on your providing me with such a document as you speak of.'

'Done!' said Velacott, as he once more sat down.

'In fact,' continued Hipcraft, 'I consider that, in the interests of justice, you are bound, if you have such a paper in your possession, to give it up; and I as a representative of the law am equally bound to bring it under the notice of the proper authorities.'

'Just so,' remarked Velacott, with a soupçon of a sneer; 'I don't care what you do, but what I want is money.'

'Ah, I thought you were a blackmailer by your very appearance,' said Hipcraft, unable longer to conceal his feelings.

'Really!' exclaimed Calvin Velacott, with a laugh. 'Well, now, I thought I had quite a respectable, almost clerical look, and that I could pass muster as being square.'

'Umph, the devil takes on many guises,' remarked the lawyer.

'He does,' said Velacott, with great point. 'But don't let us waste any more time. Just give me half a dozen lines to the effect that you will pay me the twenty pounds providing I bring the document in question, for I haven't it here.'

Hipcraft hesitated. He was not wanting in the lawyer's caution and suspicion. But suddenly he seized a pen and wrote this:

'Calvin Velacott, an adventurer and, as he confesses himself, a blackmailer, has offered to sell me certain evidence of an important character in connection with a certain criminal case; and on condition that he does furnish me with such evidence, I hereby pledge myself to pay him twenty pounds. I do this entirely in the interest of justice.

'Richard Hipcraft, Solicitor, Old Bailey.'

He turned this document down on the blotting-pad to dry it; then read it over again, and handed it to his visitor, with the remark:

'There, I think that will meet the case.'

And as he did and said this his sallow face was a perfect study in its look of cunning self-consciousness, which seemed to say: 'Aha, my boy, that licks you! You can't get over a lawyer. He's far too smart for you. And the wording of that undertaking will prevent you showing it to anyone else.'

Mr. Hipcraft expected some outburst of indignation from his visitor at the words 'adventurer' and 'blackmailer.' Therefore, he was somewhat astonished and even disappointed when Velacott read it over, smiled, folded the paper up, and put it in his pocket, with a quiet and grateful 'Thank you.' Then he rose, once more picked up his hat and stick, and said:

'I think we understand each other now.'

'Yes, I think we do,' answered Hipcraft caustically. 'When shall I see you again?'

'Oh, in the course of a day or two.'

'By the way, do you belong to London?'

'No.'

'Where do you come from, then?'

'Manchester. But, excuse me, I must go.'

And without another word Calvin Velacott opened the door and disappeared.

For some two or three minutes Mr. Hipcraft sat stock still, save that he chewed his pen as usual, while his left hand rested extended on his desk. That one word 'Manchester' was ringing in his ears. It suggested many things to him, and it suddenly suggested that it was within the bounds of possibility that something was wrong—that he was being tricked. This caused him to bring his hand heavily down on the bell, and a clerk appeared like a jack-in-the-box, for he knew that when the governor struck his bell that way 'his monkey was up.'

'Look here, go after that fellow who has just gone out, as hard as you can, and bring him back. Say I omitted to tell him something.'

The clerk disappeared. He was absent ten minutes or so. Then he came into his master's presence again panting like a coursed hare.

'I couldn't see him anywhere, sir,' he gasped. 'I've been both up and down the street.'

Mr. Richard Hipcraft growled something naughty as the clerk beat a retreat, and as Mr. Richard Hipcraft once more took up his position at the window, chewing his pen harder than ever, he felt ill at ease, and he thought that for once in his life, at any rate, he had been a fool.

XXV

EXPLAINS A GOOD DEAL

In no part of the kingdom did the 'Hastings Tragedy,' as it came to be called, cause more excitement and astonishment than in Manchester. This, of course, is easily accounted for. The firm of Vecquerary and Sons was well known in Manchester, and more or less all over Lancashire. To many scores of people Josiah Vecquerary was an intimate acquaintance, and to scores of others be was familiar by sight. To every one of these people the news came as a great shock, and it is not too much to say that without exception they all believed him guilty. Even those who regarded him with genuine friendship could not avoid coming to that conclusion, however painful it might be to them; for although he was untried, the evidence against him seemed conclusive. In fact, there were men who would have got quite angry with anyone who ventured to suggest doubt as to the prisoner's guilt. Not from any personal feeling that they entertained against Vecquerary, but because the prima facie evidence seemed to them so perfectly clear that it was an insult to intelligence to question it. The more charitably-disposed were not disinclined to admit the possibility that when Josiah shot the poor lady he was labouring under such mental excitement as to be in a large measure, if not entirely, irresponsible for his act. But beyond this they would not go.

To Mr. Vecquerary's relatives and friends the tragedy was a source of the keenest grief and suffering. And to none more so than to the unfortunate man's wife. She had during the whole of her married life regarded him with a sort of silent hero-worship. For though at times she had felt herself neglected, she nevertheless was proud of his popularity and of the attention that was paid to him. And when she heard men and women praise him, it begot in her a sense of pride that she was in a position to legally say, 'Ah, he is mine—my husband.' If, therefore, her married life had had shadows, it had certainly not been without sunshine, and it was only when her jealousy was aroused, and when she was driven almost to distraction by that infamous letter of Hipcraft's, that the sunshine entirely faded away, and only heavy, dark shadows environed her.

After that terrible quarrel, when she had accused her husband of striking her, she had suffered exquisite agony of mind; for, indeed, she realized to the fullest the truth of the poet's lines:

'And to be wroth with one we love
Doth work like madness in the brain.'

And the love she bore him rather tended to intensify the bitterness she experienced in considering herself neglected and ill-treated. But when the news came through to Manchester that her husband had been arrested on suspicion of having shot Mrs. Neilsen at Hastings, it proved the culminating point in her grief, and so violent was the shock in her case that it threw her on a bed of sickness, and brain-fever set in. The effect on Alfred Vecquerary, although it did not display itself in the same way as on his sister-in-law, was scarcely less severe. He had always looked up to his brother with the greatest possible respect and regard. He had ever been deferential to his brother, and was content to play second fiddle in every way, believing Josiah to be his superior in business capacity and in general ability, and yet, notwithstanding that he loved his brother as he did, Alfred could not believe him guiltless without doing outrage to his own common-sense, until that eventful interview with Oriel Verecourt at Hastings.

It certainly was remarkable that, out of Josiah Vecquerary's very large circle of acquaintances, Verecourt was the only one who believed him innocent. If this belief was something in the nature of a phenomenon, it was also proof that Verecourt possessed an original mind.

To those who make human nature a study, even in a casual way, it must ever be a source of wonderment that there should be such a striking resemblance between human beings and the mild-eyed sheep. If one sheep in a flock baas and bleats, all the rest will baa and bleat; and if one rushes through a gap in a hedge or through an open gateway, do not the others follow in a blind, unreasoning yielding to an impulse to do what the leader has done? And so it is with human beings. Raise but a Shibboleth, and the mob sways this way or that way, according to its leader. Point but the finger of scorn at some unfortunate individual, and will not the mob howl and yell, cry 'Stone him!' and the sinner is stoned?—make but an insinuation against a woman's honesty, and instantly there goes up a wail of horror from the flock of human sheep, not because in the abstract they are pitiless, but because in the concrete they are stupid. Now, the man who has the courage to take up cudgels on behalf of one condemned by the *vox populi* is a bold man indeed, and he is no less bold who dares to oppose his opinions to the general verdict. Such a man, in fact, must be gifted with faculties altogether out of the common. He must be an original thinker, and capable of reasoning *à priori*, and of subjecting things as they came before him to a very critical process of logical analysis. What other men are content to slur over he will examine with conscientious care, and what are insignificant minutiae to others will possess for him a value that cannot be lightly ignored. Such a man as is here depicted is certainly uncommon, and is constituted to become a leader of men, and such a man was Oriel Verecourt.

The strange and extraordinary theory that Verecourt held with regard to the murder was the result of a clear and comprehensive grasp of motives, that is, the motives which prompt men to do certain things. He did not believe that his friend had any motive in killing the woman he loved; and he did believe that Hipcraft was so relentless in his hatred of a person who had done him a real or fancied wrong that he was quite capable of charging his enemy with a crime he had never committed. Possibly, had Mr. Verecourt given expression to this theory publicly he would have been subjected to very strong ridicule, and few, very few, people—probably no one—would have shared his views. But in expressing his ideas to the brother of the accused man it was but natural they should be eagerly entertained.

Alfred Vecquerary's perception being keenly quickened by love and anxiety for his unfortunate brother, he eagerly clutched at the suggested possibility of Josiah's entire innocence as shadowed forth by Verecourt. And he felt that it was only compatible with fraternal duty and regard to take every means in his power to prove the theory right or wrong. To this end, when he arrived back in Manchester, he called upon Farabin Leedie Tindal. Of course, the reader will ask who Farabin Leedie Tindal was, and he shall be informed.

Mr. Tindal was a somewhat remarkable man, and had led an adventurous life. He had started on his career as an actor, a calling his father had followed before him. But after some years on the stage young Tindal, who was of an adventurous turn of mind, joined the foreign legion that went out to help Garibaldi, who was then struggling to free Italy. Tindal saw some very stirring times, and was twice wounded, on the second occasion so severely as to be unfitted for further military service. He next turned his attention to journalism, and wandered the wide world over as a correspondent, and during this time he distinguished himself by a remarkable ability, not only in acquiring information, but in unravelling apparent mysteries. This brought him into such notice that he received several Government commissions of a very delicate and intricate character. In carrying these out tact and skill of no ordinary kind were required, for the slightest blunder might have cost him his life as well as involved his employers in difficulties of a complicated nature. However, Mr. Tindal made no blunders, but proved that he possessed in an eminent degree all the qualities that are indispensable to the diplomatist, no less than to the clever detective.

Getting tired at last of a roving life, Mr. Tindal married and settled down in his native town of Manchester, where he adopted the calling of a detective. He would not, however, have anything to do with cases of a paltry character. He was ambitious. He aimed at being superior to his fellows. What delighted him most were cases so complicated and intricate as to baffle ordinary minds. It will be remembered that Edgar Allan Poe, the American author, maintained that no man could invent a cipher that could not be readily deciphered by someone else; and Poe himself proved a master in the art of discovering what were supposed to be locked secrets. So in his way did Mr. Tindal aver that there was no human riddle that could not be solved with comparative ease if the proper mind was brought to bear upon it. And that he possessed this mind he evidenced by the success which attended his efforts in cases that had set the ordinary inquirers at defiance. It was said of Mr. Tindal that his ingenuity, his tact, and his resources were unrivalled, and that it was almost impossible to outwit him. His reputation under these circumstances was very high, and his services were in constant demand.

When Oriel Verecourt propounded his theory to Alfred Vecquerary in Hastings, he said that 'Human brain never conceived a plot yet that another human brain could not be found to unravel.' This was not, of course, altogether an original remark, but it was sufficiently original to set young Vecquerary pondering deeply, and as he journeyed homeward he began to wonder whom he could get to take the case up, until suddenly it occurred to him that Farabin Tindal was the very man if he could be induced to lend his aid.

Vecquerary not only knew Tindal well by repute, but he had a slight personal acquaintance with him, so that he experienced no difficulty in securing an interview. Mr. Tindal listened patiently to the story. He had, of course, in common with the general public, heard of the murder, and he frankly confessed to his visitor that on the first blush it seemed to him that the evidence against the accused man was very clear and conclusive. But his interest was awakened as young Vecquerary told him the theory that had been propounded by Oriel Verecourt. When he had finished he asked Tindal his opinion.

'At present I cannot give it,' said Tindal. 'It is a matter that wants a good deal of thinking over. But I will go the length of saying that my knowledge of men and of the worst side of human nature leads me to believe that such a thing as your friend suggests is by no means so wild a theory as some people might suppose. I do not know Richard Hipcraft personally, never having met him; but I have heard a good deal about him, and I am aware that he bears the character of being a phenomenally vindictive man.'

Alfred drew hope from these words, coming from such an authority; but, though he held out large pecuniary inducement to Tindal to take the matter up, Tindal would give no definite answer then. He said he wanted a clear day, at least, to think over it. This caution was only in accord with the inborn diplomacy of the man. He would decide on nothing until he had thoroughly thrashed the subject out in his own mind. The following day Alfred received a laconic note from Tindal. It contained only this line:

'I will take the case up. Please call on me.'

In accordance with the request Alfred went, and Tindal made the most minute inquiries about Josiah Vecquerary's habits. Alfred told him everything he could, including the story of the anonymous letter that had come from London to Mrs. Vecquerary, and had led to that terrible scene between her and her husband. Tindal considered it important that that letter should be in his hands, and, fortunately, Alfred was able to secure it.

'What we have got to do now,' said Tindal, when he had read the letter, 'is to find out who wrote this. It is a shameful letter, and the writer is a poltroon and a knave. It breathes animosity in every word, and the man who could write it—for it is written by a man—might be capable of—'

Tindal paused, and showed no disposition to finish what he was going to say, so Alfred asked:

'Might be capable of what?'

'Of anything,' was the guarded answer,

As Tindal did not seem inclined to discuss the matter any further just then, Alfred took his departure, and a few days later Mr. Tindal journeyed up to London. He was absent three days; then he returned and sent for his client.

'I have had an interview with Mr. Richard Hipcraft,' he said.

'Yes.'

'It was he who wrote the anonymous letter to Mrs. Vecquerary.'

'Did he tell you that?'

'Oh dear no,' answered Tindal, with a self-satisfied smile.

'How did you find it out, then?'

'He gave me a specimen of his handwriting. You can read it and compare it with the letter. You will find the writing is exactly the same.'

As he spoke he laid a sheet of paper before Alfred, and on the paper was written:

'Calvin Velacott, an adventurer, and, as he confesses himself, a blackmailer, has offered to sell me certain evidence of an important character in connection with a certain criminal case; and on condition that he does furnish me with such evidence, I hereby pledge myself to pay him twenty pounds. I do this entirely in the interest of justice.

'Richard Hipcraft, Solicitor, Old Bailey.'

Alfred Vecquerary read this over, and was puzzled, as well he might be.

'Who is Calvin Velacott, the adventurer and blackmailer?' he asked.

'I am not aware that there is such a person,' answered Tindal, as he blew the smoke from a cigarette, and watched it disperse in a filmy cloud. I assumed that character for the nonce, for I knew that the crafty old fox Hipcraft could only be circumvented by craft. But though I have proved that his was the cowardly hand that penned the anonymous letter to Mrs. Vecquerary, there is not a doubt that he is quite innocent of any participation in the murder, either directly or indirectly.'

These words fell heavily on Alfred. Coming from such an authority, they crushed his hopes, and seemed to knell his brother's doom.

XXVI

PRIDE IS HUMBLED AND SORROW REIGNS

When Miss Muriel Woolsey returned to London after the last sad and solemn rites had been performed over the remains of poor Mrs. Neilsen, she felt so utterly cast down that not even the presence of her lover could raise her spirits. Between her and her aunt there had existed the most perfect bond of affection. The reader has already been informed that there was really no blood relationship between Mrs. Neilsen and Muriel; but the girl was not aware of that, and never having known her parents, she looked upon her guardian almost as her mother, and Mrs. Neilsen had, indeed, played the part of a mother to her. It is, therefore, not to be wondered at that Muriel should feel her loss with an anguish that refused for the time to be assuaged. Nor was it unnatural that she should cherish feelings of resentment and bitterness against Vecquerary, whom she regarded as her aunt's murderer. Verecourt tried hard to change her feelings in this respect, but his efforts were of no avail. In fact, he only raised her anger, and she went so far as to tell him that she wanted nothing more to do with a man who could 'champion the slayer of her aunt.'

It is almost needless, perhaps, to say that Verecourt did not allow himself to be affected by this. He made every allowance for the poor girl's distress of mind, and certainly did not expect to bring her all at once to his way of thinking. And so, for the time being, he allowed the subject to drop, and assured her of his love and devotion under all circumstances.

The house in which she had spent so many happy years of her life was so distasteful to her that she vowed she would not remain long in it, for henceforth it would, so far as she was concerned, be fraught with the most painful associations. Everything in it would serve to remind her of the dear woman whose cruel death had deprived her of a loving friend and tender guardian. As regards pecuniary matters, Muriel was well provided for, as Mrs. Neilsen's fortune reverted to her; and by her will the unfortunate lady left everything that she died possessed of to the girl. But, besides that, she knew that when a suitable time had elapsed she could become the wife of Oriel Verecourt, and thus her future would be secured. But, of course, in those early days of her dire distress and heavy sorrow she had no thought of anything concerning herself, and certainly not of marriage. Indeed, it seemed to her as if her life was darkened for evermore, and that nothing henceforth could give her joy. She had yet to learn, however, how time can soften the most poignant sorrow, and heal the heart-wounds that the loss of dear ones makes.

Muriel had always looked upon her supposed aunt as a widow, and she had ever been kept in entire ignorance of Mrs. Neilsen's history. This ignorance was now to be enlightened in an unexpected way.

She had been back about a week when an old, grey-headed gentleman drove up in a cab. He was a man who seemed to have been cast in a patrician mould. He had a commanding presence and a certain haughtiness in the expression of his face. But he was old now and bowed, and his silver hair and snow-white beard gave him somewhat of a patriarchal appearance. He sent up his card to Muriel, and on the card was:

Mr. Leslie Melville.

When Muriel came to him in the drawing-room he scrutinized her keenly through his gold-rimmed glasses, and then said, with a certain roughness in his manner and tone:

'You are Miss Woolsey, I believe?'

'I am,' answered Muriel sharply, for she was not indifferent to the harsh way in which he spoke.

'I understand that you have lived for a long time with the late Mrs. Neilsen?' he remarked.

'Yes. She was my aunt.'

'No. She was not your aunt.'

'Sir!'

'I repeat she was not your aunt—no relation, in fact. And it may surprise you to hear that her name was not Neilsen.'

Mr. Melville seemed to be suffering from some emotion now, and he drew out a silk handkerchief to wipe his eyes.

'It does not surprise me,' answered Muriel, finding a difficulty in keeping her voice steady. 'For when the funeral arrangements were made, my dear aunt's solicitor—I shall call her aunt in spite of what you say—came down to Hastings to superintend the arrangements, and he told me her name was Tortolini, and in that name she was buried.'

Here Muriel lost control of herself, and burst into weeping.

The old gentleman's sternness relaxed somewhat at this, though after a pause he said with warmth and anger:

'Yes, Tortolini was her name. She derived that name from the worthless scoundrel with whom she disgraced herself and her family.'

To hear her aunt thus spoken of naturally made Muriel angry, and she exclaimed with warmth:

'You have no right to speak that way against people who are dead.'

'One of them only is dead,' answered Mr. Melville. 'Tortolini still lives.'

'It's false,' cried Muriel almost passionately. 'Mrs. Tortolini was a widow.'

'You are wrong, my dear young lady; and if she told you so she deceived you, as, I am pained to say it, she deceived her family.'

These words almost deprived Muriel of the power of speech; but she did manage to gasp, as it were:

'Tell me, sir, who are you?'

'I am the father of the wretched woman whose untimely end has been brought about by her own wilfulness and deception.'

Mr. Melville was so overcome that he sobbed audibly, showing that his words belied his heart, and that he cherished an affectionate regard for his dead and gone daughter.

'Although you are her father,' returned Muriel with spirit and energy, 'you must not speak disrespectfully of your daughter in my presence. To me she was everything, and was good, noble, pure, and truthful. She stood in the light of a mother to me, and her loss crushes me with a wordless sorrow. Therefore, if you are a gentleman, spare my feelings by not saying a word against her in my hearing.'

Mr. Melville's manner underwent a change at these words. The anger and pride faded from his face. He had been trying to cheat himself into a belief that his heart was justly hardened against his unfortunate daughter; but Muriel had softened him, and he was a humbled and sorrowful old man now.

'It is noble of you to speak of my dear child in that way,' he faltered, 'and you teach me a lesson. But she was my favourite daughter. I doted on her, and she deceived me. For years my heart has yearned for her, but my pride was stubborn. It would not break; but it is broken now—broken now, when her dear face is hidden from me forever and ever. The news of her cruel death has been a terrible blow to me, and though when I thought of her waywardness I could not help feeling angry, my anger has been mingled with bitter sorrow. For some years

I have had her watched, and so I know a good deal, and this will explain to you how it is that you are not a stranger to me. I have always yearned for a reconciliation, but my pride has prevented my making advances to that end, and now it is too late, too late. But I have come now to try and make some reparation. I know that my poor daughter doted on you, and I feel sure that had she been able to express a dying wish it would have been that you might be shielded from the harshness of the world, and as much as possible from the sorrow of life. Let the duty of doing this fall upon me. I am a lonely old man, for my children are grown up and scattered about the world; while the flower of the flock, my heart's treasure, whom I have kept away from me by pride and anger, lies in an untimely grave.'

Mr. Melville was deeply moved, and sobbed almost like a child. The haughtiness that had been so conspicuous when he first entered had entirely given place to humility and grief. He had come there scarcely knowing his own mind, but he knew it now, and grief reigned where pride had so long held sway. Death had opened up the wellsprings of compassion, and the proud and angry man was now the mourning father.

Muriel was deeply touched, and said:

'I am not sure that I quite gather your meaning, sir.'

'I wish to be a father to you,' he answered. 'I know that you have no relatives with whom you are acquainted, and for my dead child's sake I ask you to accord to me the privilege of shielding you. You shall comfort my declining years, and give me an object in life. Say that you give me this privilege; the details can be settled afterwards.'

This unexpected proposal, as may be imagined, confused Muriel, and, remembering her lover, she felt that she could give no definite answer until she had taken his counsel, for though she had said some harsh things to him, and they were at variance on one point, she loved him devotedly.

'I feel that I cannot give you an answer right off,' she answered. 'I should like to take a little time to consider your proposal.'

'You shall have time,' he said, 'and while you are making up your mind I will remain in London. My house is in one of the sweetest and most romantic parts of Yorkshire, and there you shall go if you so will it. 'I want you to tell me, too, all about this, this—villain, the murderer of my daughter. I don't know that I am either revengeful or merciless, but I hope that no flaw will enable him to escape the just penalty of his crime.'

'I hope not,' answered Muriel, with great decision and warmth.

'You know him, of course?'

'Yes.'

'How long was my daughter acquainted with him?'

'Not very long. But, really, I cannot bear to talk of the subject yet.'

'We won't talk of it, then,' answered the old man tenderly, 'for it is a terrible thing—terrible, terrible! And now tell me when I shall have your answer?'

'The day after tomorrow,' she replied.

And so old Mr. Melville took his departure, and Muriel at once penned a few lines to Oriel Verecourt asking him to come to her as soon as he could. And as the day wore on, and the evening came, it brought another visitor, and that visitor was Ephraim Slark.

XXVII

AN UNEXPECTED MEETING

Slark was shown into the drawing-room, and Muriel was apprised of his being there. Of course, at this time she did not know Slark 'from Adam,' as the saying is, and she wondered who he was and what he wanted. When she entered the room she beheld a shabbily-dressed, lank man, whose oily manner, cat-like movements, and furtive glances did not prepossess her in his favour. He was the first to speak.

'Miss Muriel Woolsey, I think?'

'Yes, that is my name.'

'I have called upon you with reference to a matter that I know must be painful to you, but which, nevertheless, cannot be put on one side.'

Muriel knew to what he referred, and though, as he said, it could not fail to be painful to her, she was aware that it must be discussed, even though it did pain.

'You wish to speak of the murder of my dear aunt,' she said with visible emotion.

'Yes, miss.'

'Permit me to ask, then, who are you?'

'I am—well, marm, I'm in the law business.'

'And what is your connection with the case?'

'I am instructed to get as much corroborative evidence of the prisoner's guilt as possible,' was his equivocal answer.

'Oh yes,' she exclaimed, 'I understand.'

'I suppose, miss,' he said insinuatingly, 'you have no doubt of his guilt?'

'Not the slightest.'

'May I ask why you think him guilty?'

'Oh, because I do. Who else could have committed the murder if he did not?'

'No one, of course, miss. And surely no one can be so stupid as to suppose that he did not do it.'

'Oh, indeed, you are wrong there.'

'How is that?'

'Because I am acquainted with a gentleman who declares his firm and unalterable belief in Vecquerary's innocence.'

'Indeed!'

'Yes.'

'May I ask his name?'

'His name is Oriel Verecourt.'

'Is he a friend of yours?'

'Yes.'

'Can you tell me upon what grounds he bases his belief?'

There was some trace of anxiety in Slark's voice as he asked this question, and he watched the lady narrowly with his small eyes half closed.

'No, I cannot. But I don't think he has any better reason than that he was very fond of Vecquerary.'

'Ah, just so. And what is this gentleman's address?'

'He is in the Foreign Office.'

A smile spread itself over Slark's cadaverous face as he said contemptuously:

'Those Foreign Office gents generally have very stuck-up notions about themselves, but their opinions aren't worth much.'

This annoyed Muriel, for she could not tolerate anyone speaking disrespectfully of her lover, whatever her difference with him might be, and her answer to Slark was very caustic, and clearly proved to him that he had made a mistake.

'Well, sir, I shouldn't say by the look of you that you knew very much about the Foreign Office gents.'

'I beg your pardon, marm. I didn't mean to offend you, I am sure. But I do know something about 'em. Leastways, I've heard a good deal. But, if you please, we will let that subject drop. The law has to be upheld, and I am trying to uphold it; and, if you will permit me, I will ask you a few questions, and just write your answers down. You see, it helps one to keep things in one's memory.'

'Are you a detective?' Muriel asked, not feeling quite sure if she ought to comply with his request.

'I am, miss.'

This answer reassured her, and she could not be blamed for supposing that the fellow was there in an official capacity, and that it was her duty to tell him anything she could that might help the course of justice.

'I need scarcely say it is a painful subject to me, but in the interests of justice I shall give you all the information I can.'

'Ah, poor young lady!' sighed the hypocritical rascal, 'It must indeed be a painful subject; but I will spare your feelings as much as possible. Now tell me, please, do you know if Vecquerary and your late aunt ever quarrelled?'

'Not that I am aware of.'

'You never heard him threaten her?'

'Never.'

'You are quite sure?'

'Quite sure.'

Slark seemed disappointed as he wrote her answers down.

'Your aunt did not know, I presume, that Vecquerary had a wife and family in Manchester?'

'Certainly not,' answered Muriel quickly and indignantly. 'Do you suppose that my aunt would ever have permitted him to enter her house if she had been aware of his baseness?'

'No, of course not. But, I suppose—you will excuse this question—I suppose he did make love to her?'

'Really, I decline to answer such questions,' said Muriel with warmth.

'You see, miss,' remarked Slark in his blandest tones, 'you will be called as a witness at the trial; and these questions will certainly be put to you, and you will have to answer them anyway. Now, I am simply trying to help the cause of truth, and—pardon me for saying so—but it won't be right for you to throw any obstacles in the way of justice being done.'

Of course Muriel was impressed by this 'tall talk,' and, perhaps, she was a little awed, for she took this shabby, sleek individual to be the law's representative. So she said nervously:

'I do not want to throw obstacles in the way, but can't bear to talk of the matter, though I suppose I must. There is no doubt Vecquerary did make love to my aunt.'

'And she—she was fond of him?'

'Yes; I am sure she was, poor dear!'

'Did Vecquerary ever give her any presents?'

'He once sent her a necklet of pearls from Manchester.'

'Ah, that may be an important piece of evidence,' said Slark with an unctuous smack of his lips, as he jotted the answer down in his note-book. 'Now, it came out at the coroner's inquest,' he went on, after the manner of a barrister cross-examining a witness, 'that your late aunt was not a widow, but was separated from her husband?'

Poor Muriel's face flushed very red, but she answered curtly: 'Yes.'

'Did you know that her husband was living?'

'No,' answered Muriel, her face growing still redder, if that were possible, while her voice and manner of replying showed that these cruel questions were like knife-stabs to her.

'Umph!' muttered the wily rascal, as he wrote in his book, 'That is important. Have you any idea how long it is since she saw her husband?'

'No, not the slightest.'

'You never saw him, I suppose?'

'No. But amongst my aunt's papers is a portrait of a man who I believe is Mr. Tortolini.'

'Indeed!' exclaimed Slark, opening his ferret-like eyes. 'Could you let me look at it?'

'Oh, yes. I will go upstairs and get it.'

When she had gone Slark muttered to himself, 'I thought I might have learnt more than I have done. The governor won't think my visit has borne much fruit; but that ain't my fault. I don't know what he wants to work the case up for at all. He won't get nothing out of it, except it is seeing Vecquerary swing.'

In a few minutes Muriel returned to the room, bearing in her hand a photograph in a double case. It was the photograph of a dark, stern-looking man. Mrs. Neilsen used to keep it locked up in one of her private drawers, and whenever she looked at it, which was not often, it used to make her unhappy and angry.

'That is the photograph,' said Muriel, as she handed it to Slark, who examined it for some moments, then closed the case, and as he put it into his pocket he said:

'I will take this with me, miss. Of course you will get it back.'

'Oh no, you mustn't take it,' cried Muriel in distress. 'I don't think I ought to part with it.'

'It is all right,' said Slark. 'I must have it. I will take care of it.'

Muriel offered no further objection, believing that he was acting authoritatively and in his official capacity.

'Now I have just one more question,' said the cunning scoundrel. 'Did your aunt, to your knowledge, ever express any fear of Vecquerary?'

'No. I am sure she had no fear. On the contrary, she reposed the most perfect trust in him.'

'Just so; and of course her confidence made it all the easier for the wretch to lure her to destruction.'

Although Muriel's views were certainly in accord with his, she could make no answer, for poignant grief overcame her as she remembered how her aunt had trusted Vecquerary, and had walked blindly to her doom.

As Slark felt that he had learnt all he could learn then, he caught up his rusty hat, and, bowing, took his departure. As he reached the hall he came face to face with Oriel Verecourt, who had just arrived. Oriel was thunderstruck as he recognised the man whom he had referred to—when he was talking to Alfred Vecquerary in Hastings—as a Judas. Slark did not know Verecourt, and before the latter could recover from his surprise, the shadower had opened the street door and had disappeared into the darkness.

XXVIII

MASTER AND MAN

When Slark left Muriel he made his way as fast as a 'bus would take him to Craven Street, Strand, and to the residence of his employer.

Mr. Hipcraft had had his dinner, and was taking his forty winks preparatory to going, as was his custom at night, to the Golden Star Hotel to play billiards. His housekeeper disturbed him in order that he might announce Slark's arrival. He seemed in an unusually good humour, although he had been abruptly disturbed.

'Well, Slark, what's the news?' he exclaimed, oiling his hands with imaginary oil, and standing with his back to the fire.

'Oh, I ain't got much, governor.'

'Have you learnt anything about Vecquerary's connection with Mrs. Neilsen?'

'A little.'

'Well, you will have to learn a good deal yet. Within the last two days Sir George Jack, the eminent Q.C., has been instructed to take up the prosecution for the Crown, and as I have put a good deal in Jack's way, I applied to him immediately I heard he was appointed, and asked him to commission me to work up evidence. I told him no one was better able to do it than I. So, now that I have got a legal footing in the case,

I will move heaven and earth to convict Vecquerary. Not that there is any fear of his escaping. The evidence is too clear for that. But still there must not be the faintest possibility of a loophole. I've helped to hang a good many men in my time, but I have never felt the gratification I shall experience if I am instrumental in putting the halter round Vecquerary's neck. I shall feel then that I am revenged for the blow he struck me. I told him at the time it should cost him dear, and if he reflects at all and remembers my words, he must admit that they have been prophetic.'

'Yes, governor, you come pretty near the mark when you take it into your head,' replied the lickspittle, Slark. Then he proceeded to detail what had passed between him and Muriel Woolsey, reading her answers from his notebook. But there was one little item that Slark thought proper to withhold. It was that relating to the photograph. It may seem strange that he did not tell his master about that; but the fact is, he thought that, as Miss Woolsey seemed so reluctant to part with it, he might be able to make her pay him something for its return.

When Slark had finished his record, Mr. Hipcraft did not seem altogether satisfied.

You certainly haven't learnt much,' he remarked; 'but the fact is, I suppose this girl is anxious that the truth shouldn't come out.'

'On the contrary, she is as bitter as ever she can be against Vecquerary.'

'Are you sure?'

'Yes. I particularly asked her if she had any doubt about Vecquerary's guilt, and her answer was convincing that she hadn't.'

Mr. Hipcraft smiled. That is, he puckered his face into what he imagined was a smile, and which was certainly meant to be a smile. But this gentleman's smile was rather a grim grin, such as one sometimes sees on the gargoyles of old cathedrals.

In fact, to associate anything in the nature of laughter with Mr. Hipcraft seemed an absurdity. Laughter is the honest and spontaneous outburst of a cheerful disposition that is capable of feeling pleasure and understands mirth. But Hipcraft could not have been more indifferent to mirth had he been a dried-up mummy from one of the tombs of the Pharaohs. He was too bitter a cynic to laugh, too violent a hater to feel genuinely cheerful; gratification at the discomfiture of an enemy he certainly could experience; but it was not the gratification of a brave and heroic man, who, having conquered in fair fight, could heartily grip his foe's hand and say, 'Let bygones be bygones.'

It is doubtful if he saw good in anything or anybody. To use a metaphor, he was girtround about with an iron barrier of selfishness that nothing could break down. He lived for himself and himself alone; and the whole human race might have perished off the face of the earth and he would never have put out a hand to save one, had he thought that by doing so he would in any degree injure his own interests. The type that Mr. Hipcraft represents is, comparatively speaking, rare, but it exists unhappily, and this rascally lawyer was one of its most striking illustrations.

'Ah, we will have her in the witness-box,' he remarked in answer to his creature's statement. 'I warrant me that Sir George Jack will worry her into admissions that will be so many nails in Vecquerary's coffin. The man doesn't live who could withstand Jack's cross-examination, to leave women out of the running altogether.'

'From what I hear,' said Slark, as though he did not quite entertain the exalted notion of Sir George Jack, Q.C., that his master did, 'there will be a formidable array of talent on the other side. The Vecquerarys, you see, have plenty of money, and they'll not spare it in getting up the defence.'

'Pooh!' exclaimed Hipcraft, with an expression of supreme contempt. 'They may array all the talent in London on the prisoner's side; and what then? How the devil are they going to prove that Vecquerary wasn't with the woman on the beach; that there wasn't a flash and report; that the woman didn't fall down; that a pistol wasn't found by her side; that Vecquerary didn't bolt; that he didn't go to Hastings in a false name? Why, they might as well try to prove that the woman isn't dead and buried at all.'

'But supposing they try to prove, and supposing that they succeed in proving, that Mrs. Neilsen shot herself?' queried Slark in that soft, insinuating way peculiar to him when he thought he was saying something clever.

A sudden light flashed into Hipcraft's eyes, and a sudden flush leapt to his sallow face, as though this suggestion was in the nature of a shock to him.

'Well, upon my word, Slark,' he exclaimed with a sneer, 'I am astonished that a man of your intelligence and with your experience should talk such balderdash.'

'I'm not talking balderdash, governor. I'm only querying a possible line of defence.'

'Confound it, man,' exclaimed the lawyer with irascibility, 'how the deuce can they take that line?'

'Well, they might,' persisted Slark.

'Let them,' snapped his master savagely. 'But even if they got the devil himself on their side, they could never convince a jury, however thick-headed they might be, that the woman shot herself. Really, the idea is too ridiculous to entertain for an instant. Vecquerary killed her just as sure as I'm standing here.'

'I think so too,' answered Slark. 'But still counsel can twist things about so, and be so like truth so long as they are paid for it, that they can often convince a jury that black is white.'

'Well, they will have to convince the jury of something stranger than that if they prove that the woman shot herself,' said Hipcraft, with a decisiveness that suggested he was under the impression he had effectually clinched the argument.

'I suppose there is nothing else tonight?' asked the shadower.

'No. You may go—stop a minute, by the way. Do you know who is working up for the other side?'

'No. I have no idea.'

'Well, you must find out.'

'I will try to do so.'

'Try—hang it, man, you must. And when you've discovered him, dog his footsteps like his double.'

Mr. Hipcraft had not told his factotum about that little incident of the mysterious Calvin Velacott. He kept the matter to himself, because he could not help thinking that he had been sold—trapped—outwitted. Velacott had promised to return in a day or two with the information he said he could supply; but, like the enterprising gentleman who performs the confidence trick, he never came back again. Now, Mr. Hipcraft had such a very high notion of his own smartness and cleverness that his *amour propre* was deeply wounded at the bare idea of his having been overmatched. Hence the reason he had kept the little incident a secret. He remembered, too, that Mr. Calvin Velacott had suggested the possibility of the defence trying to prove that Mrs. Neilsen shot herself, and it seemed a little curious that Slark should have the same notion.

'I say, Slark,' he said, as a new thought struck him, 'have you heard anyone else speak of that idea about Mrs. Neilsen having shot herself?'

'No, not a soul.'

'What put it into your head, then?'

'It was simply an idea that occurred to me.'

'Ah, it's strange. Well, now, look here. If the defence should set up such a theory as you suggest, there is one thing that would utterly take the wind out of their sails.'

'What is that?' asked Slark.

'Proof that the pistol found by the dead body on the beach belonged to Vecquerary.'

'Yes, that would be a powerful link,' remarked Slark with an air of meditation.

'Yes, so powerful that all the counsel in Christendom wouldn't be able to break it. Well, now, you concentrate all your energies in trying to get undoubted proof of that. And I tell you what I'll do; if you succeed I'll give you twenty pounds.'

'Slark's eyes sparkled at the mere mention of such a sum, and he said:

'Well, governor, if it's in the power of mortal man to get proof of that I'll get it.'

As Slark wended his way towards his squalid lodgings he was dreaming of the twenty pounds; and as Mr. Hipcraft walked towards the Golden Star Hotel he thought to himself:

'Money is a wondrous power, and that wily scoundrel would sell his soul to Old Nick if he thought it would bring him money. It strikes me that the proof I want will be forthcoming.'

With this reflection the pleasant old man's spirits rose, and he was enabled to enjoy his billiards without being troubled by any qualms of conscience.

XXIX

STRIFE

The moment that Oriel Verecourt had received Muriel's letter asking him to call upon her as soon as possible he jumped into a cab—for she had sent the letter to his office—and drove straight to her house, and so it happened that he arrived just in time to meet Slark in the passage.

Muriel, who was agitated and upset, welcomed her lover very warmly, for it can easily be understood that she felt lonely and unhappy. He returned her greeting no less warmly, but his mind being full of his unexpected meeting with Slark, he asked:

'What has that fellow been doing here?'

'What fellow?'

'Why, the man I met in the passage.'

'Oh! You mean the detective.'

'Detective! He is simply a low, dirty spy.'

'Oriel, you are forgetting yourself.'

'No, dear, I am not. Do you know who the man is?'

'I have told you, he is a detective.'

'Did he give you his name?'

'No, I never thought to ask him.'

'Ah! that is just like a woman.'

'Is it, really?' said Muriel, showing anger. 'If you have such a poor opinion of women, why trouble yourself about them?'

'Now, don't get angry, Muriel. You know that I have a very high opinion of women.'

'Why do you speak so sneeringly, then?'

'I did not speak sneeringly. But I feel sure if you had known the character of that man you would not have admitted him to the house.'

'He was admitted by the servant,' answered Muriel, with decision and emphasis; 'and he represented himself to me as a detective engaged in getting up evidence against Vecquerary.'

'Against Vecquerary?'

'Yes.'

'And, of course, you told him all you could?'

'Yes, I did,' answered Muriel, with rising temper, 'and why should I not have done so?'

'Oh, well, seeing the opinions you hold about Vecquerary, of course there is no particular reason that I know of why you should not aid in every possible way the machinations of his enemies.'

Verecourt had certainly allowed his feelings to get the better of his judgment, or he would have been more guarded in his remarks. As it was, what he said not only stung Muriel, but made her very angry; and as her nerves were unstrung, and she was in a morbidly sensitive condition, she burst into tears, and displaying temper such as she had never shown before to him, she exclaimed:

'If you have only come here to insult me, the sooner you go again the better.'

'Muriel, how can you say that!' he remarked with tenderness. 'I have no intention, no wish to insult you, and I will make every allowance for your feelings; but I ask you to be just, even if you cannot find it in your heart to be generous. That man who has just gone away is Ephraim Slark, a creature of one

Richard Hipcraft, a low, scoundrelly lawyer, and perhaps the most deadly enemy poor Vecquerary has in the whole world.'

Muriel looked a little astonished at this information, but her anger was not abated.

'I know Mr. Hipcraft,' she said sharply. 'He was our fellow-passenger when we came up from Manchester, and I remember that Vecquerary was summoned for having treated him brutally in some hotel.'

'Let me set you right, Muriel,' said Verecourt sorrowfully. 'It is true that Vecquerary was summoned and fined; but he thrashed Hipcraft for speaking disrespectfully of your aunt.'

'Oh yes, I dare say!' cried the irritated girl. 'That was Vecquerary's version of the affair. But, at any rate, whatever Mr. Hipcraft may be, he didn't murder my dear aunt.'

'Muriel, I am surprised at you. Why do you talk so irrationally?'

This was only adding fuel to the fire, and Muriel's tears burst out afresh, and, stamping her foot, she exclaimed:

'You are a wretched, unkind creature, and I will thank you to go away.'

'But you sent for me.'

'Yes, I did. I wanted to ask your advice, but I would die now before I would do it.'

'Muriel, darling—'

'Don't call me darling; I won't be your darling any longer. You have insulted me enough over this unhappy and miserable business. And since I am leagued with the enemies, as you are pleased to term them, of my aunt's murderer, while you still choose to regard him as your friend, it is quite certain that we are not fitted for each other; therefore we will each go our own way.'

'Ah, Muriel!' Oriel exclaimed pathetically, and showing more feeling than he was wont to show. 'You are angry now and forget yourself, but tomorrow you will think differently.'

'Indeed, you are wrong,' she cried, her irritation in no way abated, 'for tomorrow I will return you all your letters and presents, and I never want to see your face again.'

'Muriel,' he answered, with very distinct traces of emotion in his voice, 'I will leave you tonight, as you seem to have lost control of yourself; but I cannot leave you in anger. Kiss me, at least.'

He tried to put his arm round her waist, but she drew quickly back, and with scornful mien exclaimed:

'How dare you! I am not quite the simpleton you take me for, and I will not tolerate insult either from you or any man living. All is at an end between us, and tomorrow I will return you everything you have ever sent me. And now, pray, relieve me of your presence.'

'So ends my dream,' he said with a sigh; and being sensible enough to see that argument with her in the half-hysterical condition she was in would be utterly useless, he added: 'Of course, I will relieve you of my presence, as you request; but, though you may have ceased to love me, I shall never cease to love you. And now answer me one question before I go. What did you tell Slark?'

With a certain spiteful delight in her tone she answered:

'I gave him all the information I possibly could, as well as a portrait of Mr. Tortolini, my poor dear aunt's husband. There! Are you satisfied?'

He was more than satisfied; he was surprised and hurt, but he wisely refrained from making any further remark.

'You will say good night to me, Muriel?' he said.

'I will say goodbye to you, and I hope I shall never see you again.'

He hesitated for a moment, as if debating in his mind whether he should not try and conciliate her, but he decided not to, and, drawing himself up proudly, he bowed, and without another word left the room. And when Muriel heard the street door close behind him she threw herself face downwards on the couch and wept a flood of tears. Her quarrel with her lover had torn her heart; but being proud, and believing that he was wrong and she was right, she resolved not to give in. Besides, she was not without a friend now, and presently, when she had mastered her feelings to some extent, she rose and penned a short note to Mr. Melville, saying that she had decided to accept his kind offer, and begging that he would take her away without delay. 'I shall be ready to go at an hour's notice,' she said. This letter finished, she sealed it up, and sent the servant off to the post with it at once; and as Muriel went to bed she thought: 'Mr. Oriel shall find that, though I am only a woman, I have spirit enough and strength enough to resent his unmerited contumely.'

XXX

THE RAVELLED SKEIN

Oriel Verecourt had far too much wholesome common-sense to be unduly cast down by the unfortunate quarrel between himself and the young lady he had looked upon hopefully as his future wife. If he felt it like a man, he also bore it like a man; and he made the most ample and generous allowance for her frame of mind, consoling himself with the thought that in a few days she would acknowledge to herself that she was in error; and then, when they had cemented up their difference, all would be well again. What really concerned him more than the quarrel was the thought that she had been trapped into aiding Vecquerary's enemies. It was too late then to telegraph to Mr. Farabin Tindal, who was in London; but he lost no time in doing so the following morning, making an appointment to meet at Verecourt's office at noon. He had already met Tindal by request of Alfred Vecquerary, so that they were not strangers. Tindal kept the appointment, and he then learned from Verecourt that Slark had been to Miss Woolsey's house, and had succeeded in obtaining from her a portrait of the late Mrs. Neilsen's husband, Tortolini.

Although Tindal had very decisively expressed his opinion that Hipcraft had not, either directly or indirectly, instigated the murder, he did not abandon the case. He had thought the thing out with the care and skill peculiar to himself; he had placed every detail under the microscope, figuratively speaking, and he saw things, or at any rate thought he saw things, that other people did not see. The only comment he made upon the information conveyed to him by Verecourt was this:

'Hipcraft is about as cunning a rascal as one could find in all London, and his tool, Slark, is only second to him. By the way, you know, of course, that Hipcraft has been engaged by the prosecution to get up evidence; and one of the sharpest and most unscrupulous counsel in the kingdom has been retained for the prosecution—that is, Sir George Jack, Q.C.'

'No, I did not know it,' answered Verecourt quickly, and with some change of colour in his face, for he could not fail to feel alarm for his friend's fate. 'And if that's the case, then,' he added, 'I fear it is all over with poor Vecquerary.'

Tindal smiled in his self-confident way, as he remarked quietly:

'Oh, I don't know! I should not be disposed to go quite that length. I never look upon a case as lost till it's won.'

'Well, you are more hopeful than I am. Perhaps you have something to justify your hope.'

'Not much. But I see certain possibilities.'

'Indeed! What are they?'

'At present they are so faint that you must pardon me if I decline to discuss them. I never like to commit myself to opinions until I have an inward conviction that I am right.'

'But do tell me this!' exclaimed Verecourt in an appealing way; 'do you really think Vecquerary shot poor Mrs. Neilsen?'

'You must again pardon me for not answering you. I cannot give an opinion either one way or the other.'

Although Verecourt felt disappointed, he was wise enough not to press the subject, but, like all men who hold desperate opinions that are in the nature of forlorn hopes, he would have been more encouraged if he had had support. But it was too obvious that, whatever were the views that found place in. Tindal's astute brain, no argument or persuasion could drag them forth until the man himself was disposed to reveal them. The art of thoroughly concealing one's thoughts is a rare one, but Tindal possessed it in a very high degree, and this power only served to emphasize still more his remarkable personality.

The interview ended, and Tindal went his way, returning to his lodgings in a small, unobtrusive hotel in a quiet street off Euston Road. Then he made notes for some time in his notebook, and after that he sat in pensive silence, his head resting on his hand, his elbow on the table, his eyes fixed apparently on vacancy. But probably he was conjuring up phantoms that he longed to clothe, so that he might make them actual realities and present them to his fellow-men. No one knew better than Tindal himself how abstruse was the problem set him; how tangled was the skein he had to unravel, if it was possible to unravel it at all. And, like all men who approach a duty earnestly and conscientiously, he could not fail to feel some anxiety about the success of his endeavours.

When Slark told his master that the Vecquerarys were rich, and would spare no expense in obtaining the best of counsel for their unfortunate relative, he was strictly accurate. Alfred Vecquerary, on behalf of himself and the members of the family, at once placed the matter in the hands of a firm of Manchester lawyers of very old standing and very high repute. They in turn, knowing that there was no limit to expense, gave a brief into the hands of a notable Q.C., who also secured several juniors; and with this formidable array on the prisoner's side, and the legal giant, Sir George Jack, opposed to him, the fight promised to be singularly stubborn, while all the circumstances of the case were destined to place it in the list of the most remarkable causes *celèbres* of the nineteenth century.

Mr. Tindal was aware that the little army of defence was perhaps as strong as the legal world could have furnished; but he was also aware that its strength would be as nothing if it had not powerful weapons in its armoury, and on his shoulders rested the responsibility of finding these weapons. He had accepted the responsibility, and he was fully, even painfully, conscious of the weight and importance of his trust. But he was not the man to flinch, and he had not accepted his commission until he had carefully weighed every pro and con, and had drawn inferences from the facts as they came before him.

His cogitations ended, he rose and dined—dined with almost Spartan-like frugality; his meal consisted of a humble chop, a crust of bread, and a small bottle of Bass's ale. Then he smoked a cigar, and dreamed dreams as he watched the filmy smoke rise in ghostly vapours ceilingwards. And at last he rose; changed his clothes for a suit that was tattered and torn and splashed with mud. To his closely-cropped head he adjusted a wig of tangled, coarse, dark red hair, and this wig fitted so accurately that no casual scrutiny would have detected it. Then he finished his costume with a rusty, battered hat, and thus attired it would have been difficult for a stranger to have recognised in him the neat, dapper-looking man of a quarter of an hour ago. He would have passed now for a street cadger, a crimp, a low type of bruiser, a needy adventurer—anything, in fact, but what he really was—a quiet, thoughtful, gentlemanly man, whose business in life was to solve human problems.

He slipped out of the hotel without attracting attention, and gained the Euston Road. Darkness had fallen, and a drizzling rain made the atmosphere like a wet blanket. He climbed up to the box seat of a 'bus bound London Bridgewards, and he sheltered himself with a dilapidated and battered umbrella. Presently Mr. Tindal got into conversation with the driver, who was a pure specimen of the London 'bus-driver, and as Tindal liked to know the opinions of all sorts and conditions of men, he gradually led this cockney Jehu to speak of the murder of Mrs. Neilsen. Jehu waxed warm on the subject, and it became very evident that he, after the manner of illiterate and illogical men—who, however, are far from being always wrong—had made up his mind on the subject, and that it would require something in the nature of a cataclysm to change his mind. And what his mind was may best be gathered from the following fragment of conversation—and Jehu gave vent to his feelings with a flippancy peculiar to his class. Let it first be premised that Mr. Tindal had stated that apparently it was not possible that any sane man could entertain a doubt about Vecquerary's guilt. Whereupon Jehu's purple face and red eyes were a study in disdain as he exclaimed:

'Look yer, governor, don'tchyer make any blooming error, for split me if I don't think they've got hold of the wrong bloke.'

'What makes you think that?' asked Tindal.

'What makes me think it? Well, I ain't one of them blooming mugs what cannot see a haystack when it's afore 'em.'

'But the evidence is perfectly clear,' urged Tindal.

'No, it ain't,' snapped Jehu, laying his whiplash about the near horse by way of emphasizing his distinct denial; 'it ain't nothink of the sort.'

'Why isn't it?'

'Cos I don't believe as the bloke what's in prison did it,' responded Jehu, with a lofty disdain for logic.

'But why don't you believe that?'

'Well now, look 'ere, governor,' began Jehu, with the air of a solemn judge laying down the law, 'it's this yere way. The gent what's in quod was nuts on the young 'ooman, and I don't believe as he'd agone and plugged her, seeing as how he had a misses and kids of his own, and he must 'a know'd as he'd be bowled out. Now, I'm open to bet as many pots of four-arf as yer can swaller in a blooming week that it was some other bloke as was jealous on her as shot her. But yer see the p'lice are such mugs that when once they get a hideayer can't put it outer their 'eads, they are that thick.'

Mr. Tindal was silent. Jehu's argument was forcible, even if his grammar was faulty and his language lacked polish, and as the detective descended at the Mansion House and mounted another 'bus that was going over London Bridge into the Borough he was unusually thoughtful. Up to then he had been working out a theory, which was that Mrs. Neilsen had shot herself. Now this uncultivated 'bus-driver's had knocked that theory to the wind, and his suggestion wove itself into Tindal's reasoning until it presented itself in such a feasible light that he admitted to himself that it was one of the phantom-like potentialities that he had been trying to grasp and single out from the many shadows that trooped before him, and at last fate had thrown him in contact with that rough specimen of the genus Jehu, who had been the unconscious means of giving him a new thread for his guidance.

Tindal had left his hotel with a fixed purpose, and that purpose now led him to the Borough; and when he reached the Elephant and Castle he walked down the Old Kent Road for a hundred yards or so, when he turned into an ill-lighted little street that was suggestive of squalor, misery, abject poverty, and the lowest depths of human degradation. Here he paused by a lamp-post, pulled out his note-book, and consulted it. He was evidently searching for an address, and, having found it and fixed it on his memory, he closed the book, restored it to his pocket, and pushed on. But the gloomy street, rendered still gloomier by the murky atmosphere, made it extremely difficult to distinguish the numbers of the houses, and he was compelled to ask a dirty drab of a girl who was passing to direct him, and the house he was in search of having been pointed out to him, he went straight to it, and after considerable knocking on the door his knocking brought forth an ancient beldame, her face stained with the grime of years, her rusty grey hair hanging like wind-tossed thatch about her forehead, and her tattered garments clinging like cerements to her wasted limbs. She bore a guttering tallow candle in her hand, and as she opened the door there came forth a smell of mouldiness and dirt.

Mr. Tindal stated his business, and the hag, with a scraggy finger pointing stairwards, told him to go up there to the first-floor front room. The stairs were carpetless and creaky, and seemed to have been utter strangers to scrubbing for many a year. Tindal groped his way up in the darkness until he gained the landing, and then was guided by a gleam of light that came from under the bottom of the door, which, owing to warping on the part of the door and sinking on the part of the floor, left a considerable space for the light to escape by. On this door Tindal tapped, and a metallic voice sung out 'Come in,' and Mr. Tindal, obeying the summons, found himself in the presence of Ephraim Slark.

XXXI

TELLS HOW CRAFT WAS BEATEN WITH ITS OWN WEAPON

Slark was smoking a short pipe and reading a newspaper by the light of a common dip when his unbidden visitor entered. The room was sparsely furnished, and such furniture as there was would not have brought a couple of pounds at an auction. A little square of faded old carpet covered the centre of the floor only; and a few very common and vulgar sporting prints hung on the walls, which in places were bare of paper. The ceiling was black with grime; the atmosphere of the room reeked with stale tobacco-smoke, and everything about the place was so suggestive of poverty and a struggle for existence that a stranger might have been tempted to ask if life was worth living under such conditions. Presumably Slark found that it was. At any rate, he clung to life with vulture-like tenacity, and the den and the man seemed suited. He himself represented such an unutterably mean type of human nature that it would have been difficult to associate him with any better surroundings than were to be found in that mean apartment.

Naturally he looked up in surprise as his visitor entered; the habitual cunning expression of his face was somewhat intensified, while something like a shade of uneasiness mingled with it, for he lived in a chronic state of fear of duns.

'You are Mr. Slark, governor, are you not?' asked Tindal in a voice that was an admirable counterfeit of that rusty, asthmatical wheeze peculiar to the street ballad-singer, who howls out his doggerel in all weathers, and tries to keep the cold out with drops of gin.

'Yes,' growled Slark sullenly, for he was not sure of his man. 'Who are you?'

'My name's Jim Rodgers, and I want to know if you can put me on a job?'

Slark drew his breath more freely as he asked:

'What kind of job?'

'Well, you see, I'm on the same lay as yourself. I'm a kind of jackal that provides food for the lawyers. I used to be with old Blenkinsop, of Liverpool.'

'Oh, yes; I've heard of Blenkinsop,' replied Slark. Blenkinsop had been one of the most notorious private inquiry agents' in the kingdom, and employed a perfect army of creatures of Slark's type. But he had been dead for several years. It is, perhaps, needless to say that Tindal had never been in the service of Blenkinsop, but he felt that the end he was aiming at justified the means he was taking. A strict regard for veracity cannot always be observed under such circumstances.

'But I can't do nothing for you,' added Slark to his last observation.

'I'm not so sure of that,' replied Tindal in the same rusty voice, as he seated himself on one of the wooden chairs, and placed his battered hat on the table, 'I can put you up to a wrinkle or two about the Neilsen murder case.'

These words struck home, and Slark's face lighted up with new interest.

'What do you know about it?' he asked quickly.

'A good deal, but I ain't going to tell you for nothing. I know Vecquerary, and I know a good deal about Mrs. Neilsen and her husband, Tortolini.'

'The deuce you do!' exclaimed Slark, his interest now thoroughly aroused.

'Yes; but I've been out of collar for some time, and am hard up, and if you can put me on the job I'll share the swag with you.'

'I'm open for that contract,' replied Slark, with an artful leer. 'What do you know about Vecquerary?'

'More than you, I bet.'

Slark's manner indicated that he was not quite sure of his ground, and was somewhat undecided how to act, but he asked a question that struck a keynote for Tindal. This was the question, his eagerness to obtain the information causing him to forget his usual caution:

'Do you know if Vecquerary was in the habit of keeping a revolver?'

Tindal smiled knowingly as he answered:

'I see what you are driving at, governor. I've read up all that's been published about the murder, and I ain't such a fool but that I can see this question of the revolver will be a weak link in the prosecution.'

'But that doesn't answer my question.'

'Of course not; and it's clear you've not been able to find out for yourself, or you wouldn't ask me.'

Slark felt somehow as if he had been pushed into a corner, though he had no idea how his question had delivered him into the hands of his opponent. But the remembrance of his employer's promise of twenty pounds for that missing link, and his greedy desire to earn the money, had thrown him off his guard.

'No, but I dare say I can find out,' he said, with assumed indifference.

'Perhaps you can with my help,' remarked Tindal. Slark grasped at this chance, as it seemed to him to be, and he put the point-blank query again:

'Do you know?'

'Look here, pal,' answered Tindal, with easy familiarity, 'I'm going to sell my knowledge, the same as you sell yours.'

Ephraim Slark rose, went to a cupboard, brought forth a couple of dirty glasses and a bottle containing a little gin. These things he placed on the table with the remark:

'Now, look here, old man, let's come to business. We are both in the same line, and if you will help me I'll help you. Have a thimbleful of the stuff, and then we'll talk.'

Tindal helped himself to a thimbleful, and a very small thimbleful; but it would have needed a giant's thimble to contain what Slark took, and as the sneak wiped his lips with the back of his hand, he gasped out:

'Ah, that puts life in one!'

'Well, now, I'll tell you what I'll do. If you will tell me if Vecquerary is known to have possessed a revolver, and give me proof, I'll put a fiver in your way.'

'I can't tell you now, but I'll undertake to find out.'

'How?'

'That's my little bit of business, cocky,' replied Tindal, as he laid his forefinger on his nose as a sign that he was too old a bird to be caught by having salt put on his tail; 'but you may take your affidavit I can do it, and your fiver's as good as earned.'

'Very well, that bit of "biz" is settled,' said Slark gleefully, as he helped himself to another giant's thimbleful of the "stuff" and pushed the bottle towards his visitor, who, however, declined the proffered hospitality, but accepted a long pipe and some tobacco; and the two men had soon filled the small room with a fog of smoke, and they chatted familiarly as if they had known each other for years.

Slark believed that he was hob-nobbing with a bird of precisely his own feather, and so he was less reserved than he otherwise would have been—indeed, he became quite confidential, and, as his intelligence and intellect, as compared with Tindal's, were as a rushlight to an electric lamp, Tindal probed him and drew him out, and got from him a good deal of information about his own views and the views of his employer, Hipcraft, and at last Tindal broke in somewhat abruptly with this question:

'There's no fear but what they'll convict Vecquerary?'

'Not the slightest. Three weeks after the verdict he'll be as dead as a door-nail.'

This belief put Ephraim Slark in such good spirits that, having finished the last of the gin in the bottle, he sent Mrs. Bingham, his landlady, out for another shilling's-worth; and under the influence of the fresh supply he grew pretty mellow and more confidential, for he was a weak-minded man, and, like all such men, he liked to brag of his own achievements, and he could not resist telling of his cleverness in obtaining an interview with Muriel.

This was Tindal's chance, and with assumed nonchalance he asked:

'Did she tell you anything about Tortolini?'

'No—well, that is, a little,' answered Slark, who by this time was thick-voiced and somewhat hazy in his ideas owing to the stuff he had imbibed, and, winking one of his bleared eyes, he asked: 'Do you know the fellow?'

'No. Do you?'

'No.'

'I'll tell you what I do know,' remarked Tindal. 'I know that Mrs. Neilsen had a photograph of him.'

'How the devil did you find that out?' asked Slark.

'Ah! that's my own affair,' said Tindal, with a laugh. Slark scratched his head. He was muddled, but presently his vanity got the better of him, and he said, with another wink:

'You're awfully clever, no doubt, old man, but you can't hold a candle to me. Now, won't you be surprised to hear that I've got that photograph?'

Tindal broke into a derisive laugh as he said:

'Look here, old man, you must tell that to the horse marines; I ain't quite such a mug as you think me?'

'I tell you I've got it,' roared Slark angrily.

'I don't believe it.'

'Will you make a bet?' asked Slark irritably.

'Yes.'

'How much?'

'A couple of bob;' and Tindal produced two shillings and laid them on the table.

'They are mine,' said Slark, as he grabbed the coins, thrust them into his pocket, then rose, drew out a bunch of keys and, opening one of a chest of drawers, he produced the photograph of Tortolini that he had received from Miss Woolsey.

Tindal took the portrait, examined it with critical scrutiny, then, as he handed it back, he remarked:

'Well, blow me if I thought you were speaking square when you said you had his likeness.'

'Bah!' hissed Slark, with a sneer of profound contempt, 'you ain't a match for me. I ain't been ferreting for twenty-two years without knowing my business. If I didn't, old Hipcraft wouldn't employ me. You are only a child in the profession yet. You've got a lot to learn, and I'll give you a wrinkle, pal. Don't try to best old stagers like myself. But, there, I don't want to sit on you too much. You've lost the two bob fairly, but we'll drink it.'

He was about to sing out for his landlady and instruct her to procure some more gin, when Tindal stopped him with the remark:

'No, not now. I've had enough. I'll take it out of you another time. I must go now.'

Slark tried to persuade him to stay, for he wished to make a night of it, having commenced, but, finding that his powers of persuasion were without effect, he remarked:

'Well, now, I tell you what it is; you work with me, and I'll make something of you. In six months' time turn you out perfect.'

'I know I've got a lot to learn,' answered Tindal humbly; 'but I try to learn something every day.'

A few minutes later he was groping his way down the greasy, creaky stairs, and he was glad to get into the murky street again, which, after the mephitic atmosphere of Slark's squalid apartment, seemed fresh and pure; and, as he wended his way back to his hotel, he felt that the evening had by no means been spent in a profitless manner.

XXXII

BETWEEN HOPE AND FEAR

The perversity of human nature has always been and always will be responsible for a large amount of unhappiness. That there should be differences of opinion is only in accordance with the law of our being, but when these differences arise between those who are near and dear to each other the results are often disastrous. Mr. Oriel Verecourt was to prove this in his own person, for when, a day or two after his misunderstanding with his fiancée, he called at her house, he was amazed—dumbfoundered, in fact—to find all the blinds drawn down, the place shut up, and no one there. It was manifest that Miss Woolsey had gone away, and either taken her servants with her or discharged them. On this latter point he received direct information from the next-door servant, who, seeing him there, and knowing him by sight, came out and told him that the servants had all been suddenly dismissed with a month's wages, and that the young lady' had gone off in a cab with an old grey-headed gentleman, and had taken a large quantity of luggage with her. It is needless to say that this piece of news caused Oriel much uneasiness and unhappiness. He had up to then attached no importance to his quarrel with Muriel, but it was obvious now that she had done so, and had meant what she said when she told him that she would say 'goodbye.'

It certainly did seem to him a very bitter ending indeed to his love dream, and its bitterness was enhanced and rendered infinitely more poignant by the tragic circumstances that had led up to this climax. During the time that he had been acquainted with Muriel and Mrs. Neilsen his life had known no shadow. His admiration for the elder lady had been unbounded, and his love for the younger one devout, sincere, honourable, and manly. And now one lay dead, and the other had deserted him.

How true it is, alas! that happiness in this world is but as a fleeting gleam of April sunshine; in the case of some people, more transitory even than that. We drink pleasure with a spoon; we sup sorrow from a cup.

Of course Verecourt could not get to know then where Muriel had gone to; her departure was to him in the nature of a flight, and her going and her whereabouts were alike a mystery. It will be remembered that after her interview with Mr. Leslie Melville she wrote to her lover, asking him to call upon her, and presumably it was her intention to discuss with him the offer Mr. Melville had made to her. When he did call, Slark, like a thing of evil—an ominous shadow—stood between them, and it was due to that wretched being that the quarrel arose. In consequence of that misunderstanding, Muriel did not tell her lover about Melville, and so the mystery of her going was the greater to Verecourt, who had not received the slightest information of her intention to leave London.

As he turned away he probably felt more downcast than ever he had felt before in the whole course of his life, and on arriving at his house his sorrow was accentuated by finding that Muriel, true to her word, had returned all his presents and letters. He had made her some valuable presents, and, with the ardency of the young lover, he had written her a large number of letters, but there they were now, confronting him like so many dead hopes. He could no longer doubt her determination to put an end to the engagement, and he was face to face with the fact that, after many months of sweet, and hopeful joy, a painful blow, terrible in its very suddenness, had fallen upon him, and his life was changed. One dear woman whom he had loved as a friend was dead—dead in her youth and beauty, stricken down by the hand of a cowardly and brutal assassin! The other, whom he had hoped to make his wife, had severed her connection with him, and the man whom he had come to regard with high esteem was a prisoner lying under the awful charge of murder.

It testifies in a large measure to Mr. Verecourt's noble disposition that this very fact of his friend being under such a shadow kept him up—kept him from despairing about himself; for he felt that, though he might lose his affianced wife, he must not abandon his unhappy friend until he was convinced beyond all possibility of doubt that Vecquerary was the murderer, but at present no such conviction would come to him. His faith in Vecquerary was unshaken, and that being so, he deemed it his sacred duty to do all he possibly could to prove that his faith was not misplaced. This duty kept him from dwelling too much on his new sorrow, though it was calculated to affect the whole of his life. For those who think that a true man can entirely get over a love disappointment know little of the masculine nature. Shallow and heartless some men may be, but he who loves sincerely, and loves deeply, and loses the object of his affection, feels the rupture for the rest of his days. It is no mere sentiment this, but an irrefragable truth. Verecourt, however, was destined to meet with other rebuffs, other trials of his faith and fortitude, for Tindal was as silent as the Sphinx about what he was doing and what he thought. This naturally was a great test to Oriel's faith, for he could draw but the one inference, and that was that Tindal had little hope of proving the accused man innocent; for had it been otherwise, why should he have been so reticent? Moreover, as the days sped away and grew into weeks, and the trial approached, public opinion settled into a firm conviction that Vecquerary had indeed stained his soul with the blood of the woman who had loved him. Oriel could meet with no one who shared his belief and views; and if at times he had been disposed to waver he could hardly have been blamed, for a man who can adhere to his opinion in the face of all the world is a courageous man indeed.

Vecquerary, being only a committed prisoner, and not a convicted one, was privileged to write to his friends without much restriction. He had, however, not availed himself to any great extent of this privilege. He had written a long letter to his wife, in which, with the frank honesty that had hitherto seemed to be distinctively characteristic of him, he told without reserve the whole story of his connection with Mrs. Neilsen, up to that awful moment when, on the wind-swept beach at Hastings, she sank to the ground mortally wounded. And in speaking of that awful deed he contented himself with saying: 'To me it is all a mystery. I heard the report, saw the flash of fire, and saw her fall, but mine was not the hand that slew her.'

He had also written three or four letters to his brother, but these mostly had reference to business matters; and at last, when Oriel Verecourt almost felt as if his faith would break down, the prisoner sent him the following letter:

'My Dear and Valued Friend,

'As the day for the commencement of the terrible ordeal of trial approaches, I feel as if the awful darkness in which I have been so suddenly plunged was thickening, and whichever way I turn my weary eyes not the faintest gleam of light gives me hope. Not that I fear to die. Thank God, and thank God again, I am endowed with such manhood that I regard death with indifference, but to have to die the death that seems to menace me makes me shrink with horror, for

I am innocent of this fearful deed. That I have been weak, and have erred, and wronged those near and dear to me, and whom I was in honour bound to protect, I humbly admit with sorrow and shame; but my hand did not slay dear Mrs. Neilsen, and in the sight of heaven, and before God, I swear solemnly I have not the remotest idea who did kill her. Of course, I know too well that the vows and asseverations of a man accused of such a terrible crime tell but little in his favour, for nearly all criminals when charged with murder assert their innocence. But I dare to think that you, who learned to esteem me, will believe me true; and Miss Woolsey, who knew me so well, and knew how I respected her aunt, will, I am sure, share your belief. Could I be assured that you and she regard me as a falsely accused man, I should experience a certain kind of negative happiness even in the gloom of my cell, and with the probabilities of a shameful death staring me in the face.

'But I should like to go even further than this, and, in the name of our friendship, exact from you a solemn promise that, even though I die an ignominious death, you will never rest so long as you live until you have proved my innocence. But, alas! to place such a burden upon a man who has nothing but the memory of a short friendship to sustain his zeal is too much, and I have no right to suppose that you will charge your life with any such task. I have little to cheer me in my loneliness, for though my lawyers seem indefatigable in their endeavours to get rebutting evidence, they are singularly reticent as to what is being done, or is likely to be done. So far as I understand, the line that the defence will take is that poor Mrs. Neilsen shot herself; and, as I recall all the details of that awful night so far as I can, it seems to me probable that she did, save for one thing—she had no earthly cause, so far as I know, to commit suicide. She had decided to sever our connection, but I was mad enough to want to continue it. That meeting was, as she said, to be our last. I wished to embrace her for the last time, but she refused to allow me to do so. In a confused and agonized state of mind, I turned away. Then there came a report and flash, and I saw her fall. From that moment the rest is a hideous nightmare to me.

'The shock seemed to numb my brain. I have but a confused and vague recollection of the after events. That I fled from the accursed spot is too true, and for this act you may call me coward. Condemn me as you like, I was impelled to flight by an impulse that took my reason prisoner. That is the only plea I can advance in justification of my act. I was perfectly guiltless of the crime of causing the dear woman's death, and yet I fled, and thereby gave point to the suspicions that must necessarily fall upon me; but I venture to think that few men indeed would have kept their presence of mind under such circumstances. To see a beloved friend suddenly stricken dead at your feet, to realize with equal suddenness that you will be held responsible for the death, is well calculated to deprive most men of their reason. I know it deprived me of mine. But even with death's cold grip upon me, I can take your hand. I can look steadily into your eyes, and I can say, with the full consciousness of the peril to my immortal soul if I say falsely, as God witnesseth I did not slay Mrs. Neilsen. I have learned since my arrest that a revolver was found near Mrs. Neilsen's body, and this seems to favour the theory of suicide. But though it tells against myself to say it, I cannot understand why she should have taken her own life. She was of a singularly cheerful disposition, and never once did she utter a single word to me that would suggest the likelihood of her resorting to such a means of ending her career.

'But I will no longer trespass upon your time and patience. I have told you the truth; but whether my statements will receive corroboration or not, Heaven alone knows. Be the result of the trial, however, what it may, I can but repeat again and again, until my latest breath, that I am innocent.

'Josiah Vecquerary.'

The effect of this letter on Verecourt was to strengthen his faith in Vecquerary, and to stimulate his energies to try and establish his innocence, and as soon after its receipt as possible he hurried off to see Tindal.

XXXIII

STRIKING A NEW TRAIL

Verecourt handed his friend's letter to Tindal to read, and the detective did read it with the deliberateness with which he did everything. And having read it he handed it back with a simple 'Umph,' which was capable of no interpretation, and conveyed no indication of the thoughts of that sphinx-like mind. Verecourt was distressed naturally, and he showed his distress in manner and voice as he asked:

'What is your opinion now? What do you think will be the result of the trial?'

'As regards my opinion, Mr. Verecourt, I must ask you to excuse me from giving it. If a man holds a decided opinion, he should be prepared to show that he has some solid foundation for it; otherwise, his opinion may be a mere question of prejudice or bias. Then as to the result of the trial; that is a foregone conclusion, unless very strong evidence indeed is forthcoming that the lady shot herself, or was shot by someone else other than Vecquerary.'

'But you have been engaged in the case now for some weeks,' cried Verecourt despairingly, 'and is it possible that you have failed to get hold of something that will throw doubt on Vecquerary's guilt?'

'It is not only possible, but it is absolutely so,' answered Tindal.

Verecourt's hopes sank, and his heart grew heavy.

'Poor Vecquerary!' he said, with a sigh; 'I fear there is little chance of his escaping. It's awful, perfectly awful!'

'It is,' returned Tindal, with some sympathy in his tone. 'But let me tell you this much. You see, when I first took the matter up, what I heard led me to think it was within the bounds of possibility that this crime had been instigated by some enemy of Vecquerary's, who out of pure revenge was desirous of fixing the crime on Vecquerary. If such a depraved being as this existed—and knowing human nature as I do, I knew unhappily that he was not a monster of a diseased imagination, but an absolute entity among human kind—I felt sure, all the circumstances considered, that I must look for him in the person of Richard Hipcraft. I gained an interview, however, with this man, and though I found him to be a cynic of the worst possible kind, as well as possessed of a nature that was capable of the most uncompromising hatred, I was forced to the conclusion that the suspicion that had half taken shape in my mind could not be entertained. Whatever Hipcraft may be, he is entirely innocent of Mrs. Neilsen's death. Since then I have had an interview with his creature Slark—a type of a low, cunning, vulgar, unprincipled, sordid human fox. This fellow is a perfect tool of his master, and I am disposed to go the length of saying that, if he were well paid for it, he would not have much compunction about taking the life of that master's enemy. But Slark had no hand either directly or indirectly in Mrs. Neilsen's death.

Verecourt uttered an involuntary groan, as the detective's statement only served to point more forcibly to Vecquerary's guilt.

'Having failed,' continued Tindal in his quiet, deliberate way, 'to connect either of these two men as an accessory to the fact, in even a remote degree, I have turned my attention to endeavouring to find something that would warrant the assumption of suicide.'

'Well?' exclaimed Verecourt eagerly.

'I am sorry to say I have failed there also.'

Verecourt groaned again, and said with unmistakable emphasis:

'And yet I cannot, will not believe Vecquerary is guilty.'

Without taking any notice of this remark, Tindal continued:

'I am aware that the defence is to be suicide, but I must confess that I don't quite see how that defence is to be supported.'

'But there is the pistol,' ejaculated Verecourt; 'is it not possible to prove that Mrs. Neilsen kept a revolver?'

'Ah! now you touch upon the one weak link in the chain of evidence forged by the prosecution. I know that the other side are aware of this weakness, and they have made the most desperate efforts to get proof that Vecquerary was in possession of the revolver.'

'And have failed?' cried Verecourt, with a sense of new hope rising.

'Yes, failed. I know almost every move they have made in this direction. Slark has been to Manchester; Vecquerary's house has been ransacked; his servants subjected to the most searching examination; the leading gunsmiths in Manchester and London have been visited, but up to the present not a grain of evidence has been obtained to prove that the revolver belonged to the accused man.'

'That is a grand point, then,' cried Verecourt quite gleefully, as his hopes rose still higher.

'On the other hand,' pursued the detective, 'it is as hopeless to try and prove that the murdered lady had a revolver in her possession.'

'Of course you have tried to find out if she did keep firearms?'

'Yes.'

'And failed?'

'And failed.'

'But still,' urged Verecourt, 'this weak link that you speak of must tell against the prosecution.'

'It might, other things being in accord; but I am afraid the evidence altogether is so powerfully circumstantial that one weak link will scarcely invalidate it.'

Verecourt's hopes sank again, and despair arose.

'Then your opinion is,' he said, 'that Vecquerary will be hanged?'

'My opinion is that Vecquerary will be hanged, unless something little short of a miracle turns up to save him,' was the quiet answer.

As Verecourt retraced his steps homeward he was conscious of a sense of blank despair. How, indeed, could it be otherwise after that interview? For Tindal had made it manifest that he himself was hopeless, and that he had exhausted his resources. At any rate, that was the inference Verecourt drew, and with such a man, whose nature was genuineness itself, and whose friendship was true and noble, it was terrible, very terrible, for him to have to break down his faith, and come to the conclusion that his friend was guilty. But, as a matter of fact, he found the greatest difficulty imaginable in coming to any such conclusion. To the world generally this might have seemed like perverse obstinacy, even if it had not been described by a stronger expression. But Verecourt having once made up his mind to a thing was not easily turned, and he still found refuge, so to speak, in the suicide theory, notwithstanding that no proof was forthcoming that Mrs. Neilsen had ever possessed a revolver.

So full of anxiety was he that he resolved to call upon Mr. Lewis King, the lawyer who was engaged in getting up the case for the defence. This gentleman was the London representative of the Manchester firm engaged by Alfred Vecquerary on his brother's behalf. He bore a high reputation in his profession, and was said to be a man of remarkable acumen. Verecourt knew him casually, as they were near neighbours at Kew, and Mr. King was aware how deeply interested the young man was in Vecquerary's fate. But notwithstanding this Mr. King was reticent and guarded, after the manner of his kind. He was careful not to commit himself to any direct statement until Verecourt said:

'I have seen Tindal, and he has told me he has failed to trace the ownership of the pistol.'

'Yes, I know,' said Mr. King.

'But will not that tell in the prisoner's favour?'

'To some small extent it may, but the other evidence is too strong to be materially affected.'

'Then you think the verdict will go against Vecquerary?'

'I am afraid it will, unless we can counteract the evidence.'

'Then all I've got to say,' exclaimed Verecourt desperately, 'is that if Vecquerary shot Mrs. Neilsen he was absolutely mad at the time, and not responsible for his act.'

A strange expression came over the lawyer's face. It was the expression of the sudden dawning of a new idea.

'By Jove,' he exclaimed, 'you strike a new keynote. That is a theory we have not yet touched upon, but I can see certain potentialities in it. Tell me, now, have you ever heard of your friend doing strange and eccentric things?'

'No; I cannot say that I have.'

'But you know that he was strangely infatuated with Mrs. Neilsen?'

'Yes.'

'And your own opinion is that a determination on her part to put an end to the connection might have had such an effect on Vecquerary as to absolutely turn his head?'

'Yes; I firmly believe so.'

'Well, I tell you what it is,' remarked Mr. King, musingly; I think we have struck a new trail, and I think Vecquerary may be saved from the hangman, at any rate.'

This was not much, but it was something, and it served to keep Verecourt's faith alive.

XXXIV

A NEW THREAD

Anyone who has ever had anything to do with legal cases, whether criminal or civil, will know with what eagerness the weaker side will fasten on a point that is likely to tell in their favour. This only illustrates in another fashion the drowning man and the straw. The ethics of the legal mind, it need hardly be said, are of a singularly elastic kind; improbabilities that would at other times be laughed to scorn are seized upon and advanced with all the gravity that a counsel knows so well how to assume, when he is fighting a losing cause. A lawyer understands, perhaps better than most people, the weakness of men; their impressionable side, and their vulnerable points. And as all is considered fair in love and war, so does a lawyer consider it fair to do anything and say anything, however contemptible and mean, if it only gives him an advantage over his opponent.

It has already been stated, but it may be repeated, that nearly everyone who was interested, either directly or indirectly, in the terrible tragedy at Hastings, believed Vecquerary guilty. In the minds of these persons it was only a question as to which degree his guilt should be classed in. Those who were arrayed on his side were aware that money was plentiful, and a long purse is a mighty powerful lever. Well backed up, therefore, with the sinews of war, the defenders were resolved to make as stubborn a stand as possible, though this resolve did not prevent them from seeing that their chances of winning were as small as they could be.

Mr. Lewis King, who was aged, and respectable as lawyers go, showed what his views were during his conversation with Oriel Verecourt. He sheltered himself under no ambiguous expression, but stated plainly that the verdict would be against Vecquerary unless the evidence could be counteracted. Now, that was the very point: and the question was, 'Could it be counteracted?' Mr. King was clearly of opinion that it could not. Consequently, Verecourt's suggestion that Vecquerary must have been literally insane at the time he shot Mrs. Neilsen was jumped at, so to speak, by King, who, as he himself put it, saw 'certain potentialities' in it. That is, if it could be proved that Vecquerary was suffering from aberration of intellect at the time he committed the crime, he would at least be saved from the extreme penalty of the law. It is beyond all question of doubt that Mr. King would not have thought of playing this card if he had had any hope of proving the innocence of the accused man. But he had no such hope, and so he telegraphed for Tindal.

'Tindal,' he said, when that gentleman arrived, 'it seems to me that it is a perfect waste of time trying to prove Vecquerary guiltless, and what we have got to do is to mitigate the penalty. Now I want you to set to work on a fresh track, and to get up evidence to convince the jury that the man has been subject to occasional aberration of intellect, and that he must have literally lost his reason when he killed the woman. Do you understand?'

'Oh yes.'

'Well, now, don't lose any time. Everyone who has been friendly to him, and who may be trusted to follow a lead, must be got hold of. This is really the only card we have got to play, and we must play it well, and much will depend upon you. I think I make myself clear.'

'You do,' answered Tindal, who seemed unusually thoughtful and preoccupied: 'but the fact is, I don't believe in the irresponsible idea. If Vecquerary did kill the woman he was just as sane at the time as you are or I am now.'

'If he did kill the woman!' exclaimed King irritably, laying great stress on the word if. Have you any reason to suppose that he did not, that you should speak in such a way?'

'I have no reason,' he replied.

'Then, what do you mean?'

'Exactly what I have said. It's no use attempting to split hairs.'

'What we've got to do,' replied Mr. King decisively, and with some display of temper, 'is to make out the best case we can, and we have so little to work upon that our chances are small.'

'I admit that the chances are not very good,' returned Tindal, 'but there are certain features in the case that puzzle me, and I do not like to feel that there is a puzzle I cannot solve. You may say that that is egotism. Well, I am indifferent as to what you say; but the fact is, the man who does not believe in himself seldom accomplishes much.'

'I am not indifferent to your known abilities,' remarked the lawyer in a tone of irony, for he felt a little annoyed at what he considered Tindal's want of deference. 'But however clever you may be, you cannot accomplish the impossible any more than any other man.'

'No,' answered Tindal, 'I cannot; but some people are rather given to look upon ordinary difficulties as impossibilities.'

'Well, all I've got to say is,' observed Mr. King irritably, 'if you are not disposed to work on the lines I lay down, I must, in common fairness to my clients, engage the services of someone else.'

Tindal smiled as he answered, with provoking coolness:

'You seem to forget, Mr. King, that I do not receive my instructions from you, but direct from Mr. Alfred Vecquerary, nor do I occupy the position of a mere lawyer's scout. Let us understand each other, however. The position, to me at least, is clear. You have got to make the best possible defence you can for your client; and, so far as I can, I will aid you in doing that.'

Mr. King had no wish to prolong the interview, for he felt there was a certain antagonism between him and Tindal; perhaps he was conscious that Tindal was the better man, and that would be sure to make him angry. At any rate, he said sharply:

'Very well; you know what my views are, and with or without your aid I shall endeavour to carry them out. To attempt to prove Vecquerary innocent is a perfectly hopeless task; to prove him insane will be comparatively easy; and it's no use losing the substance by grabbing at the shadow. My instructions to counsel will be to plead insanity.'

'And the plea may or may not succeed,' remarked Tindal, in a manner that clearly indicated that he had his own particular views, but did not deem it necessary to explain them then.

As he went away he was conscious that his interview with the self-opinionated lawyer had stimulated him to renewed exertions. The probabilities are that this feeling arose in some measure from wounded vanity. A pardonable vanity it may be, but he was not so obtuse as to fail to see that King had been disposed to snub him; and Tindal was not the man to be snubbed with impunity, it mattered not who the snubber might be. And there was another thing he had to admit—he had been influenced by Vecquerary's letter to Oriel Verecourt, which the latter had allowed him to read. He had made no comment at the time of reading it; but, perhaps, he did not even know then that it had influenced him. Now, however, he was disposed to say to himself: 'I would rather think Vecquerary innocent than guilty.' Then he reviewed what he had done already, and he did not feel satisfied, and he resolved to begin *de novo*. The next few days, therefore, he spent in Manchester, and had several interviews with Alfred, who, as may well be imagined, was in sore distress of mind. He asserted, too, in the most positive manner that he felt sure his brother had never possessed a revolver. Mrs. Vecquerary, who was now convalescent, though terribly weak and shattered, also vowed that her husband had never possessed a revolver during her married life.

Then, with the utmost patience, and in the most searching manner, Tindal traced Vecquerary's life so far as it was possible to do, from his first meeting with Mrs. Neilsen to his quarrel with his wife; his return to London, his going to Mrs. Neilsen's house that evening, and from thence to the theatre. From that point the movements of each of the chief actors—that is, Vecquerary and Mrs. Neilsen—were not so clear. But a new thread was obtained by Tindal in the shape of the letter which Mrs. Neilsen wrote to Vecquerary the morning after the theatre episode, and in which she appealed to him as a man of honour not to call upon her again. No doubt it will be asked how it was Tindal had not seen this letter before. The fact is, it was amongst Vecquerary's effects in London, which were seized by the police immediately after the tragedy. And it may here be stated as a broad principle that when the police arrest a person on suspicion of having been guilty of a crime they assume his guilt, and that it is for them to make the assumption good. From the very nature of their position the police must always be on the side of the prosecution; and so anything likely to tell as evidence against their man they jealously guard. Thus it came about that Tindal was kept in ignorance of the existence of that letter until he heard of it by chance from a friend who was in the Criminal Investigation Department of Scotland Yard. He at once applied for and obtained an order to see it; and its perusal raised a set of new ideas in his mind.

He asked himself why she had been prompted to write that letter. It was necessary to suppose there was something anterior to it. What was that something? Had they quarrelled at the theatre the night before? Had she been urging him not to see her again? If either of these two questions could be answered in the affirmative, the *raison d'être* of the letter would be intelligible enough. If it were otherwise, then it left a blank to be filled, a something to be accounted for; and Tindal was not the man to allow a matter of that kind, though apparently it was so insignificant, to be passed over without closer scrutiny. Now, the only person likely to throw any light upon the doubtful point was Miss Woolsey; and as she had notified her new address to the police, as she was bound to do, Tindal posted off to see her.

XXXV

THERE IS DESTINY IN ALL THINGS

The residence of Mr. Leslie Melville was situated on the border of one of the Yorkshire wolds, and far enough removed from the fret of the passionate world to be out of its roar. The house, a very old one, was known as the 'Grange,' and it had long been in the possession of the Melvilles, who were classed amongst the oldest and most honoured of the Yorkshire families. The present owner, Leslie Melville, was one of the proudest of his race; and no one but himself knew to what an extent he had made an idol of his beautiful daughter Sabena. For years it had been his dream that she should marry a favourite nephew of his, an army officer, and heir to a fortune; but poor Sabena had never taken to her cousin; and at last, falling under the sway of the adventurer Tortolini, she forgot the honour of her house and the duty she owed her parents, and secretly became his wife. There is no doubt whatever that that mesalliance darkened Mr. Melville's life, and wrecked the peace of his bright and happy home. It was a blow that his pride bent under, and though it tortured him to do it, he resolved never to see his daughter again. Whether he would have continued to keep that resolve or not, had she lived, it is difficult to say. One thing is certain—he did not lose his interest in her. He had set a watch upon her, and knew that she had been living separate from her husband.

At times he had yearned to take her back, but his pride had so hardened his heart that he could never bring himself to say in effect to her: 'Come, come to me; I am your father still, and you are my best-beloved child.' Then suddenly the news of that terrible crime at Hastings reached him, and he was bowed into the dust with sorrow. When the first effects had passed away, he began to try and think of some means to appease his conscience; for now, when too late, he blamed himself for his hardness and his pride. He was lonely and desolate. The vacant chairs in his home filled him with mourning; the silence of its deserted chambers was terrible to bear. Everything about the place seemed to reproach him for having so long estranged himself from his child; and now that the hand of death had removed her, he could no longer endure his loneliness, and so he determined that, if possible, Muriel, whom his child had loved, should be a daughter to him, and lighten his path to the grave. It is probable, however, that his hopes in this respect would have been doomed to disappointment had Muriel not quarrelled with her lover. But there is destiny in all things, and the winds that blow evil to one waft pleasure to others. Muriel's quarrel, while it caused Oriel Verecourt a bitterness of sorrow such as he had never before experienced, gave to old Mr. Melville a companion and a solace in his stricken old age. When Miss Woolsey told her lover that she would sever her connection with him, she fully meant what she said, and she determined to adhere to it, notwithstanding that it was an awful wrench to her; so much so, that for some days after her arrival in Yorkshire she was prostrated.

When Tindal went down to the Grange he simply sent his name to Miss Woolsey, but did not state his business, and so she declined to see him. But he returned a message that it was of the highest importance she should grant him an interview, and so, by the advice of Mr. Melville, she consented to do this, but only on condition that Mr. Melville was present.

With the tact and caution so characteristic of him, Tindal approached his subject in such a different manner, and with so much more grace and gentleness than Slark had displayed, that he made a very favourable impression.

Tindal's questions were directed to trying to clear up the mystery of the letter which Mrs. Neilsen had sent to Vecquerary the morning after they had visited Drury Lane Theatre. Did she know why that letter had been sent?

Muriel answered that she did not know the reason. She had not seen the letter, but her aunt had told her she had written to Vecquerary to tell him that he must not come again. Very naturally Muriel was anxious to know the cause for this request, but Mrs. Neilsen would give no reason, nor could Muriel suggest one. All that she knew was that her aunt had been suddenly taken ill at the theatre, and had left the box with Vecquerary. That night Mrs. Neilsen seemed very unhappy, and after Vecquerary had gone away she wrote the letter to him.

This information only served to deepen the mystery of the letter, and Tindal felt that some strange and sudden motive had prompted the unfortunate lady to write it; and though he attached much importance to that motive, he had to admit to himself that there did not seem much possibility then of his discovering it.

Up to this point he had not told Muriel that his interest in this dark and complicated case was to try and prove if possible that Vecquerary was innocent, but he did so now, with the result that he raised Muriel's indignation, and she told him, as she had told Oriel Verecourt, that nothing could convince her that Vecquerary did not do it. She knew that her aunt wanted to get rid of him; she knew that with that end in view Mrs. Neilsen went to Hastings, and that he followed her there; that they met on the beach, and she was murdered; and to Muriel it seemed as if it would have been an outrage on an idiot's intelligence for anyone to suggest that Vecquerary did not kill her.

Tindal was not disconcerted by Miss Woolsey's little outburst. He knew his business too well. He was far too patient to be turned from a purpose by a slight rebuff; and so by delicate argument he showed her that it was her bounden duty to help in every possible way to elucidate the mystery, and that, however much she might be prejudiced against Vecquerary, she had no business to stand in the way of those who were anxious only to arrive at the truth. His argument told so that he next asked her to allow him to inspect any letter or other papers she might have in her possession that had belonged to her aunt.

Muriel strongly objected to this at first. The papers and letters of her dead aunt were to her sacred. Her first impulse had been to destroy them, but she could not bring herself to do that; and she had allowed them to remain where her aunt had always kept them—that was, in a large, old-fashioned mahogany desk.

At this point of the interview Mr. Melville interposed, and suggested that Tindal should be allowed to casually inspect such letters as Muriel might think would help in clearing away anything that was now obscure. The result was, that Muriel brought the desk from her room, and handed such letters to Tindal as she considered he ought to be allowed to look at; but a very hasty glance served to convince him that not one of these had any bearing on the case. But at last Muriel came across a little note that was in a blank envelope, and was stowed away in a small inner drawer of the desk. This note caused the colour in her face to brighten, as though with a feeling of indignation; and after some reflection she handed the note to Tindal with the remark:

'You can look at that, but I don't know that it has any value.'

Tindal took the letter, and as he read it his whole manner changed; and his usually almost stolid features seemed to betray excitement, and yet this is all the sheet of paper contained:

'Dear Madame,

'Your husband, Mr. Tortolini, is too ill to write himself, and requests me to do so. He says that you must send him some money by the end of the week, or the consequences may be unpleasant for you. He is really in very great distress, being much pressed by duns, and as his health is very bad, he is not in a condition to endure the worry. I trust, therefore, you will relieve him from his creditors, and he will not trouble you again.

'Your obedient servant,

'Solly Williams.'

'This is an important letter,' said Tindal, as he folded it up and restored it to its envelope. It bore a date three months before, and gave an address in Boulogne. 'Have you ever seen it before, Miss Woolsey?'

'No, never.'

'Your aunt never told you about it?'

'No; but it explains a good deal now that was then a puzzle. I know that my aunt about that time was very much troubled. I remember that one day I had been out with some friends, and on returning home I found Mrs. Neilsen in a state of great distress. I asked her what had upset her, but she turned the matter off. Subsequently one of the servants told me that a strange man had called, and after he had gone my aunt appeared to be very ill. Of course, I asked my aunt who the man was, and I recollect that she seemed quite irritated, and requested me not to refer to the subject again.'

'Well, Miss Woolsey,' said Tindal, 'there may or may not be something worth inquiring into in what you tell me. At any rate, I will take the letter with me.' He spoke like one who was quite unconcerned, but there was an unmistakable expression of eagerness in his face that was altogether unusual. In a general way his face was no index to what was passing in his mind, but how it was, and what it seemed to indicate was that Tindal had made a discovery. Can you fix the date of the visit of the strange man?' he asked.

'I should think it is about four months ago.'

'Your aunt never mentioned the subject again, I suppose?'

'Never.'

'Did you not think it strange?'

'I did at the time; but Mrs. Neilsen soon recovered her wonted spirits, and I forgot all about it.'

'On the night you went to the theatre there was another lady with you, was there not?'

'Yes, a Mrs. Shenstone, a widow, an intimate friend of my aunt's.'

Mr. Tindal got the address of this lady, and then he requested Muriel to make careful search amongst the letters to see if there was anything else from Solly Williams, but nothing could be found.

The following day Mr. Tindal journeyed back to London, and that evening he called upon Mrs. Shenstone at her residence in Brompton.

This lady, who was the widow of a stockbroker, who had left her fairly well off, had known Mrs. Neilsen for a long time, and had been her confidante.

'Of course, you were aware that Mrs. Neilsen's husband was living?' Tindal asked.

'Yes, she told me that; but not very long before her death. Nor do I think she would have told me, but I was frequently urging her to marry Vecquerary, believing he was a single man. At last, one day, in sheer desperation, she said it was impossible to adopt my advice, as her first husband was living.'

'She was very much attached to Vecquerary, was she not?'

'Yes.'

'And would have married him had there been no barriers?'

'There is no doubt about it.'

'Vecquerary was fond of her, too?'

'Oh, yes. I should say he was infatuated with her.'

'Then you don't believe that he killed her?'

'Oh, indeed, I do,' exclaimed Mrs. Shenstone, tossing her head in a scornful way, as though she felt indignant at the question. 'If he did not, pray who did?'

'That is what I should like to find out,' replied Tindal calmly.

'Why, of course he killed her,' added Mrs. Shenstone warmly. 'She was determined to sever the connection, and he became desperate.'

'Do you know why she wished to sever the connection?'

'Well, yes, I think I do. But I have kept this matter to myself, because I was afraid of being dragged into the affair.'

'But, madame,' said Tindal solemnly, and in a tone of reproach, 'it is the solemn and sacred duty of everyone who can, even at the sacrifice of one's feelings, to help justice to unravel the knotted threads of crime. As you say, Vecquerary may be guilty; but his guilt must be placed beyond the possibility of a shade of doubt; and in these cases motive goes a long way. Let it be clearly shown that the wretched man had a powerful motive, and his guilt is half established.'

Mrs. Shenstone seemed deeply impressed by this line of argument, and said:

'Well, I feel so incensed against Vecquerary that he shall not escape punishment if I can help it. The fact is, the night we went to the theatre Tortolini was there.'

'What! Mrs. Neilsen's husband?'

'Yes.'

'Indeed!' exclaimed Tindal, showing more surprise than he was ever wont to do.

'Yes, I did not know it at the time. But Mrs. Neilsen became ill in the box, and Vecquerary took her out to the corridor, where she swooned. Two days after that she called on me, and said that she had suddenly observed her husband in a box immediately opposite ours; and that, while she was sitting in the corridor waiting for Vecquerary to bring her some wine, her husband, looking fierce and wicked, came towards her, and she was so alarmed that she screamed and fainted.'

'Did she know her husband was in London?' Tindal asked.

'No. Up to that night she believed he was living in Boulogne.'

'Are you acquainted with a man by the name of Solly Williams?'

'No; I never heard of him.'

'Mrs. Neilsen never told you, then, that her husband had applied to her for money?'

'Never.'

Mr. Tindal did not prolong the interview. He had no further questions to ask. Nor did he deem it necessary to show Mrs. Shenstone the letter he had got from Muriel, and which bore the signature of 'Solly Williams,' whoever he might be. Perhaps he was a myth, perhaps not, but on that point Tindal was resolved to satisfy himself before he was much older.

XXXVI

FARABIN TINDAL'S TRIUMPH

About a fortnight before the date fixed for Vecquerary's trial an evening paper, which had long distinguished itself for what is known in the journalistic world as smartness, published the following paragraph, to which it gave conspicuous prominence by means of leaded type and a large heading:

> 'THE HASTINGS TRAGEDY.
>
> 'For some days extraordinary rumours have been circulated with reference to the murder of Mrs. Neilsen at Hastings. It will be remembered that soon after the arrest of Vecquerary the question was freely mooted whether it was not probable that the unfortunate lady had committed suicide, and this theory found a good number of supporters. We are in a position to state, however, that the defence have given up the idea of suicide, and will endeavour to prove Vecquerary's entire innocence. In fact, if our information is correct, some very extraordinary revelations may be expected, and the dénouement may prove to be as sensational as anything recorded in the annals of crime.

From the influence of the journal in question, this announcement caused a flutter of excitement, and of course it put its morning contemporaries on the *qui vive*; and the note thus sounded was taken up by all the dailies, and various versions appeared. When Mr. Hipcraft read the paragraph—for, of course, it speedily came under his notice—he was, to use a vulgar but expressive term, 'flabbergasted,' and, having sent for his devoted Slark, he asked that gentleman what it meant.

'Well, I don't know,' was the answer. 'I don't think it means much. I know that the other side have been moving heaven and earth to try and get evidence to refute the charge of murder against Vecquerary; but I have not heard that they have succeeded in obtaining anything that could give them hope.'

Mr. Hipcraft was not quite satisfied with this answer; he had a somewhat painful recollection of that mysterious visit paid to him by Calvin Velacott, who had never returned, and he had long felt convinced that Velacott was an enemy in disguise, who had proved the sharper man of the two. Had he been further aware of Slark's hob-nobbing with one 'Jim Rodgers,' the wily lawyer might have been even more disturbed in his mind than he was; but, for reasons of his own, Mr. Ephraim Slark had deemed it prudent to keep that little episode of Rodgers' visit to him a secret. The reminiscence was not a pleasant one for Slark to dwell upon, because he had come to the unalterable conclusion that he had been sold; and there are few things that make a man feel smaller in his own estimation than a knowledge that he has been outwitted. Slark knew that he had been outwitted, but he was ignorant to what extent—had he really known, he would have been more uncomfortable than he was. But whatever his thoughts were in this respect, it was perfectly manifest that he had no shadow of idea that his side would not triumph. That the defence would make a desperate fight for their man was known by the forces they had arrayed, but that they would carry their man triumphantly out of the fray seemed too preposterous to be looked upon as even a remote possibility. But the adage that it is the unexpected that always happens was to receive a striking confirmation in this instance; and Farabin Tindal was to uphold his reputation as a born genius in the way of solving abstruse problems of human wickedness.

After his interview with Mrs. Shenstone, Tindal began to feel that the scent was getting stronger, and acting on the letter signed 'Solly Williams,' which he had obtained from Miss Woolsey, he proceeded to Boulogne, to the address given, and he found that Solly Williams was by no means a mythical personage. Mr. Williams turned out to be an adventurer in the most objectionable sense. It is not relevant to this history that his career should be followed step by step, although it would have made a story in itself; but it may be briefly stated that, coming from a fairly good family, he began life as a midshipman in the navy and, having risen to the position of lieutenant, he was tried by court-martial for 'mutinous conduct, drunkenness, theft, and assaulting his superior officer while in the execution of his duty.' This formidable charge being fully substantiated, he was sentenced to be dismissed his ship in disgrace, and to suffer two years' imprisonment.

At the expiration of his sentence this enterprising gentleman resolved from that day forth to live by his wits. He knew that the world was full of fools, who could be easily preyed upon by anyone who laid himself open to do it; and Solly Williams, being young, good-looking, plausible in his manner, of good address, with a glib tongue, and a most dangerous element of cunning, succeeded in making victims, especially amongst women, until he met with an accident. However remarkable it may seem in connection with such a character, it is, nevertheless, a fact that he had a passion for chemistry, that he might have turned to good, honourable, and profitable account had he been possessed of application. But there was his weak point. He loved ease, he hated work; he was a devotee of all those pleasures that minister and pander to the flesh. But still it came about that he dabbled by fits and starts in his favourite science, and one day, while trying an experiment with some highly dangerous gases, an explosion occurred and sent the experimenter a senseless mass into a corner of the room. After this he was six months in the hospital, and was at last discharged cured. But his face was frightfully disfigured; one eye was entirely gone, and his left arm was so crippled that he had little use in it.

This misfortune served to embitter and sour his nature, and he took up swindling as a fine art, until it became necessary for him to retire to France to escape making the acquaintance again of an English prison. At last he drifted to Boulogne, where Mrs. Neilsen's husband, Tortolini, was residing. The two men met, and at once an attachment sprang up. Tortolini was the more brilliant, the more accomplished, and the cleverer adventurer of the two, and Williams, recognising this, tacitly gave evidence that he was prepared, metaphorically, to sit at the feet of the other and worship him. Williams, in fact, became Tortolini's factotum and willing tool. It was strange that it should be so, but it was true; and the connection presented one of those striking psychological peculiarities which are constantly cropping up in connection with our common nature. In due time Williams learnt from Tortolini of his marriage, and at the bidding of his master he tried to find out Mrs. Tortolini's address. But in this effort he was not successful until the police-court affair between Richard Hipcraft and Vecquerary. Though this would not have helped him, had it not been that Tortolini remembered that his wife had some relatives named Neilsen. Putting this and other things together, he thought it probable that the lady was his wife, and he set Williams to work to find out, with the result that Tortolini was proved correct, and his wife's retreat was discovered. Williams visited her, for Tortolini at the time was lying dangerously ill at Boulogne, and at his request Williams wrote repeatedly for money. Mrs. Neilsen usually destroyed these letters, but in accordance with some inscrutable law of destiny she either purposely kept one or overlooked it, and that one fell into the hands of Farabin Tindal, and thus Williams and Tindal were brought together.

At this time Williams and Tortolini were no longer together, having quarrelled about money matters, and Tindal ascertained many interesting facts about Tortolini. Amongst others, that the unprincipled Italian had been living in London, and that when he went away he had in his possession a revolver belonging to Williams, and marked with the initials 'S. W.'

This fact was a powerful link in Tindal's hands, and no man could have known how to use it better than he; taken in connection with Tortolini's presence at Drury Lane Theatre on the same night that his wife was there, it was doubly powerful. With the skill and perseverance that were his characteristics, Tindal, having got hold of the threads, never let them go; and he ascertained that Tortolini's companions in the box that night were a young married couple, Italians, resident in London, whose acquaintance Tortolini had made. They were highly respectable people, and knew nothing of Tortolini's career, but as a compatriot abroad they took to him, believing him to be a gentleman and honest man.

It was surely a cruel fate that on this particular night, when Tortolini and his Italian friends occupied a box at Drury Lane, Mrs. Neilsen, Tortolini's unfortunate wife, and her friends should have been in the theatre at the same time.

'Fate is inscrutable and destiny a riddle,' says an old writer, and surely it was so in poor Mrs. Neilsen's case. Her husband saw her leave the box with Vecquerary, and he went out intending to have an interview with her. But when his presence caused her to scream and swoon, he got alarmed, and went back. But all the fiery jealousy of his nature was aroused, and from that hour he dogged his wife's footsteps as if he had been her shadow. Jealousy and hatred of and for the woman he had so foully wronged made him as cruel and unerring as the bloodhound that scents blood. He ascertained her movements; he found out that Vecquerary had been in the habit of visiting her; he learnt that she had gone to Hastings, and he followed her.

His precise object in this, as was subsequently ascertained, was to extort money from her if he could prove her guilty of an intrigue. But on the fatal night when she left her hotel to meet Vecquerary, her husband dogged her. Her movements and the direction she took to the beach suggested to him that she had an assignation, and silent and sure as death itself he was behind her. Concealing himself under the pier, amongst the heavy shadows, he witnessed the meeting; and the fierce, fiery jealousy of his nature overpowering all other considerations, he shot her with Solly Williams's revolver, which for some time he had carried about with him. As soon as the crime was committed he threw the revolver beside the body and fled.

This was the story that, word by word, piece by piece, inch by inch, as it were, Farabin Tindal was to be the means of giving to the world. It was not without difficulty that Tindal secured the arrest of Tortolini; for the police were averse to confessing themselves in error, and losing their grip on Vecquerary. But the proofs and circumstantial evidence that the able detective brought forth left them no alternative; and the wretched Italian, who was lying sick unto death, was pounced upon in an obscure foreign hotel in the neighbourhood of Leicester Square. The news of the new arrest came upon the public like a thunderclap; and those who had been the loudest in their denunciations of Vecquerary now turned their coats, and exclaimed that they had always believed him innocent.

XXXVII

TRUE LOVE ENDURETH FOREVER

Of course Vecquerary was put on his trial, and seldom, indeed, had a criminal case caused such intense excitement. The public mind had been prepared for a *coup de theâtre*, and the scramble for seats was terrific; while the people who could not obtain admission to the necessarily limited space of the court-house filled the street leading to it, until there was a perfect block. Seldom before, either, had counsel for the defence in a great criminal trial 'come up so smiling,' to use a sporting phrase. The material placed in their hands by Tindal gave them powerful weapons to fight with; but the prosecution had to confess at the outset that their case against Vecquerary had broken down, and they stated that the husband of the deceased lady had been arrested, but that he was then in the prison infirmary, helpless, in the last stage of consumption. A verdict of 'not guilty' was entered against Vecquerary, for there was no other alternative; and he left the court a free man, but alas! a terribly changed one. The fearful ordeal through which he had passed had blanched his hair, whitened his face, and entirely crushed the youth out of him. He was bowed and prematurely aged, with a pitiable look of frozen sadness in his once bright eyes.

In allowing himself to fall so completely under the fascination of the beautiful and unfortunate Mrs. Neilsen, he had been guilty of an outrage against the proprieties, and he had so far wronged his wife and children, and all belonging to him. But it is not often that men who do wrong as he had done wrong pay such a fearful penalty; for as long as he might live his life would ever be darkened by the ordeal he had passed through, and by the remembrance of the awful death of the dear woman who, but for his weakness, might have lived to a green old age.

His wife, although still weak and ill, had travelled from Manchester in company with her brother-in-law, Alfred, to be present at the trial, for she knew that it was a foregone conclusion that her husband must be set free. And when in effect he felt the shameful shackles of the prison fall from his limbs, and heard the shouts of the multitude echoing with a mighty roar the verdict of not guilty, he was dazed and stupefied like one who had long been kept in darkness, and then suddenly thrust into a blaze of sunlight. His wife received him in her arms, and, remembering the painful scene that had occurred when they last parted, she murmured: 'Husband, forgive me.'

His friends led him away to an hotel; and then Oriel Verecourt, who had been content to remain till the last to offer his congratulations, came forward, and grasping both hands of his friend, he wrung them with nervous energy, and in a voice full of emotion exclaimed:

'God bless you, old fellow. It is an additional comfort to me in this hour of our triumph to know that I never believed you guilty.'

Vecquerary could make but a feeble reply by words, for his voice was choked by the sobs that he could not keep back.

While Vecquerary's friends were thus congratulating him on his acquittal, and welcoming him back to the sweetness of liberty, Mr. Richard Hipcraft was sitting in his office in gloomy silence, with a strange, confused expression on his sallow face.

For days the rumours of Vecquerary's innocence, and finally the arrest of Tortolini himself, had affected Hipcraft in a very marked manner. It preyed upon his mind, for he felt that he had erred as he had never before, perhaps, erred in his life. Miserably mean and contemptible as his character was, he had in his own peculiar way, keen sensitiveness with regard to what he would have termed 'his professional reputation;' and he had in a large measure staked that reputation on Vecquerary's guilt. Therefore, his pride was wounded. But, more than that, vexation of spirit that the man he had hated with such an intensity of hatred had escaped irritated him to an extent that was quite unusual with him; and when his clerks came to him on business matters, he answered brusquely, or snarled at them with that peculiar snarl which he always gave vent to when he was in a sullen humour.

It was his custom, when he left his office in the afternoon, to walk home. He used to say that he liked the walk, and that the exercise did him good. But on this particular afternoon he took a hansom, as he did not feel well, and was unequal to the walk, although the distance from the Old Bailey to Craven Street, Strand, was not very great.

When he did reach his home he was, as the saying is, as irritable 'as a bear with a sore head,' so much so that his housekeeper exclaimed to the kitchen wench:

'Well, I don't know what's a-coming over him. He ain't like the same man, he ain't; and he looks that awful in the face that I am just frightened at him.'

Half an hour later he rang his bell, and told the woman to go for Dr. Turner, as he felt very unwell. She went, but returned with the message that the doctor had gone to a case some distance away, and would not be back till late. Hipcraft was annoyed. He had some sort of vague notion that it was Turner's place to always be at his beck and call. As he began to feel a little better, he thought that a game at billiards would pick him up, and so he went round to the Golden Star Hotel, where he played three or four games, though not with his usual verve and go, as was noted by those who knew him. He drank two or three glasses of brandy and water, and attempted a cigar, but, though an inveterate smoker, he gave the cigar up, saying that he was so out of sorts that he couldn't smoke.

'Why, what's put you wrong, Hipcraft?' exclaimed a crony. 'Has the result of the Vecquerary trial gone against your grain?'

This was the keynote for an argument. Hipcraft waxed warm. He said that he believed there had been a miscarriage of justice, and that if Vecquerary did not murder Mrs. Neilsen she was not murdered at all. Of course, there was a strong discussion, during which Hipcraft got very excited, when suddenly his voice became thick and ropy; a peculiar expression was in his eyes; he put his hand to his head as if he were bewildered; and at last he pitched forward against the billiard-table. Men rushed towards him and grasped him; and he murmured brokenly: 'Take me home! Take me home!'

And they took him home, where he became unconscious, and when Dr. Turner did come he shook his head gravely and ominously, as well he might, for his patient had been smitten with 'a fit of happleplexy,' as the good housekeeper termed it. He had long shown a tendency to such a seizure, and it had been accelerated by the excitement. He rallied a little the next day, but only partially regained consciousness, and towards midnight was seized with another fit, from which he rallied no more; but as the daylight was dawning over the great city and stirring its pulses into feverish life again, the Angel of Death entered into Mr. Richard Hipcraft's dwelling and wrote 'finis' on the last page of his life's history, so that the book was closed forever. It was a mournful history, with not much to redeem it from its story of sordidness, of hatred, and all uncharitableness. The man had lived unloved, at any rate in his later years, and no tears fell when he was borne to the eternal silence of the grave.

Little is left to chronicle in connection with those who have played their parts in this drama of real life; but that little is not without importance. Smitten into helplessness and hopelessness by that rapid disease of the lungs, the wretched Tortolini drew rapidly near his end in the prison hospital, and, shuddering with horror as he approached that awful brink which overhangs the abyss of impenetrable darkness and mystery, he asked to see a priest, for he was a Roman Catholic, and to this representative of his faith he made the fullest confession of his crime with a request that when he was dead it might be made public.

Vecquerary returned for a time to Manchester, but he felt that he could never again know happiness there; and realizing his share of the business, he sold up his house, and went abroad with his wife and children.

Muriel Woolsey for some time after Vecquerary's acquittal remained silent in her Yorkshire home: for she was ill, and crushed with a sense of a lost love, until this became so unendurable that at last she wrote to Oriel Verecourt one line:

'Can you forgive me?'

He answered her with one word:

'Yes.'

And a few hours later he was on his way to Yorkshire.

The reunion of these young hearts that had for a time been estranged was very sweet; and, as Oriel held his affianced wife to his breast, and kissed the face that was upturned to his, the beautiful eyes filled with an expression of thankfulness and hope, he said:

'Darling, true love endureth forever.'

THE END

August
Derleth
In Re: SHERLOCK HOLMES
THE ADVENTURES OF SOLAR PONS

August
Derleth
THE MEMOIRS OF
SOLAR PONS

August
Derleth
THE RETURN OF
SOLAR PONS

August
Derleth
THE REMINISCENCES OF
SOLAR PONS

August
Derleth
THE CASEBOOK OF
SOLAR PONS

August
Derleth
THE NOVELS OF
SOLAR PONS

August
Derleth
THE CHRONICLES OF
SOLAR PONS

August
Derleth
THE APOCRYPHA OF
SOLAR PONS